DAVID DONACHIE was born in Edinburgh in 1944. He has always had an abiding interest in the naval history of the eighteenth and nineteenth centuries as well as the Roman Republic, and, under the pen-name of Jack Ludlow, has published a number of historical adventure novels. David lives in Deal with his partner, the novelist Sarah Grazebrook.

An Ill Wind

DAVID DONACHIE

Allison & Busby Limited
13 Charlotte Mews
London W1T 4EJ
www.allisonandbusby.com

A CIP catalogue record for this book is available from
the British Library.

Hardcover published in Great Britain in 2009.
Paperback first published in 2010 (978-0-7490-0870-3).
Reissued in 2011.

10 9 8 7 6 5 4 3 2 1

ISBN 978-0-7490-1098-0

Typeset in 11/16 pt Sabon by
Allison & Busby Ltd.

The paper used for this Allison & Busby publication
has been produced from trees that have been legally sourced
from well-managed and credibly certified forests.

Printed and bound in the UK by
CPI Bookmarque, Croydon, CR0 4TD

To Bella & Oscar Jeffs,
and, of course, their
willing slaves,
Caroline & Alex

CHAPTER ONE

The evacuation of Toulon left no time for anyone to be shy when it came to being active; the defences were falling to the French revolutionary armies in increasing numbers, the forts being abandoned, blowing their stores of powder, and the general situation was deteriorating by the hour. Even if Lieutenant John Pearce, a naval officer by accident rather than design, thought himself free from the need to respond to orders, to refuse to serve under such circumstances when the fate of the entire garrison was at stake, would have been churlish in the extreme.

Thus he found himself, along with those men for whom he had taken responsibility, aboard the fireship HMS *Vulcan*, heading past the Grosse Tour and into an inner bay known as the Petite Rade, his destination the naval harbour of Toulon, intent on adding to the destruction. Beneath his feet the ship was being primed, which meant the barrels of powder and pitch with which it was equipped were being linked to the fuses and highly inflammable liquids which would turn the vessel into an explosive fireball.

HMS *Vulcan* was leading a small squadron made up of manned galleys under the command of Captain Sir Sidney Smith, tasked with ensuring that when the port finally fell to the enemy, little of military value would be left for their use. The fireship was to be laid alongside the capital ships of the French fleet, those not fit for sea or vessels that could not be manned and sailed out. Once ignited, HMS *Vulcan* would turn into the torch that destroyed them and they in turn would fire the rest of the vessels tied up to the naval quays.

Not content that such measures would be sufficient, it had been decided that fires must be set on the vessels themselves, to ensure ruin, just in case the French sought to save them. While Pearce agreed that the service was necessary, there were friends with him who did not: the group of fellows, of which he was one, who knew themselves collectively as the Pelicans.

'They are short of men,' Pearce insisted.

'Short of men,' grumbled Charlie Taverner, the least eager to undertake the service. 'How can a whole fleet be short of men?'

'There are not enough hands to crew all the ships in the French fleet, and according to Admiral Lord Hood scarce enough to man the vessels he already commands, given the losses he has suffered.'

'Old Hood must be desperate to send for you, Charlie.' That jest got Michael O'Hagan a queer look, which only made the huge Irishman laugh more, his eyes narrowing in that massive head, yet still able to twinkle from the reflected light of the fires that surrounded the bay. 'Even Rufus here has at least the virtue of being willing.'

'No I ain't,' Rufus Dommet protested: he had been agreeable when asked, but as ever when challenged, wanted to side with Charlie.

'Well,' Pearce sighed, 'we are here now, so unless you're in the mood to swim, it would be best to get through with it and then get back to the hospital to load the wounded afore that too is overrun.'

That was the duty he had been drawn away from. The hospital in question lay on the St Mandrier Peninsula and was extremely vulnerable to enemy attack, protected as it was by a poorly manned and equipped redoubt where the narrow neck joined the mainland; indeed, it would have fallen if its strategic position had been of value. Luckily the French attack was not one designed to take territory but to render the anchorages of Toulon untenable: in short, to drive out the combined fleets of Britain, Spain and Naples, because to stay within range of the shore-based enemy cannon would be too costly.

The name of the man directing this assault was known to all now: not the general in command but the artillery officer, a fellow called Buonaparte, who had cleverly eschewed infantry assaults and instead moved forward his guns in calculated steps that took no account of casualties sustained, creeping ever closer to that inner bay. He knew, as did those he fought, that to command the entrance to the Petite Rade was to trap inside every vessel that remained. Lord Hood had reacted as he should: there were no more British or allied ships to ensnare now, they had all upped anchor and fled to the safety of the wide outer bay known as the Grande Rade.

HMS *Vulcan* was towing several boats, passing first a steady and departing stream of overloaded fishing and coastal trading vessels, then, within sight of the commercial waterfront, a quay densely packed with people intent on desperate flight, people who knew what was coming with the revolutionary armies: the guillotine and the representatives on mission from the Committee of Public Safety, men driven by a bloodlust that would see it employed for day after day to decapitate those they saw as the enemy of their murderous political philosophy.

'Look at them, poor souls,' Michael said.

As the Irishman said this the press became so great that several of those at the front, hoping for a boat, were pushed into the water, their distressed cries echoing over the rumble of the mob. The few boats left at the quay were loading only those with the means to pay, their chattels with them if they had enough funds. Those without means were left to pray or fall; indeed, the harbour was already awash with the floating bodies and possessions of those who had suffered and could not swim.

'We should be lookin' to them, not setting ships afire. We's about the wrong duty.'

'Who speaks there?' came a loud and commanding voice. 'Am I leading traitors to do their duty?'

'Quiet, Michael,' Pearce snapped: he knew his friend well enough to guess there would be a response and an impolite one. Then he turned to face the officer commanding the ship, a long-serving lieutenant called Hare, whom he had only met when coming aboard that evening. 'My man speaks from humanity, sir.'

'Humanity be damned, sir, when necessity calls. Tell him to mind his tongue or, by God, he'll feel the lash when this is over.'

That the ship's captain meant what he said was evident by the look on his face, made more menacing by the fact that it was lit in orange and red by the flames from ashore, these reflecting off the dense, low cloud as well as the still harbour water. Raging along the hills that led up to Mont Faron, the ridge that dominated the port, the fires were caused by the burning defence works, the redoubts and small forts, which had been built since the allied fleets had taken possession of the anchorage in August. Below, the town itself was being bombarded by revolutionary cannon, setting building after building ablaze. The task set for this little flotilla was straightforward: anything that might be of use to the besiegers, soon to be the owners of this premier naval port, was to be torched – the arsenal, the rope-walk, sail lofts and warehouses full of stores.

Given they were almost the first words Hare had addressed to John Pearce his impression of the fellow was based only on what he could see. There was

11

arrogance in his posture: hands behind his back, feet spread to anticipate any slight roll of the ship and a sort of sneer on his heavily pockmarked face.

'You do not see the need, sir, to offer succour to these poor unfortunates?'

John Pearce should not have spoken, he knew that even as he said the words: regardless of how he perceived his status, to take issue with a fellow officer and one ranked as a master and commander, much senior to him in years served, was inadvisable at the best of times and this was far from that. Yet he was incapable of allowing roughshod authority to rule his behaviour.

The response was a bark. 'I see the need, sir, to serve my king.'

'Then perhaps, sir, those of Naples and Spain are more Christian sovereigns.'

'Damn you, sir, what do you mean?'

'I mean, sir, that if you look yonder to the outer mole you will observe Neapolitan and Spanish warships taking off the refugees, an act which shames those like us who serve their royal cousin.'

Hare stalked up to him and looked Pearce right in the eye, his nose an inch away. 'You dare dispute with me, sir?'

Pearce held both his ground and the man's eye. 'Not dispute, sir, I merely point out what I see.'

'Well, sir, I will take note of what you do, and if it does not satisfy, you may well find that a court decides you are not fit to hold a lieutenant's commission.'

'They can have it now, sir, given it is not something

'I value so highly that I will not speak as I find.'

'Gentlemen, please,' said another voice, gentle but authoritative, that of their titular commander, though given he was clad in rating's clothing, check shirt and ducks, it would have been hard to identify him as a post captain. 'We are not lacking in enemies to dispute with, I see no virtue in arguing amongst ourselves.'

'We cannot have troublemaking, Sir Sidney.'

The man actually laughed. 'Then I am in the wrong place, Mr Hare, for I am bent on that very thing.' He then looked at the other party to the dispute. 'Lieutenant, I confess I do not know your name.'

'Pearce, sir.'

'Then, Lieutenant Pearce, your concern for these poor folk is to be commended.' That brought a hiss from Hare. 'But so is the captain's love of duty. If we do that, which I confess must be our primary concern, perhaps then we will have time to look to our compassion. Captain Hare, I require to be put ashore with the men designated to join me, so that I may supervise the destruction of the port facilities.'

As he uttered those words a cannonball landed right alongside the ship sending up a great plume of water, which, on a windless night, rose to a great height before dropping straight back down again, soon to be followed by a second. Seeking the source, it soon became obvious that some of the vessels chosen to be destroyed were manned and a few of their cannon were being employed to defend them.

'I see the rats have emerged from their cellars,' Smith said. 'Toulon is full of men whose loyalty is attached to a weathervane, for the monarchy one minute and the Revolution now the tide has shifted. Captain Hare, I require that your guns be employed to keep those fellows honest.'

'With the men you propose to take ashore, sir, I am light on gun crews.'

'Then let us oblige, sir,' said Pearce. 'My men and I will happily help work one of your cannon.'

'Well said, Mr Pearce. Now, Captain Hare, let us have the boats alongside and see to what we are about.'

Pearce, Michael, Rufus and Charlie found themselves helping to work a long nine-pounder with the rest of the gun crew made up by a trio of men from *Vulcan* and, if they were unfamiliar with each other, so common was the discipline of the Royal Navy that they were soon serving the weapon handsomely, knocking, at near point-blank range, lumps out of the enemy bulwarks and seeking to silence any counterfire.

Other cannon were playing along the shore, to keep the enemy clear of the route to the arsenal, or to be more precise those Toulonnais who had reason to seek to stop the destruction, the folk who earned their livelihoods in that facility. Already flames were beginning to lick around the major buildings and there was the constant crack of musketry as the detachment of soldiers sent to defend the firing parties went about their duty, albeit with many a returned discharge from the French workers.

Coat and hat off now, John Pearce was on the lanyard, both aiming and firing the weapon, peering through the gun port to do the former, this while the weapon was levered round and the elevation wedged at his command. He stood well clear once the gun was loaded and primed, to haul hard on his line and fire the flintlock, the discharge sending the huge lump of black metal, as well as the trunnion on which it ran, jumping hard back on to its restraining tackles. Powder monkeys raced to and from the magazine with charges taken from the gunner, sat, hopefully safe, behind his wetted screens, this while the more useless ratings fetched balls from the lower-deck storerooms to keep regular the bombardment.

Much as they were playing hard on their enemies, along with the other vessels in the flotilla, the Pelicans were under return fire and shots were striking home, either slamming into the hull and rocking the whole ship or, aimed better, taking out great chunks of the bulwarks or raking across the deck to land in the water behind, having sliced through rigging and ropes, while all around and beneath him there were men working flat out, still priming the ship.

Pearce never knew what set off one part of that: an enemy shot striking a deadly spark or a piece of foolishness by one of those employed in the task; all he felt was the result. The dull boom coincided with the planking beneath his feet rising up as if forced skywards by a giant's hand. It then began to crack open as the first flames emerged with the rest of the blast, the gun they were working, just run in and unstable, tipping over on its side on the suddenly uneven deck.

He was thrown to his knees, while Michael O'Hagan

was blasted backwards to roll along the deck. Rufus Dommet – a terrified look on his young, freckled face – was slammed into the bulwark, while Charlie Taverner, seemingly unaffected, stood still and shocked. Then his tricorn hat went sailing through the air and Charlie dropped down to his knees, holding his ears. John Pearce had felt the same pressure, but he was able to turn to see where the real damage had been done.

The explosion had come from under the quarterdeck, at one time full of people but now utterly empty, with the wheel gone, the front of the poop shattered and the cabin behind it ripped open, the bulkhead shredded to expose a scene of devastation in what had been Hare's quarters. Getting to his feet with some effort, Pearce headed aft, able on the way to help raise a shocked and bewildered Michael, though in grasping to pull him up he nearly fell over himself.

'What in the name of Holy Mary was that?' Michael shouted, though all a deafened John Pearce could hear was a muffled sound that seemed distant. The ship was rocking like a see-saw and it was with some difficulty they made their way across the splintered planking to join men equally bewildered and equally deaf, all shouting at each other and all unable to properly hear what was being said. Looking through the gap that had once been the starboard bulkhead he saw in the water two blue coats, one on his back and another face down.

There was no time for hesitation, no time to issue any orders, he just had to hope the men left standing would show some sense. Kicking off his shoes he dived in, hitting the waters of the harbour, so cold it made him gasp. In an instant he struck out to get to the second blue coat and turn him face up lest he drown and as he reached him a rope landed in the water by his arm. Looping it round the body was not easy but Pearce did manage to get enough of a knot on the man to allow them to haul him back to the ship.

That done he swam over to where Hare lay on his back, his eyes closed, his mouth open. There was no time to see if he was alive or dead, only time to get underneath him and grasp his shoulders, then kick out for the ship's side. Hands were there as he reached the rough scantlings, ready to haul the captain out, then reach down for Pearce and help him back on deck, where he found an anxious midshipman leaning over the comatose bodies, examining them.

'They're alive,' he yelled, into the cloth ears around him, looking to see if they had heard, reassured by the eager nods.

Pearce, dripping wet, was quick to realise, after a searching glance, he had to be the most senior person left aboard. He also knew that if there had been one unwanted explosion there could very easily be a second and third which would rip them all to shreds. Issuing the orders that followed his conclusion was a nightmare of endless shouting, always facing the person he was addressing so at least they would have his lips as an aid to comprehension, this while he got back into his shoes and his uniform coat.

'Prepare a boat. We must get any wounded to St Mandrier, while all the other boats are to be made ready to abandon ship.'

The midshipman mouthed the need to get the cannon loaded and run out, so they would go off as the fire took hold of the ship, helping to demolish whatever they were aimed at. A party had to be organised to man the relieving tackles below decks, given the ship's wheel had been shattered in the explosion. Those who could handle muskets needed to get them loaded so as to play upon the decks of the two capital ships between which he was going to jam HMS *Vulcan* and keep them clear of renegade French sailors.

'Do you know where the main fuses are to be lit?' he shouted to the midshipman, relieved when the lad nodded. 'Then get to them and stand by to ignite them on my command.'

He turned to a quartermaster's mate who had not been on deck at the time of the explosion but had rushed to the station immediately it had occurred. 'Stand by the companionway to shout down the orders to steer.'

That directive was followed by a stream of others, calling for sails to be set by men who seemed to move as slowly as bearers at a funeral. There were no specific commands, anything that would serve to give them steerage way would do, though with no wind to speak of that led to limp and useless sails. Instructions were sent to the men who, on his orders, had piled into the boats, to get up ahead and take tow. Their efforts brought round *Vulcan*'s bowsprit, damned slowly but round all the same, with Pearce shouting to the quartermaster's mate the orders that would ease the rudder to aid them and, once on course, to get the men from below to lash off their tackles and be ready to disembark.

Onshore he could see the results of what Sir Sidney Smith was about, though he could only hear muffled evidence of the explosions. The arsenal was alight from end to end, the flames seeming to lick the low clouds, creating a glow that lit up everything around the naval harbour in a sort of hellish montage. HMS *Vulcan* had drifted into position, the towing boats having got enough way on her to get her heading to where Pearce needed her to be, her bowsprit right between the bow and stern of a pair of French seventy-fours.

It had to be well timed: Pearce had to get himself and the remainder of the crew off the ship after the fuses were lit but before they took hold and exploded the powder, he having no true idea of how long that was. So he ordered everyone into the boats and went below himself to join the midshipman, who now stood over a tangle of fuses, long trails of primed cord, with a piece of slow match smouldering away in his hand. Sign language rather than words told Pearce that, once ignited, they would be required to run like the devil. After a nodded acknowledgement, the lad touched the fuse ends and they immediately began to splutter and trail off in a cloud of acrid smoke, progressing towards the various charges.

He and the midshipmen were no longer there. The boy was racing ahead of Pearce, taking the companionway three steps at a time, but he had to be grabbed and directed to where the last boat, manned by the Pelicans, lay rocking and waiting. As soon as they had one foot on the cutter, the oars were dipped and they began to pull away from the ship's side.

Pearce should have sat down, but he was keen to see what the result would be and it was impressive: HMS *Vulcan* went up like a volcano erupting, a great sheet of flame shooting from her deck, that followed by a boom as the powder barrels went up. It was as though she grew to twice her size for a second, but that was blotted out by the mass of flames that engulfed her, great streams of burning pitch shooting out to run along the scantlings of the French seventy-fours, some rising high enough to set afire the standing rigging, that rapidly catching fire.

Taking his naval officer's hat from Michael, who had had the presence of mind to gather it up, Pearce jammed it on his head just as the debris from the explosion began to fall. Had he not been wearing it the lump of wood might have done him serious harm. As it was, landing on the crown of his scraper, it was hard enough to fell him and knock him unconscious.

'Row for St Mandrier,' Michael O'Hagan ordered, a shout that included the boat carrying the two wounded officers. In doing so he completely ignored the bemused midshipman who should have issued any command.

CHAPTER TWO

It was a groggy John Pearce who landed on the hospital jetty, still wet from his dip in the harbour and shivering, helped by Charlie Taverner and Rufus Dommet to stand upright while his boat was secured and the two wounded officers Pearce had rescued were unloaded from the other and taken to be attended to. A quarter of an hour later, inside the building, trying to dry out by the heat of a blazing fire, he was sought out by an anxious Heinrich Lutyens, the surgeon, who, having seen to his new patients, was eager to inform him that there was as yet no sign of the transport supposed to be coming to take off the wounded, as well as those who ran the hospital. Getting a mumbled response, he demanded of Pearce's companions what was the matter.

'If you look at this you'll see, Mr Lutyens,' said Rufus, handing him a hat, the crown of which had been flattened. 'Lump of timber did that, your honour.'

'And he had only just donned the bugger,' Charlie added. 'God must love him.'

'Sit him down,' Lutyens ordered, and once that had been done he began to run his upright finger back and forth across Pearce's eye line, before running his fingers through the thick hair on the top of his head. 'A touch concussed, for certain, but no sign of any abrasion.'

'Why no transport?' Pearce asked, in a low voice.

'I have no idea. It was promised but has yet to arrive and I have to tell you time is of the essence. Word has come from the lieutenant manning the battery protecting us that the French may be massing for an assault, one he fears he will struggle to contain, and I would remind you the marines, too, need to be taken off.'

Pearce heaved himself to his feet, slowly shaking his head to clear it. 'Then there is no time to sit and ponder. Charlie, where is that mid we had with us?'

'Still sat in the boat with the men from the *Vulcan*.'

'Get him here. Heinrich, a pen and paper, I must send word to Admiral Hood and inform him that we face capture, and I would appreciate a tot of your medicinal brandy to clear my damned head. Rufus, fetch Michael; you, he and Charlie are to gather every man in this hospital who can fight, or even walk, and any men in the boats not needed to row. We need bodies in that redoubt to give the French pause.'

'What about you?' Lutyens asked.

22

'Me?' Pearce replied, picking up his wrecked scraper. 'I need a new hat, I think. It wouldn't help if the French saw that.'

'I'm sure my husband would not begrudge you his.'

The female voice made everyone present turn, to see Emily Barclay standing in a doorway.

'With respect, madam, I think I am the last person he would wish to gift anything to.'

If the pause that engendered was short, it was enough to remind those who heard the exchange that bad blood existed between Captain Ralph Barclay, her husband, and Lieutenant John Pearce. It had been Barclay who had illegally pressed the Pelicans into King George's Navy, Barclay who had survived the travesty of a recent court martial for the offence, the verdict of which, that he was innocent of the charge, being one Pearce was determined to overturn.

'Then accept it from me, sir.'

'I do not think your husband would be grateful to you for that offer.'

'You must leave, sir, my husband's opinions of my actions to him and me.'

Again no one was minded to mention that she was discussing a relationship that had undergone much recent strain, enough for her to leave both her husband and her floating home on his ship, the frigate HMS *Brilliant*, and take up residence here in the hospital. They had been brought back together because Captain Barclay had ended up as a patient, having required his left arm to be removed after a musket ball shattered his elbow during a failed assault on one of Buonaparte's most dangerous batteries.

Emily Barclay had not waited for a reply; she had gone to the room in which her wounded husband lay, returning, his hat in her hand. 'Take it, sir, I beg.'

Pearce had been joking about the hat, but he stepped forward to do as he was asked, not wishing to make light of her gesture. Up close he was struck, as he had been the first time he had clapped eyes on her, by her beauty. Even now, in a mob cap, a stained apron and showing signs of a lack of sleep, she looked striking: luminous eyes in a face of flawless skin, with just a wisp of her auburn hair escaping to stick to her cheek. The temptation for Pearce to reach out and brush it away was almost irresistible, yet resist he must, there were too many people present.

'Is Devenow still with your husband?'

'He is.'

'Then please tell him he is needed, and if he shows a mind to object, tell him he best come if he does not want his captain to end up, once more, a prisoner of the French.'

The way she pursed her lips then amused him. Was it a reminder of the unpleasant fact of her own confinement after HMS *Brilliant* had been taken in a hot frigate action off this very coast in midsummer, or was it that Devenow probably loved her husband more than she did? He was a man Pearce loathed, a lower-deck bully who generally made the lives of those he messed alongside hell, but if his devotion to Captain Ralph Barclay was absolute, his other quality, that of being a fighter, was of more moment in the present crisis.

Pearce spun round to find the young midshipman, a slip of a lad who could be no more than fifteen and was probably younger, awaiting his pleasure. On the table Lutyens had placed an inkwell, a quill, a shaker of sand and the wax and candle necessary for the seal. Sitting down, Pearce began to write as he spoke.

'I do not know your name, lad.'

'Niven, sir,' the boy responded, with a distinct Scottish accent which had Pearce wondering if he should claim national kinship. Deciding that would only delay matters he issued his commands.

'Well, Mr Niven, this is to go to HMS *Victory*. Try to get it to Lord Hood or Rear-Admiral Hyde Parker, at the very least into the hands of the C-in-C's secretary. Do not, and I say this at your peril, be fobbed off by anyone else.'

The reply of 'Aye, aye, sir' was tremulously delivered.

Pearce smiled. 'Have no fear. You will find, young fella, that admirals are human and their bark is very much worse than their bite. You can command the boat crew, I hope?'

'I can, sir.'

'Then go and God speed.'

As the boy dashed out of the room Pearce wondered,

not for the first time, about a service that entrusted so much to people so young: had he died or been incapacitated in that explosion, a lad like Niven would have taken command and, no doubt, have done his duty. He was also aware that his head was throbbing like the devil, but that had to be set aside.

'Heinrich, I need some dry clothing and I want the use of anything that can pass as a weapon down to the meanest broom handle. Meanwhile, make sure everyone we do not take with us is ready to leave, for when that ship arrives we must embark with haste, lest the French come on our tail when we spike the cannon and abandon the redoubt.'

'They will not harm the wounded, surely?'

'When it comes to the Revolution,' Pearce replied grimly, for he had had more experience of its terrors than most, 'I would not want to discount any barbarity.'

Midshipman Toby Burns, not much older than Niven, sat alone in the midshipman's berth of HMS *Britannia*, noting the passing of time through several bells, alternately fingering the despatch he had been given to convey and the bandage he still wore around his head. Handed to him by Admiral Sir William Hotham in person, he wondered at the quietly delivered order that went with the written communication, the intimation that it was not to be immediately delivered.

He knew what it contained, given he had been present when the admiral dictated the contents to his clerk:

an instruction to the commander of HMS *Hinslip*, an empty transport presently lying no more than a cable's length from the flagship, to proceed to the St Mandrier Peninsula and once there to take off combatants and non-combatants alike. It was that which was said afterwards, when the clerk had departed the great cabin, that hinted at trouble.

'It would be best, Mr Burns, if this were delayed for several hours. I trust you will see to it.'

Toby Burns could still sense Hotham's breath on his cheek as the admiral leant close to whisper those words. The look in Hotham's eye, when he stepped back again, was one that implied Burns would understand the need, but he was not absolutely sure he did and that rendered him fearful. Not the brightest of young men, he nevertheless knew, even if he could not discern the purpose, when he was being used. He also worried that someone would enter this berth and ask what the devil he was doing here skulking, given every other midshipman in the fleet had been sent away and was now occupied in some harrowing duty to do with the evacuation.

Quickly he checked his bandage again, to ensure it had not slipped from his head; it would be fatal if anyone saw there was no wound beneath. The subterfuge was necessary, given Toby Burns carried a hero's reputation gained when this new war was barely two months old. He knew only too well it was based on false evidence, indeed it was a status that had come to hang like a weight around his neck: he was expected to be brave and reckless when in truth he shied away from conflict of any kind. There was a brief flash of anger as he imagined himself telling Sir William Hotham to do his own dirty work, but that did not last: dread of a tongue-lashing resurfaced all too speedily.

Locked in his own gloom, he dreamt, as he had for months, of being free of the King's Navy. Before joining, sea service was something he had seen in the romantic light in which it was always portrayed: how different the reality from the tales with which he had grown up, of glory and pride in naval service within England's wooden walls. He only had to look around the grubby berth – this being a flagship – an overcrowded home to twenty-four midshipman, had only to smell the bilge that permeated the whole ship, to recoil from the rats that infested the lower decks or eat the monotonous diet and reflect on the character of the men he shared it with, be they mids, officers or ratings, to know the depth and inaccuracy of the myth.

The screen that shut off the berth from the Orlop deck was pulled back and there stood another vision to render worthless any romance: the skinny young urchin who went by the title of mess steward. A youngster who never went on deck unless ordered and certainly avoided fresh air when it rained, he was as black as ever with the filth that covered him from head to foot, dirt ingrained into his very pores.

'What the devil do you want?' Burns demanded, in a

harsh tone, for, if he was fearful of those who were his naval or physical superiors, he was not one to show any kindness to a creature below him in the pecking order.

'Now't,' the lad replied, showing white uneven teeth that only accentuated his dirty face, a part of him only marginally cleaner than the sleeve with which he constantly wiped it.

'Come to rummage, I daresay, while the berth is empty,' Burns snapped. 'Well, you can carry on for all I care, I have nothing left to steal, all my supposed shipmates having beaten you to it.'

'I ain't a fief,' the lad protested. 'I came to tidy.'

'Then,' Burns barked, standing up, 'you are singular in this vessel.'

'What is you about, 'en?'

'None of your damned business,' Burns said, pushing past him.

Head down, angry and sick of this imposed prevarication, he made his way up to the main deck and along to the entry port, calling to the sixth lieutenant of the ship, the man on duty, that he required a boat.

'Require, sir, require?' Beddows enquired, with an arch expression. 'What day is it that a midshipman requires from a commissioned officer?'

'I carry a despatch...'

'So you say, Burns,' the officer growled, interrupting him. 'But carrying a despatch, if indeed you are, does not mean you give up all manners and all courtesy to rank.'

'I require a boat, sir.'

'Better, young man, but I think I need a please, as well as a couple of fingers to your hat.'

'And I think I must tell Admiral Hotham how much you facilitated his instructions.'

Terrified of the words he had used, which due to his underlying anger had come out unbidden, Burns was about to apologise, but then he saw the change of expression on the sixth lieutenant's face: it went from hauteur to fright in a flash.

'You are on an errand for the admiral?'

'I am,' Burns replied, before adding, in a way that threw caution to the winds, 'and a most pressing one that you delay, sir, at some peril to your position.'

The feeling he had then, as Beddows rushed to call in a boat, manned by poor unfortunates obliged to lay off the ship in the cold and swell for this very eventuality, made him feel warm for the first time in an age. The sixth lieutenant might not outrank him by much – had he not been a midshipman himself until only a few months previously? – but he had the power to evoke the admiral, the ability to induce fear and that made him top dog. He almost cooed his next words.

'I will be sure to tell Sir William how you reacted with such alacrity, sir, once you were appraised of his interest.'

'Obliged, Mr Burns, much obliged.'

* * *

'Damn it, what is the man about?' yelled Lord Hood. Aimed at the captain of the fleet, Rear Admiral Hyde Parker, it had a terrible effect on young Mr Niven, who visibly began to shake in his shoes. 'Part of the orders I gave at six bells this morning was to get HMS *Hinslip* to St Mandrier with all despatch. Everyone should be off the peninsula by now!'

Parker, round and smooth of face in contrast to his craggy, grey-haired superior, felt the need to look put out, yet he was far from that, this being just another example of Sir William Hotham, Lord Hood's second-in-command, acting to thwart his superior's wishes. As the administrative officer of the fleet he not only had onerous duties to perform in keeping it up to scratch, he was required to act as a lightning rod for the C-in-C.

'God rot the fellow,' Hood barked, before he cast an eye back to the shivering Niven. 'What's amiss with you, lad, got the ague?'

'No, sir, begging your pardon, sir.'

'Well, there's something amiss with you.'

'Perhaps he fears to be yelled at,' said Parker.

'Who's yelling at him?' Hood bellowed.

'I suspect he thinks you are, milord.'

'Stop shaking, lad, I don't bite.' Hood then furiously waved Pearce's letter, his voice rising once more. 'Excepting when a poltroon does his best to make a fool out of me.'

'I think it would be best to act, milord. Loss of temper will not serve.'

The eyebrows came down to a glower. 'Mind yer manners, Parker, remember who you are addressing.'

'Of course, milord,' Parker replied, not in the least contrite.

'You see what I have to put up with, lad?' Hood asked a still-quivering Niven, his voice gruff but low. 'No respect from men who should know better. I daresay you know how to obey an order. You eaten at all?'

'Yes, sir, dinner, sir.'

'Dinner, that was hours ago. See that chafing dish on the table yonder?' The boy nodded, his eye drawn to the highly polished mahogany of a dining table, set with several silver dishes, one of which had a small candle underneath. 'There's sausages in there, French mind, and too full of garlic for my taste, but filling. Help yourself.'

Niven did not move until Hood added. 'Do you know how to obey an order, boy?'

Hood watched as the youngster approached the table in a wary fashion, amused by the way he gingerly opened the dish, but that diffidence did not survive the smell that greeted him. Hood had to actually suppress a laugh, as he saw Niven begin to stuff his mouth to the point where speech would have been impossible.

'Never met a mid that weren't starving,' he said. The humour evaporated when he looked back at Hyde Parker, again waving the letter. 'This is downright insubordination.'

'I agree, milord, but it is an indication of how Admiral

Hotham feels about the strength of his position.'

Hood began to pace back and forth, evidence of his mood audible by the growling noise emanating from his throat. His political master, King George's first minister, William Pitt, trying to hold together a fractious coalition, one that would wholeheartedly prosecute the war with revolutionary France, had warned him to be guarded with Hotham, who had friends amongst the faction known as the Portland Whigs. Indeed the leader of that group, the Duke of Portland, was a strong supporter of Hotham and would no doubt like to see him in command of the Mediterranean fleet.

Hood was a Tory from his greying locks to his silver shoe buckles and had been a member of Pitt's government, the senior naval lord on the Board of Admiralty, before the outbreak of hostilities. He hated Whigs and, of that entire breed, he hated the slimy Sir William Hotham the most. But he was hamstrung by instructions, which had come to him by a private and secret letter from Downing Street delivered to him by the man who had written the note he was holding, Lieutenant John Pearce. Abruptly he stopped both his pacing and his growling, to look at the signature appended to the message young Niven had brought him.

'Ain't Pearce charged with clearing the wounded from the hospital?' Parker nodded, which received a knowing look from his superior. 'And then he's supposed to be on his way back to England?'

'I believe, sir, the idea was that, with the evacuation

33

complete, he would take passage on the first available ship with his companions, the men he calls the Pelicans.'

Hood moved closer to Parker, looking over his shoulder to ensure the midshipman was still intent on filling his face, before speaking softly. 'Would Hotham go to such lengths to dish one man, Parker, and interfere with my orders?' Hood's captain of the fleet declined to reply to that, though his look was significant. 'Strikes me only London can deal with Hotham and it also strikes me that we have, taking passage home if we can get him off in time, the very fellow to go back to Billy Pitt with my concerns.'

'Unofficially,' said Parker.

'You know I dare not damn the sod in my official communications, they are read to the cabinet. But a private letter...' Hood stood slightly hunched thinking for a moment, before calling to Niven. 'You, lad, what ship are you in?'

'*Windsor Castle*, milord,' Niven replied, wiping a greasy set of lips on his sleeve.

'To which you should now proceed.'

'Yes, sir.'

'Well, you won't be. I have a chore for you. I daresay your captain will not mind if I borrow you for a bit. Parker, I need your help in this, you being better at the political game than ever I will be.'

'I'm not sure I take that as a compliment, milord.'

'It ain't,' hooted Hood, 'it's as close to damnation as

34

it comes. We must get an order direct to HMS *Hinslip* to weigh for St Mandrier immediately, to supersede any instructions to the contrary. Then I need you to help me compose a true account of affairs in this command for our political master.'

'Might I remind you, milord, you require Pearce to agree to both carry and see it delivered. He might refuse.'

'Refuse!' Hood barked, 'I'll see him keelhauled if he tries.'

Niven, his belly full, sat on the footlockers that lay below the line of nine casement windows that ran the full width of HMS *Victory*'s stern, marvelling at the space and the accoutrements afforded to the high and mighty. A sleeping cabin and a personal privy, a public cabin and a private one that could be combined to entertain several dozen people, the room to walk about, good furniture and even paintings, which stood in contrast to his own meagre berth, a cubbyhole aboard HMS *Windsor Castle*, shared with a dozen of his fellow mids.

He was enthralled: this was worth working for, worth risking life and limb to achieve, and it took no great leap of his tender imagination to see himself striding back and forth across the chequered canvas that lined the floor, as Lord Hood was doing now, dictating something to the fatter admiral. How grand it must be to have someone of such high rank to write your letters for you! When they had finished, Hood strode back and forth once more, handling without effort the swell of the ship, reading in his hand a letter of several pages, while Admiral Parker penned another. That finished, Niven was called for and handed the second missive.

'You are to return to Lieutenant Pearce and give him this and tell him I beg he read it, which has an order that he attend on me as soon as possible and the reason therein. Now, having done that he may well say words to the effect that he is damned if he will. You will then pass to him this verbal message with my authority. If he refuses my request, I will haul him and his so-called Pelicans into the first ship I can find and send them off to the East Indies. Have you got that, boy?'

'Yes, sir,' Niven replied, nervously.

'Then repeat it.'

He had to be coached and he stumbled over the words several times, but eventually Hood was satisfied that he had the threat off pat.

'Right, young fella, on your way back to St Mandrier and be assured I will inform your captain of your exemplary conduct. You're a credit to the service.'

Niven nearly made five foot as he stretched in gratitude.

CHAPTER THREE

Wrapped in his boat cloak, at least in dry breeches, Pearce led his party of Pelicans, Vulcans and barely ambulant men, two dozen in number, out of the tiny fishing port of St Mandrier, heading towards the neck of the peninsula, to the earthwork redoubt which had been thrown up to house the battery of four cannon facing the French counterpart on the mainland. The crossing of the wooded hill in between was hard going and required the likes of Devenow and Michael O'Hagan to assist some of the patients, but once the summit had been reached, things eased somewhat as they headed downhill, and on the flat and narrow spit the going was good.

With him, to see them through the darkness and the wooded paths, he had brought flaming torches soaked in pitch, yet they had a double purpose: he hoped they would serve to tell the enemy, if they were gathering for an assault, that rather than being abandoned the redoubt was being reinforced. At all costs it had to be held till that transport arrived, and Pearce was acutely conscious it would be not only the likes of the Barclays who would face captivity if this bluff did not work: he and his friends would too.

A party of marines under a Lieutenant Driffield manned the battery. Pearce, being naval, outranked the lobster, but there was no accepting responsibility when the fellow, with palpable relief, tried to pass on to him the supervision of the position. As Pearce was quick to point out, he was here to bluff, not to fight. Having climbed to the top of the earthwork and seen nothing but the fires of the French encampment, he had retreated back to ground level to enjoy the heat of the blazing bonfire that lit up the British position.

'Give me the situation?' he asked.

'We have been here for months with practically no activity, but as of yesterday men have been filing into Les Sablettes.' Seeing Pearce raise a flame-illuminated eyebrow at the name, Driffield explained. 'That's what the Crapauds called their position, which at least has the virtue of being a reference to its geographical name. This Buonaparte fellow everyone is talking about is much given to romance when it comes to christening his creations. He named one "The battery of men without fear", in French, that heathen tongue, of course.'

A fluent French speaker, John Pearce forbore to point

out that to the men of Les Sablettes the heathens were defending this redoubt. 'Your Buonaparte fellow is also much given to outflanking and suppressing our guns, Mr Driffield, which is why we are being obliged to abandon Toulon. Do you think they will attack soon?'

'Only if they are mad, sir! It is flat open ground, narrow, with sea on both sides, and we have four cannon loaded with grape, which anyone leading them would reckon to be the case. No, they will either try to suppress us with shot and shell, to dismount our guns and break up the protective embankment, or they will gather boats and seek to get round behind us. You coming up, and the sight of your torches, may well give them pause.'

'As long as they have no sight of the unfortunates bearing them.'

Driffield pulled a face: even in the poor light he could see that several of those present were wounded men. Two, sat in front of the tents that housed his marines, were missing arms, while another, who had insisted on joining, had had a leg removed, though some time previously, since then becoming, with his wooden peg, a sort of orderly in the hospital.

'What is the likelihood of boats?' Pearce asked, aware that if they could outflank this battery they could very well go right on to the hospital jetty.

'They will be cautious there, sir, for it is where we have all the advantage. The smallest of our warships could sink them and once they are out in the bay they would be sitting ducks.'

'What preparations are there for disabling the guns?'

'Spikes are ready and I have rigged lines to overturn the carriages, alongside sledgehammers to shatter the wheels. I would double- or triple-shot the barrels and seek to blast them, but that would endanger my own men. Besides, these are new cannon and have not been fired much, so they are still very sound.'

'Good. I take it you have ample food?'

'Only if we are not to be here too long.'

'I don't think we will be, Lieutenant Driffield. Either we will be hotfooting it back to the hospital or we will be hauling up a white flag. Let us get everyone fed and I, for one, could use some sleep.'

'I have commandeered a fisherman's hut, sir, which I am happy to share, and though it is not luxurious it is at least shelter.'

'Pickets?'

'Two hours on, four off and set for the night, sir, I will make sure they stay alert.'

'Good,' John Pearce replied, feeling, as he often did, like a military fraud: this marine would know more than him about both attack and defence, though he might match him in gunnery. That was because Driffield wanted to be in his chosen profession, one into which John Pearce had been forced. 'We must be up at cock's crow and get a look at their preparations.'

'What is actually happening in Toulon, sir?'

'Surely you have looked across the anchorage, Lieutenant, and seen for yourself.'

The marine looked past Pearce to the distant flames engulfing much of the furthest part of the port, made more hellish by being reflected in the calm black sea. The arsenal and naval warehouses were located there, while individual fires were raging, flickering points of red and orange light, all along the harbour frontage, leaving Pearce, when he too chose to look, to wonder at the fate of all those people he had seen lining the quays.

Just then, a huge explosion rent the air, sending up hundreds of feet into the night sky a sheet of bright flame as well as visible debris. Seconds later they felt the blast, much diminished, but at such a distance evidence of its stunning power.

'What the devil was that?' Driffield demanded.

'There are a pair of French frigates in the harbour full of powder,' Pearce said, knowing this from Sir Sidney Smith's briefing. 'We were supposed to sail them out and I doubt we have succeeded with at least one of them.'

'We're safer here, Mr Pearce, I reckon.'

'Let's hope you are right.'

Tobias Sidey, captain of the fleet transport, HMS *Hinslip*, had seen the same explosion and, being closer to the seat of it, felt even more the blast. He weighed as soon as he got the order to do so, or to be more precise, two sets of orders telling him to do exactly the same thing, a verbal one from Lord Hood and another from Sir William Hotham, that being a normal written instruction. The message from *Victory*, however, left him in no doubt of the need for extreme haste. On a windless night, to obey such a command was a tall order: the sails, once dropped and sheeted home, hung limp, flapping occasionally as a slight zephyr did something to trouble the canvas.

Toby Burns was standing off, on his way back to HMS *Britannia*, wondering if he should tell Admiral Hotham of the renewed orders from Lord Hood and deciding on silence, when Captain Sidey put his own boats in the water and began the wearisome task of towing his ungainly ship towards the St Mandrier Peninsula, a vessel he knew would be too deep of draught to enter the inlet in which the hospital jetty lay. Those same boats would be required to take off the people he was tasked to collect, and the whole could be at risk of fire from the enemy batteries if they had been pushed far enough forward.

At the same time, Midshipman Niven was arriving at that very jetty, in search of Lieutenant John Pearce, only to be told that he would have to traverse the hills to the west in order to go and find him. Bolstered by the good opinion of the commander-in-chief and still feeling well fed, he set off with enthusiasm, soon plunging into the Stygian darkness of the wooded hillside, struggling to stay on the path and losing his way more than once.

* * *

Emily Barclay sat by her husband's bed, really that of Heinrich Lutyens, which he had first given to her when she left HMS *Brilliant*, a couchette she had passed on to her husband after his amputation, the ever-faithful Devenow carrying him from the operating table. He had been unconscious then, through a combination of laudanum and shock, but had since fallen victim to a dangerous fever. She was obliged to frequently mop his sweating brow and wipe off the excessive perspiration, caused by both his condition and the heat from the blazing fire in the grate. She was also called upon to press down hard on his remaining right arm to restrain him from time to time, as whatever deep dream he was experiencing made him wrestle with his demons.

To be sitting here nursing this man was to induce in her a series of deeply ambivalent feelings. Captain Ralph Barclay, twenty years her senior, was her husband, but she had come to comprehend she had agreed to marry him as much to satisfy family needs as through any affection. Indeed, she knew now that the pressure from her parents as to the suitability of the match had probably weighed more heavily on her than she had realised at the time, flattered as she was by the attentions of such a person, a seeming man of the world, who had all the *gravitas* of his thirty-seven years and his senior naval rank.

Ralph Barclay had not turned out to be a man of the world after all: he had proved both to be given to falsehood and to be a narrow-minded naval officer, a post captain of more than three years seniority and one who abided religiously by the codes of a profession known to be harsh. At home in Somerset he had seemed avuncular and wise, but once aboard his ship he had been exposed as a hard horse captain and one with whom she had come to dispute. What she saw as cruelty he saw as taut discipline, and more recently she had been given cause to question both his character and his probity, all of that overlaid by what appeared to be blatant and shameless avarice.

While she had accepted on their wedding day her new husband was not rich, Emily had no idea of how pushed he was for funds, given he had no ship and the country was at peace. Ralph Barclay had been obliged for five whole years to live on half pay, a stipend that supported not only him, but also his two twittering, older sisters. Only slowly had she realised how much he had needed to avoid the pressing demands of the local tradesmen.

Certainly the joy of getting a frigate at the outbreak of the war had been exciting, but she had watched with some trepidation how difficult it had been for him to pay for the very necessary things required to properly carry out his duties: the food and wine to entertain, the new uniforms and items of basic furniture needed to turn his cabin into something approaching comfort. She also knew, now, he had taken her to sea with him, in truth a breach of regulations, though much ignored, in order to avoid the expense of maintaining his new wife in her own household.

Even ignorant of the rules which governed the behaviour of naval officers, Emily Barclay was aware her husband had stretched them to and beyond their limits: she had seen the pressed men brought aboard at Sheerness, some bearing the effects of being taken by force, and had, out of loyalty, held her tongue when she heard them described as volunteers and averted her gaze when they were painfully struck with a starter, a short, knotted rope. The taking of a couple of prizes, one in a very questionable way, might have eased the financial concerns, but Ralph Barclay's behaviour continued to trouble her, the whole coming to a head at his recent court martial.

She had sat through that and had heard the lies uttered by not only him, but also her nephew, Midshipman Toby Burns. The likes of Devenow and her husband's slimy clerk, Cornelius Gherson, uttering falsehoods, bothered her not for the fact that they were spoken, but more by the certain knowledge that it was her husband who had induced them to lie to support his case. All these thoughts piled in on her and swirled in her mind; what she did not have was a solution as to how they were going to affect her future.

'My dear, you must get some sleep.'

She had not heard the door open; in fact, she suspected she had drifted off into a reflective, if troubled doze, aided by the heat of the fire.

'I will sleep here in the chair.' Seeing Lutyens frown,

she added, nodding to the bed, 'He has to be restrained, as he is much troubled in his fever, hardly still. If he pulls out the ligature it may lead to an infection.'

Lutyens approached the bed and bent to sniff at the piece of thin cord which protruded from the angry wound of the stump, where once there had been an elbow. Once the mortified flesh had healed around it, to the point where it and the swab attached to it could be easily pulled free, that would indicate the arm was healed.

'I smell no corruption,' he said, 'and the fever will pass or carry him off in the next day. It will hardly serve if you make yourself ill in the same period.'

Did she want the fever to carry him off, for that would solve the dilemma of her present discontent? That she had never loved this fevered man she now knew: the emotions she had felt as a seventeen-year-old bride had more to do with admiration and respect. Also, Emily had been raised to think, as had most girls of her age and class, that security was a better grounding for a happy life than deep passion. Yet she was not, again like her contemporaries, immune to the dream of a great romance: had she and her girlfriends not speculated endlessly on such a thing every time they gathered in a group, imagining some Prince Charming would come and carry them away to a life of connubial bliss in a sparkling palace?

How Emily wished Lutyens, in his insensitive way, had not said those words! What was it that made a man of such a tender and sympathetic character, as he was, become so brusque when it came to matters medical or the prospect of death? Did he have any idea of the train of her thoughts? Did he know that part of her very being, fighting with her deep sense of duty, longed to be free of an attachment which had revealed itself to be founded on sand?

'Mr Lutyens, sir.'

'Yes?'

The ship's boy, a recovering patient who had fallen from the rigging of his vessel and broken an arm, was hanging round the door.

'There be a big bugger of a ship—'

'Mind your language,' Lutyens snapped. Emily just hid a smile; once she would have been shocked to be witness to such blaspheming, but months aboard her husband's frigate had cured her of the touchy hearing of her more tender years.

'Savin' your presence, Mrs Barclay, but there's a ship a'warping into the entrance of the bay, bein' towed like, and I reckon it has come for us.'

Just then they heard the sound of the second massive explosion of that night, albeit the exterior walls of the building muffled the sound and fury. Captain Ralph Barclay sat bolt upright, eyes open and blazing, throwing out his good right arm, finger pointed straight at the doorway, his voice at top pitch as he shouted, 'Seize him up and tie him to the grating, he'll feel the lash or I'll see him damned.'

'Holy Christ in heaven,' cried the boy, as he fled from that accusing finger.

Emily was on her feet in a flash, speaking in soothing tones, pressing her husband back onto his pillows.

'The fever approaches crisis,' Lutyens said, 'but I must see to this ship and, if it is our transport, send word to Lieutenant Pearce.'

'The damned cheek of the man,' Pearce said, as he read, in the gloomy morning light, the letter from Lord Hood, in which he was required to call upon the admiral to receive private letters, which must be returned to London and William Pitt. 'Does he think I am his valet?'

Midshipman Niven, who, covered in scratches and earth, looked, in the cold light of dawn, as if he had been dragged through a hedge backwards, was shocked, given he knew to whom Pearce was referring, but he did not utter the words he had been coached to say, simply because the man to whom he would have to address them looked angry enough to box his ears for his temerity.

'Is there any other message, Mr Niven?'

'Only, sir, that Lord Hood was most anxious you do him a service.'

Weighing the letter in his hand Pearce was minded to tell Hood to go to the devil, yet he was also aware that there might be some advantage in this. He needed to get Ralph Barclay into a court of King's Bench on a charge of perjury and he had the evidence of the lies

48

to make his case, falsehoods which had been aired at the travesty of a court martial set up by his patron, Admiral Hotham. Lord Hood, as his payment for a previously rendered service, had gifted him sight of the entire transcript and allowed him time and the means to make a fair copy.

Yet he had few illusions as to how difficult it would be to get Ralph Barclay into the dock: the navy, or rather the Admiralty, always defended the press gang and would very likely seek to protect one of their own. Barclay was politically insignificant so those in power would do nothing to advance Pearce's cause. Yet here he was being offered an entrée into the highest office in the land outside that of the monarch himself. The letter Hood referred to would likely guarantee him a private audience and, given Hood was a strong supporter of Pitt's government, the king's first minister might very well see the need to repay the favour on the admiral's behalf. At the very least it could do his cause no harm.

'Very well,' he said, more to himself than to the midshipman, as he pushed the letter into one of his deep pockets. 'Is there anything else, Mr Niven?'

'HMS *Hinslip* should be on its way, sir. Lord Hood was most irate that it had not come already.'

'So, young fella, were the folk at the hospital.'

'Seems he gave the order yesterday at six bells in the morning watch and he was raging that it had not been obeyed.'

'Gave the order to whom?'

Niven's tongue was suddenly trapped in the corner of his mouth, evidence of contemplation. 'I think it must have been to Admiral Hotham, sir. There was another mid came to *Hinslip* with the earlier order and I heard his boat being hailed as from *Britannia*.'

Pearce just grunted; Hotham would not have known he had left St Mandrier to aid the Toulon evacuation, while he knew very well how he stood in that quarter: he was seen as a menace, or perhaps even more, a danger, for if he could get a conviction against Barclay there would be repercussions that would affect the man's superior.

'Back to the hospital, Mr Niven, and tell them to send us a messenger as soon as the ship arrives.'

'French are stirring, John-boy,' Michael O'Hagan called softly, from the top of the earthwork where he lay, only the tip of his curly-haired head showing above the parapet. 'Might be an idea to rouse out that marine.'

'Let him sleep yet, Michael,' Pearce replied, crawling up to join him. 'He was up half the night checking on the pickets, not to mention all the fireworks from over yonder.'

Reaching into his pocket, Pearce produced a small spyglass, property of the slumbering Driffield, and aimed it at the French position. He could see the men lining up, moving away from the embers of their night-time fires with no great élan: a motley bunch in no recognisable uniform, instead clad in a variety of garments, the only common feature the red, white and blue cockades on their various headpieces, the sky, a uniform grey, doing nothing to render such adornments colourful. Yet he was very soon aware that he, too, was under observation, from a short fellow out in front, in a long blue greatcoat and a fore-and-aft hat worn crosswise, it too with a huge tricolour cockade at the brim. He also had a proper telescope to his eye.

'Do you see him, Michael?' Pearce said, passing the little telescope. 'He must be the fellow in command.'

Peering through the glass, Michael scoffed. 'There's not much to see, John-boy, given he's a short-arse. I could piss over him and he'd feel only the drips.'

Looking around in the morning light at a prospect new to him, Pearce took in the narrow, scrub-covered spit of land before him, a mixture of stunted dark-green bushes and sand, the whole barely above sea level, and the still, grey sea visible on both banks. Driffield was right: it would be a murderous piece of ground across which to mount an assault. His eyes ranging further on, Pearce spotted something of a different hue to the south-west, newly disturbed earth. Taking back the little spyglass he examined it with some concentration, sure that what he was seeing were the outlines of an embankment of the kind raised to protect artillery. If it was another battery, and it had cannon in place, it was one that could enfilade the British position and render it untenable. What to do: this had to be held until the hospital was abandoned, or...

'Mr Driffield,' he said to the sleepy marine a few minutes later, 'you said nothing about that artillery position over yonder.'

Taking the glass, the marine followed the line of Pearce's finger, and once he had adjusted the magnification he swore. 'By damn, we've been humbugged; that is new.'

'Is that position as dangerous as I think it is?'

'Lethal if it is manned and equipped, sir, for we cannot withstand the shot that two separate batteries can pour into us, especially from that angle of fire, and hope to reply effectively. We would be obliged to shift fire from the causeway as well, and we would need round shot to seek to suppress this new fellow, which would reduce the effect of our grapeshot and make an infantry attack very much easier.'

'As I suspected,' Pearce replied.

'How in the name of the devil did they get it up without us seeing anything?'

'Don't take it to heart,' Pearce replied, peering at that solitary figure in the pale-blue greatcoat, who was still examining them. 'Their artillery specialist has done it all over the perimeter. Do you think that might be the very fellow standing there?'

Swinging the glass round, Driffield replied, 'It could be. He's certainly a new face to me.'

'How long could we hold, given this situation?' Driffield looked at him strangely and it was clear he saw no need for the question, just as Pearce suspected he was supposed to know the answer. 'I ask only for clarification.'

'Sense dictates we spike the guns now, sir, and run, if we do not wish to be buried in the earth we threw up to protect ourselves, to then be bayoneted, if we can still have breath.'

Pearce's response was acerbic. 'With the less than fit men I brought up last night, that is not an attractive option.'

'My marines and I can hold for a time, Lieutenant Pearce, but we will spill much of our blood doing so.'

'Bravely said, Mr Driffield, but hardly a pleasant alternative.'

'It is a necessary one, sir.'

'No,' Pearce snapped. 'Michael, find me something white and a pole to attach it to.'

'You are planning to surrender?' Driffield demanded, clearly shocked.

'No, Mr Driffield, I am planning to talk.'

CHAPTER FOUR

Making his way forward, Pearce could not avoid observing the smoke rising from the town of Toulon, his eye drawn to the tall and very obvious masts of ships still in the harbour, wondering why they had not been destroyed. The operation of the previous night, a joint Spanish and British affair, had that as its purpose: to render useless, by burning, the remaining elements of the French fleet before they could fall into revolutionary hands. If those masts were still visible, it was likely the hulls beneath them were also intact, which would mean that somehow the exploit had failed. For all he might like to, he could not continue to look at that and wonder: he must deal with what was at hand.

Being tall, John Pearce had been acutely aware since reaching adulthood that, when it came to relations with his shorter brethren, it was best, if he had no desire to cause an upset, not to stand too close, lest in towering over them he set their hackles to rise. The man he was approaching – Michael O'Hagan and the truce flag at his heels – was small of stature, anyway, and slim of build, but that was accentuated by his bicorn hat, and even more by his open greatcoat, long enough to touch the toecaps of his knee-length boots. Underneath that he wore a uniform jacket over white breeches, with tabs identifying him as an officer of artillery.

Behind him, in ragged lines, stood the unkempt French infantry, muskets at the rest, with another cockaded officer, bearing a sword, at their head, this one with a tricolour sash as well. To the rear of that stood the redoubt of Les Sablettes, with the snouts of six cannons poking out through the sandbagged embrasures.

'I hope in this white flag lark, John-boy, we will not be putting ourselves at the same risk as the last time.'

Pearce smiled. 'You're not frightened of a few Frenchmen, are you?'

'No, by Jesus, it is you who scares me.'

Close enough for the laugh that induced to be seen and heard by the man they were approaching, it got a raised eyebrow added to a look of curiosity in the dark eyes. Pearce reckoned from what he could see of the fellow's olive skin colour that he was a citizen of the southern part of France. And he was young, younger than he appeared from a distance. Stopping well away from him, he spoke in French to name himself and his rank, noticing as he did so that another French officer had come forward to stand a few paces behind what had to be his superior, albeit he looked to be the younger of the two.

'Why have you come under that flag?'

'To whom am I speaking?'

'Does it matter?'

Arrogant little sod, Pearce thought, but he did not let that thought colour his speech: he kept his tone neutral, while also registering that the fellow had a strange accent to an ear schooled in Paris. 'It helps to know.'

'It may help you, monsieur.'

Pearce looked past the diminutive fellow to the other, older officer, and received for his pains a look of utter disdain. 'Well, we have come to prevent a useless effusion of blood.'

'Yours.'

'Not only ours, monsieur,' Pearce replied, jerking his head towards the spit of land he had just crossed, flat and featureless. 'Your men cannot cross that without suffering many casualties.'

'From your cannon?'

'Yes.'

'I might destroy them before they are obliged to even leave their positions.'

'You will have noticed, monsieur, that the position has been reinforced. I brought forward a party of soldiers last night, I presume you saw our torches. Each has a musket and is well trained to use it.'

That got a sneer. 'Are they prepared to die where they stand?'

Suddenly Pearce recalled what Driffield had said about the way the French artillery commander was naming his batteries. He dropped his pleasant manner and spoke in a determined tone. 'It is not only your country who can produce men without fear. They will stand if I say they will stand, and so will I.'

'So you are a brave man, Lieutenant Pearce?'

'I know how to do my duty, monsieur.'

Short-arse, as Michael had continued to name him, turned to talk quietly to his older confrère, which gave the Irishman a chance to ask how they were faring. Pearce, not knowing if they could be overheard, or if either of these French officers spoke English, just shook his head, this as the smaller fellow turned back to speak to him.

'And you propose?'

'Our position was constructed to defend the Ile St Mandrier and the hospital upon it.'

That point raised a smile on what was actually quite a handsome face. 'Not to mention the approach to Toulon harbour from the south-west.'

True as that was, Pearce ignored it. 'As of this moment we are awaiting the arrival of a transport to remove the wounded from the hospital and, as soon as that is complete, my instructions are to follow them aboard and abandon the place.'

Suddenly a loud cheer came from the British redoubt

and Pearce, looking towards it, could see a nipper with his arm in a sling running towards them. He obviously had a message and there could only be one that could cause such excitement. Pearce waved at him to go back to safety.

'I think that moment may have arrived, monsieur,' he said, facing the Frenchman once more.

'My colleague here, eager for glory, wishes to drive you into the sea.'

Pearce looked past the speaker to the other officer, taller and grizzly-looking, who had in his eye the glare of the revolutionary fanatic. 'Then tell him that I will ensure every musket is trained on him as soon as he gets within range. I am sure his tombstone will tell those who gaze upon it he died a glorious death. You and I will know it was a foolish and unnecessary one.'

The head dropped and Pearce found himself looking at the top of the bicorn hat; clearly the man was examining the possibilities. Suddenly the head came back up again, the voice sharp. 'You have one hour, monsieur, to abandon your position.' The other fellow started to protest, but Short-arse held up his hand to silence him. 'You will, however, leave the guns. My colleague here can have the glory of capturing them. Do you agree?'

'Yes, you have my word on that, but do you not wish that honour for yourself?'

The eyes lit up then, as did the face, and the accent, which Pearce could still not place, was even more pronounced. 'What are a few cannon, monsieur, when I have kicked the whole allied force out of Toulon?'

'Would your name be Buonaparte, by any chance?'

The question was wasted, for the recipient had already spun on his feet to limp away, leaving Pearce to wonder if he might be carrying a wound, calling over his shoulder, 'One hour.'

Driffield looked positively petulant when Pearce told him what had happened. 'It is a disgrace to leave the guns, sir.'

'It would be even more of a disgrace to die here to save them and I would point out to you we have no way to remove them.'

'Let us at least spike them, Mr Pearce.'

'Mr Driffield, I take responsibility and I gave my word. You may tell your fellow marines that I ordered you to leave them.'

'What about the powder?' Driffield demanded, pointing towards the planking-covered trench in which the barrels had been stored to protect them from heated shot, on top of which, for added security, was laid the ammunition for the cannon, barrels of grape and piles of round shot.

'It was not mentioned, so you can salve your military conscience by blowing it up. Now, I must get my fellows out of here immediately, given they will take a lot longer to get back to the hospital jetty than your own. Strike your tents and gather your equipment, Mr Driffield, but do not delay, for there is a fellow over yonder who is dying to thrust his sword blade into someone. Michael, Charlie, Rufus, Devenow, gather up our charges and let's be on our way.'

He looked at the nipper with the broken arm. 'You, lad, run back and tell them we are coming and they must, at all costs, wait for us.'

Driffield delayed giving the orders that would see the camp struck; instead he watched as the stumbling patients made their way up the hill that blocked off the small fishing port from the neck of the peninsula, keeping his eye on them as they wended their way up the twisting path, waiting till Pearce and his party were well out of earshot. Then he called to his sergeant.

'As soon as they can no longer see us, I want the shot moved and the cannon hauled over the powder store.'

'Did I not hear the officer say they was to be left, sir?'

'They are being left, sergeant. They are not being spiked or having their wheels smashed.' The look that got was, to the marine officer's mind, larded with potential insubordination, and his response was harsh. 'We cannot expect a bluecoat to comprehend the loss of honour attendant on abandoning the guns to the enemy. I intend, when I rejoin my fellows, to be able to look them in the eye.'

'We'll not have time to do that and break the camp of all of our equipment.'

'Equipment, sergeant, can be replaced. Honour, once lost, is gone for ever.'

* * *

Getting the wounded from the hospital into the boats, given their numbers, would have been a hellish task if it had not been for the sailors from HMS *Hinslip*. With that natural ability British tars had to overcome obstacles, they had ordered some spars brought ashore and jury-rigged a hoist so that the more serious could be lowered to lay across the gunnels of the ship's boats. On *Hinslip* itself, another hoist was ready to haul them inboard, as steady as you like, so that excessive movement did not aggravate their wounds.

Emily Barclay was only made aware that her husband had come out of his fever when his time came. She found him, pale, obviously weak and looking wasted, trying to sit up in the bed, struggling with only one arm, an attempt he abandoned as she filled the doorway. Husband and wife looked at each other, neither wishing to be the first to speak. Only then did Emily notice that his eyes were red, as if from weeping; or perhaps it was a result of his fever.

'There is a ship lying off the bay, a transport. We have to get you aboard.'

'Where is *Brilliant*?' Ralph Barclay demanded, struggling to sit up again.

'I have no idea, husband,' Emily replied, moving forward to restrain him. 'There will be some orderlies here presently with a stretcher to carry you to the jetty.'

'I can walk,' he insisted, trying to get out of bed and failing.

'You cannot, husband. You have had a fever, a bad one, after your...'

She could not finish it, so he did it for her, his face as pained as his stump must be. 'The loss of my arm?'

'Yes.'

'Who took it off?'

'Surgeon Lutyens.'

'Did he try to save it?'

There was bitterness in the way that was spat out, and Ralph Barclay's face bore an expression his wife had seen before, one which implied that the whole world was against him, implied that perhaps Lutyens had set to with knife and saw out of spite, not necessity.

'You were carried in unconscious, Captain Barclay, and it was obvious to Heinrich—'

'It is Heinrich now?'

'It has been for some time,' Emily snapped, her eyes flashing at the implication of over-familiarity. 'I challenge you to stand over men in distress as well as poor souls who are dying and still hold to formalities.'

'You were in a place you should not be. You should have been where you belonged.'

'Captain Barclay,' Emily said, in a tired voice, 'I no longer know where I belong.'

Two orderlies appearing at the door stymied any response, one carrying the canvas stretcher, the other a pair of trestles that, at bed height, would ease the transfer of the patient. Once more Ralph Barclay struggled to stand on his own, the effort being too much, and it caused him to fall back on to the end of his stump, bringing from his throat, even if the contact was cushioned by the bedding, a loud wail of pain. Emily heard it in the corridor, on her way to the next patient.

Pearce was within sight of the hospital when he heard the dull explosion of Driffield's powder, wondering what had taken him so long; the fellow was, by his calculation, cutting it fine. He would have been even more discomfited had he seen the remains of the redoubt. The earthwork was intact, but the cannon, dragged from their positions, were shattered, especially the wheels, while the barrels lay hither and thither amongst the tattered tents and scattered cooking implements that had once been their encampment, the whole scene of destruction observed from a safe distance by Driffield and his men.

They and their red coats were out of sight when the French, led by Colonel of Artillery Napoleon Buonaparte, crossed the top of the earthwork, to see before them the scene. Aware that the accusing eyes of his inferior officer were upon him, Buonaparte said, in an angry tone, 'This Pearce has ensured that I will remember his name.'

It was a grubby Sir Sidney Smith who sat making his report to Admiral Lord Hood, black from head to foot, this caused by a combination of smoke, sheer scrabbling in the dirt, and the various substances from tar to expended powder to which he had been exposed. Aware that his mission had not been a complete success, he was trying to gauge how the older man was taking the news that many of the French capital ships were still intact, awaiting only rigging and sails, as well as crews, to be ready for sea.

'This will not go down well in London, Sir Sidney,' said Parker, the other officer present.

'I am aware of that, sir, but my men did all that they were asked to do.'

'Hardly that, sir,' said Hood, softly.

'In that, milord, I mean all that was possible. The Dons were tardy, when they were not downright unhelpful.'

The accusation of treachery hung in the air, the notion that the Spaniards had not pursued the policy of destruction of the French warships with the necessary zeal. It took no great imagination to discern why: Spain, in every conflict since the Armada, had been England's enemy, often in alliance with Royal France. To have them, in this present war, as allies, had always felt odd, though up till now Hood could not have faulted the desire of their sailors to defeat the ogres of the Revolution.

If their soldiers had been less than wholly supportive, the senior Spanish naval officer had backed whatever plans Hood mooted to the hilt, deferring to him as the commander of the allied force because the British had the most powerful fleet. Yet a man would have had to be blind not to see such a policy did not always sit well with the more junior officers: they still saw Albion as the traditional enemy, smarted daily about the occupation of Gibraltar, now ninety years a British thorn in the pride of Spain.

'I suspect they blew the two powder ships, milord,' said Smith. 'They did not want us to have them any more than the French.'

'A couple of powder-filled frigates are neither here nor there, Sir Sidney,' Parker responded, 'but those ships of the line they failed to burn will come back to haunt us.'

'They feared to make us too powerful,' Hood snapped, causing both of his other officers to look at him. 'We are strange bedfellows, you know that and so do they. The last thing they want is a British fleet in the Mediterranean so powerful that it would be unassailable by Spain alone.'

'Are you saying they will desert the alliance, milord?'

'I am saying they have taken precautions to ensure they are not at a disadvantage if they do. Sir Sidney, I require from you a despatch regarding your exploits of last night, to go with mine in due course back to London, where I daresay another nail will be manufactured from my words to seal my coffin.'

Sam Hood had never looked young, he was after all in his seventies, but he had, up till now, looked sprightly. He did not appear to be that now: he looked worn down with the cares of his command.

'We must find another anchorage, Parker, and since we still have French capital ships to contend with it will have to be one close enough to cover Toulon. Let's send out some more sloops and frigates to see what they can find.'

'Corsica, sir?'

'Yes, Sardinia at a push.'

'If you recall the despatch Lieutenant Pearce brought in during the summer, milord, he has noted the main ports, such as Calvi and Bastia, are held by strong garrisons.'

'Then we might have to boot them out, Parker,' Hood retorted, with some of his old fire. 'You would do service in that, Sir Sidney, would you not?'

'Happily, sir, as would every officer in your fleet.'

'Right, Parker,' Hood commanded. 'Once all is settled signal the combined fleets to weigh for Leghorn.'

The hospital was empty now, and Heinrich Lutyens walked the rooms to ensure that nothing had been left behind, at the same time wondering what a fate had ensured he ended up here, doing that which he had sought to get away from in London, the exclusive practice of his profession. His sea chest was already aboard, but over his shoulder he had a satchel containing his notebooks and the ledger into which the hurried scribblings he had made these past nine months had been copied. Were they complete? Could he, from what he had already, compile that treatise he had set out to compose, an academic study of the stresses and strains of naval life on the human mind?

Idly he wondered if he would decline to serve on, and go back to what he had left behind, a highly successful and lucrative practice based on the twin facts that, not only was he highly thought of by his peers, but he was socially well connected, through his father, to the court of King George. Serving as a ship's surgeon was beneath his standing, a post normally occupied by men little above the old station of barbers, but it had not been without pleasures.

The men he had studied on HMS *Brilliant*, including those pressed by Ralph Barclay, had provided him with much material – not least, because he was educated, John Pearce. And Lutyens had been in a proper battle, albeit below decks in the cockpit and out of sight of the action, had been taken prisoner when Ralph Barclay was forced to strike his colours, so he had that experience, though it had been a benign confinement, given he had taken on the task of looking after the wounded from that sea fight.

Wherever they were bound for now he still had charges who required treatment and he might be afforded further opportunities for study. After all, HMS *Hinslip* was a ship, another floating and confined world, where all the things that interested him would once more be on display: the interaction of humans with each other in a constrained wooden hull; fears, bravery perhaps, the disputes that happened with men living cheek by jowl in damp conditions and eating a diet so boring that their most common complaint was a compacted bowel. On top of that there was the relationship between Emily Barclay and her husband; how would that work out? Plus he still had close and observable John Pearce and his Pelicans. Yes, there was still much of interest.

'Do you so enjoy being a prisoner that you fear to leave that estate?'

Heinrich Lutyens turned to face John Pearce, a haughty look on what had been described as a fish-like face, his fine nose in the air. 'Given the lack of culture of the alternative, John, it has its attractions.'

'Come,' Pearce said, 'the last boat is ready to cast off.'

They walked out and made for the jetty, past some very forlorn-looking locals, the fishermen, their wives and children who eked out a living in this tiny bay. They would fear what was coming, even if they had, being poor and ignorant folk, done nothing to deserve to suffer from revolutionary retribution.

'Can we not, John—?'

'No,' John Pearce said, cutting right across Lutyens, his face clouding into anger. 'I tried to persuade the captain to take them off with us, but he has strict orders from Hood. No civilians.'

'Then may God bless them.'

'As long as Doctor Guillotine does not.'

CHAPTER FIVE

The sight of smoking Toulon had long disappeared over the stern as HMS Hinslip cleaved her way through a heavy swell, under lowering clouds that threatened worse weather to come, surrounded by the overladen ships of the combined fleets, somehow the attitude of gloom making itself felt over the intervening sea. On the quarterdeck stood Captain Sidey, in his foul-weather gear, oilskin coat and hat, legs spread to cope with the motion of the ship, his square, weather-beaten face set and determined, eyes narrowed to keep out the flying spume.

John Pearce stood on the leeward side, his arm hooked round a stay, well away from the water shipping in over the weather beam. Here the heavily canted deck took the bulwarks close to the grey, foam-flecked waters of the angry Mediterranean. He was wondering what the future held, there being something about staring at the shifting seawater to invite introspection, for once they had landed at Leghorn he would be looking for the first vessel home.

He had, quite naturally, looked for HMS *Brilliant*, likely to be somewhere out there on the vast expanse of sea, but had gained no sight of the ship into which he had been originally pressed. It had been a long journey from Sheerness, full of incident: of initially seeking to avoid those with whom he had been taken up, only to become close to many of them; of being pressed not once but twice; of surviving being wrecked on a Breton shore; being raised more by malice than favour to the rank of midshipman, then, due to good fortune and the advice of better men, to success in battle and his present rank, that a gift from King George himself that ignored the requirement that a naval lieutenant must not only have six years sea time, but should face an examination by a panel of senior captains.

None of it would have come about if he had not ducked into the Pelican to avoid a pursuit determined to put him in prison: one sojourn in the Fleet as a youth, sent there with his father by a vengeful government seeking to shut up a radical voice, was enough to make anyone desperate to avoid repetition. Of course, not even that inadvertent slipping into the Thameside tavern would have occurred if he had not come back from Paris in the hope of getting lifted the warrant for sedition, outstanding against both him and his father, far from well and still in the French capital.

'A penny for your thoughts.'

Pearce turned just in time to see Emily Barclay, in her hooded cloak, stagger, taken off guard by a suddenly much sharper tilt of the deck. Instinctively he held out a hand to stop her falling over, catching her wrist and pulling her towards him, only to find that she put out an equally determined hand, firm on his chest, to stop that resulting in more bodily contact.

'Always give one hand for the boat, Mrs Barclay, I thought you would know that by now.'

It took no effort to get her wrist out of his hand, Pearce was not seeking to keep hold of it, and she did that which she should have done before, stretched out to secure herself with a grip on the hammock netting.

'Thank you, Lieutenant Pearce, I fear I spent enough time ashore to forget.' Aware that he was staring at her she looked quickly over the side. 'It is all so grey, not what they tell us about the wine-dark sea.'

'There are spots of brightness even in such a dull aspect as this.'

'Do you know Homer?' she asked, avoiding what was clearly a compliment.

'I do, both the *Iliad* and the *Odyssey* and I have struggled to think what kind of wine the ancients drank that turned it the colour of seawater, whatever the state of the sunlight. I cannot countenance blue wine any more than grey.'

'I think, sir, it was a poetic allusion.'

'There are moments when poetry cannot do other than come to mind, for instance the presence of a beautiful woman must have inspired Homer to write of Helen.'

Her voice took on a sharper note and she looked into his smiling face. 'Please, Lieutenant, can we put aside this gallantry?'

'I shall if you will stop calling me Lieutenant.'

'You are not, I hope, suggesting I use your given name?'.

'You do for Heinrich Lutyens.'

'With whom I have shared experiences that...' Emily Barclay stopped then, the words she was about to say too close to those she had used with her husband.

'Perhaps, given that I have no duties and yours will ease as the wounded recover, we might get to know each other better. I have an impression that such a thing would not displease you.'

'I must go below,' she insisted, beginning to turn away, an act stopped by Pearce taking hold of her wrist again.

'No. I have spoken too openly and I promise I will not cause you any more embarrassment.'

'Why Lieutenant,' Emily lied, seeking to look innocent, 'I have no idea what you mean.'

Pearce grinned: she looked prettier than ever when she was dissimulating. 'You asked what I was thinking about?'

'You were, you must admit, in a brown study.'

'I was thinking of the first time I saw you and how I got to be there.' Seeing he had upset her again, he spoke quickly. 'And since you are wearing the same hooded cloak you were wearing that day, it had brought back to mind even more unpleasant memories.'

'My cloak?'

'No, not that, but the circumstances in which it was observed. If you recall, your husband struck me a blow with his fist.'

Emily could remember that blow just as easily as John Pearce and she could also recall that she was the cause of it, or rather the fact that he had stared at her as he was brought aboard the ship and she had matched the look. 'I am sorry he did that.'

'Do not apologise for him.'

'I didn't.'

Both had spoken too abruptly and it rendered them silent, yet both had in mind the same image, albeit from different perspectives: he, in seeing a strikingly beautiful woman where it was least expected, acting out of habit, not sense, to make sure he had marked her out; she, observing the line of bedraggled pressed men, poor of appearance in the main – then he appeared, so obviously different in look and bearing, albeit he was followed by a giant she now knew to be the Irishman O'Hagan.

'In truth, you caught me when I was recalling what had brought me back from Paris.'

'Which was?' Emily asked, although she had a very good idea: her husband, in the first days of Pearce's enforced service aboard HMS *Brilliant,* had intercepted a letter which he had sought to send to a famous radical politician in an attempt to gain his freedom. That, even coded and in French, had mentioned Paris and a sick parent and she, better at the language than her husband, had been reluctantly persuaded to translate it.

'My father's illness.'

'What were you doing in Paris?'

'Avoiding prison.' That brought her head round to look at him directly. 'My father and I fled to Paris to avoid a writ for sedition issued in the name of King George, a King's Bench Warrant against what he had written about the exploitation of the people by the monarchy and the government.'

'Your father was a Leveller?' she asked, staring out to sea again.

Pearce smiled, thinking that given her probable upbringing such a notion would be anathema. 'He would have been proud to have been called that. Folk named him the Edinburgh Ranter and those who disliked his words and his works blackened him, but a kinder soul you have never met.'

Now she had to look once more at Pearce: the way his voice had softened with remembered affection made it inevitable.

'And your mother?'

'Died bearing me. I was brought up by my father, and in a way that has made me feel different to other men.'

'Hardly surprising given what you say of his opinions.'

That being delivered with some pique, Pearce was tempted to rebuke her, to demand how she, no doubt the product of a comfortable upbringing, with food always on the table, could possibly comprehend what life was like for the majority of her fellow Britons; but that would be to drive her away, so he stuck to reminiscing.

'I did not mean that. My father was a man who saw the whole of his country as his home and everyone in it as his brother. As soon as I was weaned he took me on his travels, the length and breadth of the whole nation. I saw more in a month than most of my fellow countrymen will see in their lifetime, and not just places, but people from the lowest to the highest.'

'Highest? In the company of a radical?'

'Not every wealthy man sees disputing with a radical thinker as a crime. I have had many a happy time in great houses, and if we were invited to stay for long enough, I even went to school, though that was generally less pleasant. But enough of me, tell me about you.'

'There is nothing to tell that would match that which you seem to have enjoyed.'

'Why did you marry your husband?'

He should not have said it and he knew that, but he could not help himself. From the first time he had realised that Ralph Barclay and she were wed he had wondered at such an unlikely connection, a curiosity

77

only reinforced as he had come to see his character and the way she opposed him: he was a callous man; she was a humane woman.

'That, Lieutenant,' she snapped as, one hand firmly on the netting, she turned to leave, a signal gun sounding as if to mark the movement, 'is none of your business.'

'All hands to wear ship.'

Pearce knew that where he was standing he would be in the way as the sails were loosed and reset, but rather than follow Emily Barclay towards the quarterdeck he made his way forward, cursing himself and ignoring the water that, blasting over the bowsprit, covered him and soaked his legs.

Captain Sidey had notified all who came aboard that his birthday was imminent and he clearly had a desire they should celebrate it. He had formed a choir aboard *Hinslip*, and given they were approaching the festive season, he was intent on their practising for the forthcoming Nativity as well as celebrating his name day; if he made an error it was inviting his passengers to join in, or at least one of them. The weather had moderated somewhat, the sky clearing as the wind swung away from the westerly towards the north, turning colder, so with the ship running steady, the seasonal songs were sung under what was slowly turning from bright blue into a starlit sky, loud enough to be heard by those ships sailing close enough in company. Sidey had a stentorian voice and was a hearty chorister, and it was soon apparent, given the quality of the rendition, that he had schooled his men, for they sang without books, knowing the words.

'Heathen songs to my ears, Charlie,' Michael whispered, 'but there's no doubting the skill.'

Unlike Pearce, stood by the binnacle, book in hand, trying to sing along with the crew, the Pelicans had avoided the warbling, thankfully in the eyes of most of those they were messing with given they would have upset the harmony. Heinrich Lutyens was the problem: he seemed to be managing that without assistance, his high reedy voice was rarely in proper tune, leading Emily Barclay, standing by his side and singing sweetly, to occasionally and quite visibly wince.

'I used to look forward to Yuletide,' young Rufus said, in an equally soft tone. 'There was always a fair in Litchfield and folk were generous to us youngsters.' Then he shivered, it being far from warm. 'Not sure I'm doin' that now, sat here.'

'It was a time for profit to me, lads, shamed as I am to admit it. This week in London it were full of visitors come for the season, easy marks most of 'em and with bulging purses to boot.'

That got Charlie Taverner a look from Michael. 'Holy Mary, Mother of God, Charlie, do you know what shame is, to be robbing folk at a holy time?'

'You shamed yourself enough,' Charlie hissed back, 'holy time or nay, but you were too drunk to ever recall it.'

'You were, Michael,' Rufus said, more in sorrow. 'Blind drunk.'

'Seems a long time since I was in that state.'

'Always ended with your wanting to fight some poor soul,' Charlie complained. 'With those damn great fists of yours.'

'Did I ever get round to you?'

'Never, mate, I was too nippy on my pins and you was too drunk.'

'So I tried.'

'You did.'

'Now, would that be over your touching up sweet Rosie?'

'I never did.'

'Yes you did, Charlie,' Rufus insisted, which got him a hard look for his honesty.

'Can't say I miss the Pelican much,' Michael said. 'Her excepted.'

'Belay that noise, you lot,' one of the sailors muttered. 'We's trying to sing.'

It was Charlie who responded; he hated to be checked even if the fellow doing it was in the right. 'You sound like a bunch of crows to me, mate.'

'From what I hear of you, mate, rooks is more your style.'

Charlie made to move forward, an act arrested with ease by Michael O'Hagan.

'Damn cheek.'

'There ain't none of us saints, Charlie,' Michael said.

'No, Michael, or we would not have been stuck in the Liberties, wondering where the next fill of ale was coming from.'

As the singing soared, the trio fell silent, each still thinking of that. The Pelican had not been a place of much joy to the likes of Charlie and Rufus or their mates, Abel Scrivens, now dead, and Ben Walker, captured by Barbary pirates and, as Pearce had discovered in Tunis, a slave of the Mussulmans. The quartet had eked out a precarious existence on the Thames riverbank, not too bad in summertime and damned near too deadly for the cold and starvation in winter, often reduced to hot bedding with others to just have a place to lay their head and never sure where the next meal was coming from.

They were bound to the place by their past, each one subject of some warrant for crimes committed, locked in the Liberties of the Savoy where the writ of the tipstaffs did not run, free to roam only on the Sabbath. London and the teeming Strand was yards away at times, but they dare not step into that great thoroughfare or beyond for fear of being collared by the law on a weekday, Charlie least of all, he being a sharp who had worked nearby Covent Garden.

Michael was one to come and go from the Pelican as he pleased – he was a free man – his reasons for being there more to do with the aforementioned Rosie than anything other. An apple-cheeked serving wench of ample proportions, she had been Michael's squeeze, due to his always having coin in his purse and a manner of emptying it often, given that, as a man who could seriously wield a shovel, there was always more to be earned in a city forever expanding.

Charlie had hated him for his easy spending, but more for Rosie, on whom he had designs, thinking that he being a handsome cove, and he was that, was more appealing than the Irishman's copper and silver. Rosie would have none of it: Michael O'Hagan paid for her favours and if Charlie wanted to share them, to which she was not averse, then he must shell out for them likewise.

'I dreamt about us being pressed again last night,' said Rufus, whose only crime was to have run from a bonded apprenticeship in the leather trade. 'Woke up a'trembling.'

'It would be Irish snores that would wake you, Rufus,' Charlie whispered, 'and they are loud enough to shiver the timbers.'

Michael grinned at that: he was proud of his snoring, which was loud enough to drown out all the others doing likewise, each, with one watch on deck, in their twenty-eight inches of hammock space.

'I don't recall that night, as you know,' he said.

'You were so drunk you tried to belt Pearce when he told you to run,' Charlie cackled, but that did not last, given it was not an occasion to remember fondly. 'We should have spotted them tars eyeing the place.'

'And young Martin.'

The boy they were speaking of, Martin Dent, a growing lad now and a skilful topman on HMS *Brilliant*, had been a drummer boy then, in a red coat that stood out a mile even in that smoky, crowded place.

'We was too busy dunning Pearce for ale,' said Rufus.

'I don't recall you getting him to shell out for drink,' Charlie snapped, adding a finger gesture to one of the captain's choir. 'That were me, mate.'

'You got a silver tongue, Charlie, an' no error.'

'But now't but air in his breeches,' Michael scoffed.

'When I'm dreaming,' Rufus insisted, 'I sees them tars burstin' in with clubs the size of spars, with us runnin' all ways to no purpose.'

Not only had Barclay's men rushed the tavern, they were outside the doors front and back, waiting to catch hold of anyone trying to run. All three of them, Abel Scrivens and Ben Walker too, had, with John Pearce and more than a dozen others, found themselves bruised and battered, trussed like chickens before being thrown into the boats and carried down the Thames to Sheerness.

The singing of a hymn had reached a crescendo, the voices rising to a swelling sound that filled the gathering gloom, then stopping abruptly, to leave Captain Sidey beaming with pleasure, that is until he looked sideways to the surgeon.

In a cut-down part of Sidey's cabin, Ralph Barclay swung in his cot, aware that he was well enough now to have joined in the choral observance of Sidey's birthday and just as aware of why he had declined. Every attempt he had made in the last few days to catch hold of his wife and ask her what she meant by saying she had no idea of where she belonged had been thwarted by her insistence that she carry out her nursing duties; she was avoiding him, of course, but there was little he could do about it in such a crowded ship without making obvious to all and sundry the depth of their rift.

The decks below were lined with cots full of the seriously wounded, others were fit enough to use hammocks like the crew. Where he was accommodated was not spacious, and in cutting off part of his own cabin for a post captain – Sidey was an elderly lieutenant, he being a man without the interest or patronage necessary to see him elevated in rank – that too was much constrained. No one, it seemed, had seen anything untoward in Emily taking quarters elsewhere, in a screened-off cabin near that of Lutyens; they saw her as a nurse, not his wife, and, besides, he was an invalid.

When it came to nursing, the one man he had remaining from his ship, the ruffian Devenow, was a better attendant: it was he who had helped Ralph Barclay take the air the day after they weighed from Toulon, he who had caught hold of his collar when, reaching out a hand to steady himself against the roll of the ship, he had stuck out a stump and nearly fallen to his knees. How had he managed to forget his missing arm when the pain was a constant, occasionally relieved with a dose of laudanum?

How would being a one-winged bird affect his career? That he did not know, though there were plenty of precedents of officers having suffered amputations going on to serve their full term. He knew he must see Admiral Hotham, the only senior patron he could rely on, for the one constant in the King's Navy, just as it was in normal life, was the need for the application of interest, the ability to call upon the intercession of a powerful patron to help secure advancement.

'How you farin', your honour?'

Devenow, a big man with a brutish face, had entered without knocking, and Ralph Barclay was about to damn him for insolence only to check himself: he needed this fellow to care for him so there was no sense in making him sullen.

'I am in pain. Perhaps Mr Lutyens will spare me a little more tincture.'

'I'll see to it right off, your honour.'

'Did you take part in the singing, Devenow?'

'Me, your honour, sing?' the sailor replied, with a smile that showed the gaps in his teeth. 'I only sing when I is full of grog, as you know. I'll see to that laudanum.'

How did I end up being cared for by the likes of him? Ralph Barclay thought, as the door closed, showing how little he understood Devenow, a man he had caused to be seized up for a flogging more than once.

A fellow who hoarded his grog until he had enough to get insensibly drunk, and a bully to boot who stole the grog off his messmates, or caused them to hand it over without protest at the implied threat of a beating, he inevitably sought to use his fists on those sent to restrain him. Yet he held no grudge against his captain: in a mind not much given to notions of fairness, he saw it as Ralph Barclay's right to regularly flog, in the same way as he saw it as his right to get habitually and stupidly inebriated.

Needless to say, in the copious notes Heinrich Lutyens had made regarding the odd habits of the lower-deck ratings, Devenow and his ilk, for he was not alone, occupied several pages.

CHAPTER SIX

Ralph Barclay's desire not to attend Captain Sidey's feast was thwarted by the need to use the whole of the great cabin to accommodate his guests: the temporary bulkheads erected to form the convalescent cabin had to be struck down so that all the leaves of the dining table could be put in place. Though not by any means a wealthy man, Sidey was determined on a good spread, raiding those stores he had acquired in Italy, for his duties prior to this one had taken him back and forth to Genoa. This allowed him to conjure up a substantial, if plain, meal and, of course, from that source the cheeses were excellent, while the wine was plentiful and of a better quality than the usual blackstrap served on a daily basis.

There was no question but that Emily Barclay had to sit next to her husband: he required assistance to cut his meat, the 'Roast Beef of Old England' as it was termed, even if it was part of an Italian cow. As accompaniment there was a brace of chickens from the coop on the deck and part of an elderly sheep that provided mutton to feed them, the rest, in truth nearly the whole carcase, being given as a birthday treat for the ship's crew.

At the table, sat as far away as possible from the one-armed man, was John Pearce, given his greatest desire was to put a knife into Ralph Barclay, not into the overcooked fowl on his pewter plate. He had challenged the man to a duel once; if the law did not incarcerate him for his perjury he would do so again. That thought, surfacing as often as it did, was inclined to tempt him to glare, obliging him to take refuge in his goblet of wine.

Lutyens was present, as was Lieutenant Driffield, who had scarce spoke a word to Pearce since coming aboard: their sole conversation had been to confirm that the orders the marine had been given had been carried out, that followed by the impression that the fellow was avoiding him, which Pearce assumed was because he was still smarting about surrendering the cannon to the enemy.

Also attending were two army officers, their wounds of the kind to allow them to be present, as was HMS *Hinslip*'s premier, Mr Ault, a very new naval lieutenant who had a serious problem with his blush: no words of any kind could be addressed to him on any subject without his cheeks going a deep red, and that was also the case if Emily Barclay, the only lady present, caught his eye, not hard given he was totally smitten and looked at her from under his long, soft eyelashes with the mistaken impression that no one noticed. Sidey, using to the full his right as host to dominate the conversation, was regaling them with his previous service, naming captain after captain who had thought him an excellent subordinate.

'As for fame, sirs, I served with Captain Arthur Philips and a finer seaman there never was, this being prior to his voyage to New South Wales, of course.'

'A hellish journey, according to the accounts of those who returned,' said Lutyens. 'You do not see, Captain Sidey, anything to gainsay the sending of convicts to such a far-off location.'

'Got to send them somewhere, Mr Lutyens. After we lost the Americas it was that or hang 'em.'

'Which you are not in favour of?' asked one of the army officers, the question slightly garbled by his wounded jaw. 'Or so I sense by your tone.'

'Ain't me, sir, but the juries. They will not convict a felon if they fear he or she faces the rope, so the judges are reluctant to place on the black cap, and as for nippers...'

'Would you hang a child, captain,' asked Pearce, 'for the theft of a loaf of bread when they are starving?'

'Starving, sir?' Sidey demanded, forking a large gobbet of greasy mutton into his mouth. 'They all claim they are starving, Mr Pearce, but how is we to know when and where it is the truth?'

'Generally a look at the ribs provides a good indication,' Pearce replied, pointing to those on the beef, visible where it had been carved. 'If it has the appearance of those on your table, then it is proof enough.'

Having been in prison, John Pearce had seen the kind of undeserving folk that ended up there, just as he had seen the kind of dregs the human race could well do without, the sort that would steal your eyes given half a chance, then come back for the holes. He and his father had been obliged to take turns at sleeping in their original cell, a space so crowded with humanity there was scarce room to lie down, the straw on the floor full of vermin as well as the filth that overflowed from the communal bucket. Thankfully their stay had been brief: Adam Pearce's friends, fellow radicals, had got together the funds to procure them a private cell and food to eat, before raising a bond for their release.

He had been brought up by a singular man, a peripatetic widower maybe, but a caring parent and, as he had told Emily Barclay, they were rarely still as Adam Pearce journeyed all over the country preaching his solutions to the evils of the existing system of governance, one in which the rich had too much and the poor too little. John Pearce had been taught to wonder how men and woman of means could walk or ride by people dying in the gutters, without asking themselves if their Christianity obliged them to do something about it.

That had been one of his father's favourite stump

topics, the hypocrisy of religion: Adam Pearce earned his soubriquet of the Edinburgh Ranter on those occasions, as he castigated his audience, churchgoers all, for their indifference to the suffering of others, this while his son, carrying round the hat to collect the funds needed for food and board, kept a weather eye on those who would rob him if they could, too often the offspring of the very people Adam Pearce was demanding his listeners support.

Life had improved in '89 when the French Revolution sent radical British hearts soaring, more, it turned out, once the dust had settled and the Revolution revealed its true colours, from the fall of the Bourbons than any love of liberty. That bright dawn, as the poet Wordsworth had called it, brought prosperity to Adam Pearce and a degree of fame of the kind he had not previously enjoyed. His opinions had been sought by men of stature, his written pamphlets eagerly purchased and read by folk who thought they would welcome change making life comfortable if not outright wealthy; then a frightened government had reacted a second time to his blasts against privilege, obliging both Adam and his son to flee to France.

'I see you have a soft heart, Lieutenant,' said Ault, his cheeks turning bright scarlet as he broke the train of Pearce's thoughts.

'Let me say that I would prefer that the needy be taken to somewhere they might prosper than hung up on a gibbet.'

'From what Captain Phillips has written to me they will not prosper in New South Wales, sir. By all accounts the place is not fertile.'

'There are parts of it which are, Captain Sidey, for I too, or rather my father, had news of the colony, but they are all in the hands of those who supervise the convicts, not of the convicts themselves.'

'Do tell them who your father is, Pearce,' growled Barclay, with a face that matched his tone.

Hitherto silent, Ralph Barclay was suffering from a combination of laudanum and good Italian wine, as well as his proximity to his wife; thus, in his manner and his form of address, he breeched the convention in a naval setting that officers were polite to each other at all times, regardless of personal feelings, for the very simple reason that on voyages that could last for six months or more, not to do so would lead to mayhem and very likely murder.

Pearce's tone was equally cold. 'You make it sound, sir, as if I should be ashamed of the connection.'

'I would if it were me.'

'But you are not me, Captain Barclay—'

'Of course not,' Emily Barclay cut in, a rather forced smile on her face. 'I am sure you are as proud of your parentage as is my husband.'

'A toast,' called Sidey, lifting his goblet high. 'To our dear mothers and fathers.'

That was not an injunction anyone could gainsay and it was a shrewd ploy by a man who plainly knew when an argument might brew up to ruin any chance of conviviality. Collectively everyone murmured the words and drank deep. It was young Ault, too stupid or inexperienced to see what his superior had stopped, who asked the question.

'So, Mr Pearce, is your father someone famous?'

'Infamous, more like,' snapped Barclay.

'Does your wound pain you much?' said Sidey quickly, seeking an abrupt change of subject, while glaring at his premier. 'I have often wondered at how one would feel after an amputation.'

'I have observed, Captain Sidey,' said Emily, speaking before her husband could respond, 'that not only does it give great pain but the memory clouds the loss. You will observe, if your manners allow you the curiosity, that my husband constantly reaches for his knife as well as his fork only to be cruelly reminded that he cannot simultaneously lift both.'

'I am sure, Mrs Barclay, that with you to care for him, your husband has much to comfort him and a striking compensation for his loss.'

Well intentioned, it was precisely the wrong thing to say, which Captain Sidey realised as he saw the thunderous look which crossed Ralph Barclay's face. Yet his fears that an outburst of foul temper was imminent were groundless: there was no way this particular guest was going to air his marital difficulties in public. Indeed, had Sidey been present more often at Toulon, and mixed with his fellow captains, he would have known to say nothing: the fact that Emily Barclay had moved from her husband's cabin to the hospital had been a subject of gossip, just as those who had seen them together in public, for instance at a ball they both attended when it looked as if the allies could hold the port, had observed that it was a less than amicable relationship.

The problem for Sidey and his dinner was that Ralph Barclay had to take his rising anger out on someone, and that had to be John Pearce, the last person to respect his rank or his opinions, and to do so he chose to assuage Mr Ault's curiosity.

'His father, young man, is a certain Adam Pearce, who some would name as traitor to his king and country.'

It was instructive to look at the faces around the table: to see who knew the name and who, like Driffield, were ignorant; not that such an obvious lack of knowledge prevented him from then looking aggrieved. If a post captain implied something was deplorable, a lowly marine lieutenant would see it as advantageous to take his part.

'Was, Captain Barclay,' Pearce said, in a calm voice. 'My father is dead, and as for his loyalty, it was to his fellow humans, and in that he never wavered.'

The whole table fell silent, no one looking in Pearce's direction except Ralph Barclay; it was hard to know who was blushing most, the young premier, or his wife, now looking at her hands, but eventually it was Lutyens who spoke.

'My father is the pastor of the Lutheran Church in London.'

'And very well connected, I believe,' exclaimed Emily, quickly.

'Oh yes, Queen Caroline often comes there to worship and brings both the king and the princes to do likewise. She does like her masses said and sung in German.'

'You have been to court yourself, Mr Lutyens?' asked the jaw-damaged army officer.

'I have.'

'Then, sir, you must describe it to us, for it is not a privilege given to many.'

That intervention had everyone sitting forward and saved the dinner, as the conversation moved around Lutyens's descriptions of Windsor and Buckingham House, as he fielded questions about protocol, the questionable behaviour of the various princes, King George's health after his bout of madness many years previously; would the Prince of Wales gain the Regency he so badly desired, bringing his Whig friends into power and deposing William Pitt? The only two people who did not take part were John Pearce and Ralph Barclay.

Below decks things had started out jolly enough: Captain Sidey had issued an extra tot of rum to each man and the fresh mutton was a welcome change to the unrelieved diet of salted pork and beef, leavened with slush and peas. But it soon emerged there were tensions, not amongst the crew but between the Pelicans and Sam Devenow, this emerging as the bruiser, with his scarred face and beetle brow, began to show signs of being drunk. From laughter and good cheer, the atmosphere slowly turned guarded.

As usual he had been hoarding his grog and, unbeknown to the rest of the crew, for those affected did not want to admit it, he had been up to his old tricks in the article of persuasion, which amounted to a close-up sight of his great fist and a request that the victim should forgo his ration and hand it over, something he had once tried on John Pearce. As the rum began to take hold, Devenow's eye fixed on Michael O'Hagan, a man he had fought and lost to in a bare-knuckle bout; typically, he had since then seen some hidden advantage the Irishman had enjoyed, in short his defeat had been a fluke.

'You can never trust a Paddy, shipmates, for he allas do something underhand.'

Though not quite shouted, Devenow made his claim in a carrying voice, taking no notice of the fact that there were several Irishmen in the *Hinslip*'s crew. The men who sat at his mess table adopted various ploys to avoid complicity in the statement, either looking hard at the table or, if they were really fearful, fixing the speaker with a blank and non-committal look they hoped would pass for agreement.

'It's in their blood, see, and if they are papists it is worse, for they are stupid too.'

'Sure, it's a pity,' Michael said, 'that jaw of his ever got mending.'

The mess tables, at which they sat, on the gloomy

main deck, were not so far apart, the result being that, even over a quiet babble of conversation, the remark was overheard.

'They say they has luck, mind,' Devenow responded. 'But I reckon they cheat.'

Michael was about to respond, hands on the table ready to raise himself, when another voice spoke, one of the ship's crew, an older fellow and no Paddy. 'We have a way with trouble aboard this barky, don't we mates, an' I ain't never met the man that will keep his feet on the deck one dark night when half the crew are intent on chucking him into the briny.'

That was a warning even Devenow was not daft enough to ignore: he was being told to hold his tongue or face being chucked overboard, the fate of many a bully that had gone too far aboard ship.

'An' I would say, when it comes to grog, a man should be satisfied with his ration.'

The deck was crowded, but there was no doubt who was isolated.

'Well said, that man,' called Michael.

That was not the only dispute that took place on HMS *Hinslip* that day. Once the dinner was complete and the cabins put back in place, Ralph Barclay had a chance to berate his wife.

'You took his part, madam, against me, your own husband. How am I to hold my head up in such a circumstance?'

The voice was slurred due to that combination of liquid opium and wine, and his jaw seemed uncommonly slack as he fixed his wife with a look best described as hangdog.

'I did not, husband, I merely tried to prevent you from making a fool of yourself.'

'A fool, damn you?'

'Moderate your language, sir,' Emily hissed, 'as well as the sound of your voice. There is but a thin wooden bulkhead between us and Captain Sidey's cabin.'

'Moderate, you say. Am I to be that when you do nothing but traduce me?'

'You are allowing your imagination to run as fast as your tongue.'

It was with bleary eyes that Ralph Barclay gazed at his young wife, once so obedient, once so in awe of him that she would scarce raise her voice, wondering where it had all gone wrong.

'You need rest, Captain Barclay,' Emily insisted. 'You have overtired yourself.'

'Damn it, if I only had two arms I'd make that swine pay for the way he insulted me.'

'Of course you would,' Emily replied, easing off, with great gentility, his heavy uniform coat, before helping him get into his cot so that he did not trouble his wound. This was no time to remind him that John Pearce had challenged him once already to a duel, and he had used the excuse of his superior rank and a forbidding royal ordinance to avoid it.

'You must stand by my side, Mrs Barclay,' he said softly but vehemently, 'It is nothing but your duty. Love, honour and obey, madam, that is the vow you took.'

'Rest now.'

Ralph Barclay closed his eyes; he was indeed weary and with his wife watching he quickly fell into a slumber, his face relaxing as he did so, making him look less the stern naval captain and more like a benign uncle. Gazing at him, Emily wondered at what would become of them, for she knew that the way she had behaved in Toulon was challenging in the extreme to the social order of which she was a part. The wound might take him home, her also, and she knew that to do the same in England would damn her in the eyes of everyone in polite society, and that probably would include her own parents. Her now sleeping husband was right about those marriage vows she had taken: they were held to be sacrosanct and to be obeyed.

'Mr Pearce, I am sorry to call you onto the deck to have this conversation, but I wish it to be a discreet one.'

It was already dark, so Captain Sidey's square and ruddy face, in the light from the binnacle, had an ethereal quality. John Pearce had a very good idea what was coming and he was not sure how to react.

'As you know, Captain Barclay holds post rank,' Sidey said. 'He is, in short, my superior officer.'

'And mine,' Pearce responded, just to add to his thinking time.

'Of course, as my superior, I am in no position to check him.'

'I would not say that, Captain Sidey. If a man displays a lack of manners at the dinner table I think any other guest is well within their rights to haul him up with a round turn. Rank bestows many privileges, the freedom to insult is not one of them.'

Even in the faint glowing light, Pearce could see the look of disbelief on the captain's face: he was employed in a service where rank gave his superiors the right to be as rude as they liked, one they frequently exercised.

'Perhaps it would help, sir, if I afforded you a little history.'

The affirmative reply lacked conviction: Sidey did not want to be drawn into what smacked of complicity, yet having broached the matter he could hardly refuse this man an explanation. He listened, chin on chest, as Pearce told him the background to his dispute with Ralph Barclay, but not about the case he intended to bring against him: he did not trust him not to speak of it.

'So you see, Captain Sidey, my position, the method of my recruitment, plus my lack of a desire to advance myself in this profession, gives me the grounds to speak as I find, one I have exercised on men of higher station than our wounded post captain.'

'Surely you must make allowance for his wound?'

'You, sir, do not know him and so ascribe his manners to his affliction. I can assure you I do know him and the loss of his arm and the consequent pain have nothing to do with his behaviour. That is how he is.'

'Then think of my position, sir,' Sidey insisted, moving his head further into the light to make his point. His voice had in it a hint of desperation; elderly he might be, but there was still a flicker of ambition in the man, the hope common to all naval officers that by some stroke of good fortune or chance meeting with someone of influence, he might make that great leap from his present rank to the post captain's list.

'The best way to avoid compromising that, sir, is never to have us both at the same board again.' Sidey was relieved, he could see that: Pearce was giving him a way out, but there was a sting in the tail. 'Mind you, sir, I would be most put out if I discovered that I was the only one whose attention this problem was drawn to. I fully expect you to ask Captain Barclay to mind his conduct. After all, we are bound to meet in places other than your cabin: on this deck, for instance.'

'I had intended to speak with him, of course,' Sidey said.

'Good,' Pearce snapped, for he did not believe him. 'I daresay when we are both taking the air on deck, the fact that you have done so will be plain for all to see.'

'We will be in Leghorn soon,' Sidey said, with an air that told Pearce he would be glad to see the back of both of them.

CHAPTER SEVEN

The Tuscan port of Livorno had been a base for English sailors for half a century. Why it had been translated into being called Leghorn by those same mariners was lost in the mists of time; John Pearce asked but received no answer that satisfied his curiosity. Built on marshy ground the ancient port was a mass of canals, to rival Venice, running around the fortified walls of the city, the harbour itself dominated by an old red-stone fortress falling into disrepair, with the main defensive bastion long since moved inland, making it less vulnerable to cannon fire from seaborne attackers.

Lord Hood had chosen it as the place to land his refugees simply because it was an Austrian fief: the Grand Duke of Tuscany was the brother of the present Holy Roman Emperor. It was one of the three main trading ports of Italy along with Genoa and Naples, and had, for decades, in times of war, been used as a base for British privateers, ships and crews granted letters of marque from the Crown to prey on the trading vessels of the enemy.

Naturally, at this time there was a strong, if less than upright colony of fellow countrymen waiting to greet the British elements of the arriving armada, not with much joy since, when it came to taking prizes, the two elements of British sea power, being in direct competition, loathed each other. The privateers' captains also knew the risks they ran by having so many king's ships and men close by, even if their crews had protections that saved them from being pressed: those that did not see it as prudent to get quickly to sea would stay out of harm's way in their own part of the port.

There was nothing elegant about the way the combined fleets entered the anchorage: the wind was foul and the swell heavy enough to make even anchoring the larger vessels a trial, and it was certainly too strong to allow the capital ships, stuffed with so many souls that scarce an inch of planking was free from bodies, to warp themselves into the quays. Added to that there was an element of continued alarm.

Unbeknown to those aboard HMS *Hinslip*, which, bearing wounded, was allowed to tie up to the harbour wall – albeit with a line of marines under the command of Lieutenant Driffield to ensure no desertions – a rumour had circulated that the port was already short of food, so non-military personal would be refused permission to land. That turned out to be false, leaving as a mystery how such a story had been concocted and, even more puzzling, the notion of how it had swept through a fleet at sea.

The scenes on the quays, as boats plied back and forth with dishevelled refugees, were reminiscent of Toulon, if in reverse, as the exiles taken off by the allied fleet were landed. Many came from British warships, given that, once the soldiers and sailors Hood commanded had been taken aboard, he had opened his vessels to those fleeing the Revolution. Some kissed the stones of the harbour upon landing, never having felt safe afloat, only gaining any sense of security on land. Other frantic souls rushed around asking questions of the newly disembarked or searching every arriving boat for the face of a loved one, a husband, wife or child.

Those who had lost relatives had also lost most of their possessions and were thrown upon the mercy of the young grand duke. Fortunately for them, he was, like his father before him, an enlightened ruler and a good Christian: food was made available and his officials were on hand to seek suitable accommodation for those in distress. Added to that, Livorno had a good, modern hospital, so that the more seriously wounded could be brought ashore to beds, better for recovery given they would not be subject to the vagaries of vessels riding at anchor on a disturbed winter sea.

'Lieutenant Pearce, is it not?'

Supervising the loading of the less seriously wounded

men onto a sprung cart, which was acting as an ambulance – the more serious cases had gone by boat using the extensive Livorno canals – John Pearce turned at the sound of the high-pitched voice, to find himself looking down at the smiling face and diminutive frame of Captain Horatio Nelson; being very aware of the major difference in height, he took a step backwards before replying, touching his hat to a man he respected.

'Good to see you, sir.'

'Not, I think, in these circumstances, Mr Pearce,' Nelson replied with a pained expression as he looked around him. 'We are surrounded by tragedy.'

'They are alive, sir, and there is no certainty they would still be so if they had stayed in Toulon.'

'Do you think so, Mr Pearce? It is hard to believe the French Jacobins are as barbaric as they say.'

'They are just that, Captain Nelson, believe me.'

Nelson nodded: he had been gifted a brief outline of the past of the man with whom he was conversing and knew that when it came to knowledge in that quarter he could not gainsay a fellow who had actually witnessed their behaviour at first hand.

'I have just encountered the Comte de Grasse, poor fellow. He got his frigate out of Toulon but at the price of not knowing what has become of his wife and small children. To think that the grandson of one of France's greatest admirals could be so distressed.' Looking along the teeming quay once more, Nelson asked. 'Was it as bad as they say, Toulon?'

'I should think worse. What we saw from our boats was terrifying, so ashore it must have been like hell to be amongst it.'

'I have heard only garbled accounts.'

Pearce left the *Hinslip*'s crew and Driffield's marines to carry on with the loading while he informed Nelson of some of the things he had witnessed, noticing the pain his tale caused in a man who gave the impression of being too sensitive a soul for the occupation he followed. But then he recalled this pint-sized captain had a reputation for being an ardent fighter, always to the fore if a fight was expected – hard to believe, since looking at him, Pearce was left to wonder if he had the strength to lift a cutlass.

'The last time I saw you, Pearce, you were bound for Naples.'

'I was, sir.'

'And I asked you to convey my compliments to the ambassador, and my letters, of course.'

Pearce kept his face expressionless then: he had garnered at their last meeting, anchored off Tunis, the distinct impression that Nelson was more interested in the beautiful Lady Hamilton than her husband.

'They were delivered, sir, as you requested.'

'And Lady Hamilton, you found her well?'

'I had no opportunity to talk with her, sir. Sir William came out to meet us with a most urgent message for Lord Hood.' Seeing the crestfallen look, Pearce changed the subject. 'Your mission in Tunis, sir?'

'A farce,' Nelson barked, for the first time showing a trace of that fiery reputation. 'I am of the opinion that Britannia should negotiate, of course, but I am also of the view—'

'That a little gunnery concentrates the mind,' Pearce said, smiling as he interrupted him.

That humoured look did not anger Nelson; if anything it pleased him. 'You read my thinking most accurately, Mr Pearce.' Then looking past him to the *Hinslip*'s gangplank he added. 'This was not the ship in which you last sailed? You are no longer serving on HMS *Faron*?'

'No, sir, in fact I am, in truth, no longer serving anywhere.'

'We's ready to be off, your honour,' said Charlie Taverner, to Pearce's back, cutting off any response from the captain and careful, as were Rufus and Michael, to always address him properly when another officer was present. It was only if you looked into the eyes you could discern the twinkle that hinted at something less than outright respect.

Looking past him at the loaded cart, Pearce asked. 'What of Captain Barclay?'

'He wishes to travel alone, your honour,' Charlie replied, 'or with his wife, not wishing to share the transport with ordinary soldiers.'

Or any transport under my command, thought Pearce.

'Barclay?' asked Nelson. 'He is a casualty?'

'Lost an arm, sir. Left one, just above the elbow.'

'Poor fellow, is he still aboard?' The word 'obviously' formed, but sarcasm was inappropriate, so it was the word 'yes' that was said. 'Then I must visit with him.'

'His mood is somewhat – how should I put it? – truculent, sir.'

If Nelson wondered at the way Pearce said that, or the grin it produced on Charlie Taverner's face, he was not about to enquire. If he had he might have been told that in refusing to give his true name on being pressed into HMS *Brilliant*, 'Truculence' was the name under which John Pearce had been entered in the ship's muster book and it had been, since that day, a private joke between the Pelicans.

'Are you advising I should not call upon him, that his wound is too serious?'

'No, sir. I am saying, however, that his mood is likely to be standoffish.'

'I can live with that, Mr Pearce. A man has that right if he has suffered such an affliction.'

With that, Nelson, executing quick strides, was off up the gangplank. Pearce was watching him, shaking his head at the notion that anyone would call upon a man like Barclay, when Michael, having crept up behind him, whispered in is ear.

'John-boy, if you look along the quay you will see that devil Gherson.'

'Has he spotted us?'

'Sure, he's staring hard enough.'

Pearce turned slowly and nonchalantly, seeking out Gherson's face in what was a crowded vista, but the man was easy to spot, as much by his faux discreet manner as anything else. Then there was his absurdly handsome face, under that near-white hair and the very obvious glare of dislike. They had been boating down to Sheerness that night they were pressed when they first met the lying, toadying swine, if 'met' was the right word for a body in nothing but a long, flapping shirt coming off London Bridge, tossed over by human hands, Charlie reckoned. He landed right by the cutter as it was negotiating the strong currents created by the bridge pillars, to be hauled in by his collar, saving his life, if not pleasing him by the outcome.

'He's dressed in gentleman's garb, Michael, those clothes he is wearing are of fine quality.'

'Would be, John-boy, given Barclay took him on as his clerk.'

'Then he best watch his funds, for if Gherson is close to his strongbox they won't be his for long.'

'Why's he a'hoverin' round here?' asked Charlie, speaking out of the corner of his mouth.

'Maybe he still has business with Barclay.'

'Then it'll be bad business with that shite,' Michael spat.

'Whatever business it is, lads, it is none of ours. Our task is to get our wounded to the hospital.'

As soon as he showed a sign of moving, Driffield appeared and signalled to some of his marines to accompany the cart: with so many privateers' vessels in the port, the temptation to run was a strong one for tars, known to be a body of men given to going absent without any excuse.

Ralph Barclay did not have to be in a bad mood to be short with Horatio Nelson, given he despised the man. Standing before him, looking sympathetic, was a fellow post captain whom he saw as damn near an enemy, and certainly a rival. Where he had been obliged to press men to man his ship, Nelson, who arse-licked Hood, to Barclay's way of thinking, had been gifted a full complement of hands from the volunteers gathered at the Tower of London. Worse than that, the pint-sized poltroon, barely ahead of him on the captain's list, had been given command of HMS *Agamemnon*, a line of battleship of sixty-four guns, while he had been given the smallest frigate commensurate with his post rank.

Resentment came easily to Ralph Barclay: he begrudged the fact that Nelson was held in high regard by Lord Hood while he was not, resented that his previous patron, Admiral Sir George Rodney, had died and left him without a senior naval sponsor at a critical time, albeit he was now well in, he thought, with Admiral Hotham. He and *Brilliant* had been tied up to the quay at Toulon, like a damned guard ship, while Nelson went a'whoring all over the Western Mediterranean on special missions and no doubt got a chance to line his pockets by gathering in a few valuable prizes.

'You must tell me how you got your wound, Captain Barclay.'

The reply was very nearly a snapped 'Fighting the enemy while you were swanning around as Hood's bumboy.'

But his wife was present and, given he was between doses of laudanum, and thus in pain, he took part of his ire out on her, once he had given Nelson the bare bones of the event. A force had been assembled to attack one of the French batteries that was causing too much trouble, given it had an especially large cannon that could land its balls in the harbour. He was looking past Nelson to Emily when he spoke on, outlining with one hand where the nuisance lay and also the position of the redoubt in front of the one he commanded, which he had been exchanging fire with for weeks.

'The assault took my opponents in flank, drove them from their position and the troops moved on to the major target. My wife's nephew, Midshipman Burns, had brought up from HMS *Britannia* a party of tars to spike the abandoned French cannon once captured, but when it came time to do his duty he failed to carry out his orders.' Seeing that his wife was stung, for he had not told her of this, he added, 'And not, I am sad to say, for the first time. The boy is shy.'

'Shy?' Nelson asked, as if the notion that a midshipman might not do his duty was unbelievable.

'He is too young to carry such responsibility,' Emily protested, though she did wonder why she was defending a relative she now sought to avoid. Toby was her nephew, but what her husband was saying was no less than the truth. Then she realised what he was about: paying her back for the slights she had laid upon him by attacking her blood relative. That she would not let pass, and it was with a biting tone she continued.

'He was forward enough, husband, when it came to doing your bidding.'

That gave Ralph Barclay pause: he had coached Toby Burns to lie at his court martial, to take upon himself the blame for the fact that the crew from HMS *Brilliant* had pressed men who were not seamen by profession, as they should be, but had been in a part of London on the River Thames, the Liberties of the Savoy, where to press anyone was forbidden by ancient statute.

'He supported you, husband, when you demanded it of him. Perhaps if you trained him more assiduously for the duty you say he failed to carry out he might have done better.'

The look of confusion on Nelson's face was obvious: he was in the middle of a family spat with no way to politely leave without making the knowledge obvious. It was Barclay who saved him by continuing his tale, suddenly more willing to talk of that than whatever was the cause of the dispute with his wife. He also put his good hand to his stump and let a look of pain suffuse his face.

'I am tiring you, sir.'

'No, Captain Nelson, allow me to finish my tale.'

Knowing Emily was glaring at him he was in no position to further damn her nephew. 'I went forward to do the spiking, with the lad, who may have got lost on the way.'

'More likely, you must admit, Captain Barclay,' Nelson proposed with some feeling, turning to look at his fellow captain's wife with some appreciation. 'I am sure that any sprig of your tree, Mrs Barclay, would be a stout one indeed.'

Emily had to just nod at such idiocy, much as she wanted to do otherwise, given she was not fond of this little fellow either, seeing him as given to tittle-tattle of the kind that had got her into trouble in Sheerness. She had gone to an assembly dance the night her husband was out hunting for men and had taken pleasure, as she had all her life, in the dancing. This Captain Nelson had told her husband how much she had enjoyed it and, given he was not one to take pleasure in such pursuits himself and given to jealousy, had caused her no end of trouble.

Ralph Barclay was annoyed at being interrupted, and spoke tersely. 'Do you wish, sir, to hear this tale?'

'Forgive me,' Nelson responded, turning back, while cursing himself for so openly admiring the man's wife, a fault to which he knew he was prone, and not just here in this cabin.

'Well, we did as was required, then General O'Hara, who planned the assault, came up and, stupidly to my mind, went too far forward. Anyway, he was wounded—'

'I heard he was taken prisoner.'

That got Nelson another hard look: he had ordered Devenow, who was with him, to take the wounded general back to safety. The man had ignored him and saved his comatose captain instead, leaving O'Hara to be taken by the enemy.

'He was, but I took a musket ball from the French counterattack just as I exited the redoubt, which, we having set charges, was blown to perdition. I was saved from capture myself by one of my own ratings.'

'Who is to be commended, sir.'

'Of course,' Barclay replied, totally unaware he had signally failed to do anything of the sort. Suddenly he wanted shot of Nelson, so he said, 'You must forgive me, Captain, I am somewhat fatigued.'

'Of course, Captain Barclay,' Nelson replied. 'It only remains for me to wish you a speedy recovery and a return to service soon.'

The stump moved. 'This may hinder any employment, sir.'

'Nonsense, Captain Barclay, I am sure you will soon be in command of a ship once more. Mrs Barclay, I bid you good day.'

'You could not wait to shame me, could you?' Ralph Barclay said, as the sound of Nelson's heels faded.

'In that, sir,' Emily snapped, going out of the door, 'I cannot begin to compete with you.'

She ran straight into Cornelius Gherson, with a sheaf of papers under his arm, who gave her the kind of smile with which she had become familiar, one that told her she was an object of his unwanted attention, and not just that, desire.

'What do you want?'

'Ah, Mrs Barclay, we could perhaps stand for some time to outline that, but I fear I would keep your husband waiting.'

'I certainly have no yearning to delay you!'

The calculating look on the face was infuriating and she would have been even more upset if she had known the train of his thoughts. Cornelius Gherson saw himself, and in truth with some evidence, as an accomplished seducer. Was it not that very ability which had got him chucked off London Bridge by the thugs hired by an irate and cuckolded husband, who just so happened to also be his employer? To him, the likes of Emily Barclay presented a challenge, one he felt certain he had both the charm and the looks to overcome and, once he had achieved that, to make her his willing slave. That she had rebuffed him so absolutely turned attraction into deep dislike, while his spiteful nature looked for revenge.

Emily Barclay loathed him and had done from the very first time he had sought to use her husband's empty cabin to carry out his clerkish tasks. Annoyingly he did not move to let her past, but forced her to squeeze past him, feeling her body through both their garments and emitting a soft sigh that made her want to turn and slap his face.

'Gherson,' she heard her husband bark as the man went in to him. 'You took your damn time in coming.'

'I had some difficulty, sir, in getting away.'

'Is Glaister still in temporary command of my ship?'

'Yes, sir,' Gherson replied, pulling an unhappy face, 'and awaiting a new captain.'

'And our little enterprise?'

If Ralph Barclay had been glum before Gherson entered his temporary quarters he was a sight more so once he heard what had happened in Toulon harbour. The scheme he and Gherson, anticipating a forthcoming evacuation, had concocted to sell supplies stolen from the French warehouses had come to naught. His premier, Glaister, who had been brought into the scheme, seemingly fearful of being found out, had thought it best to rid the ship of a dangerous cargo worth several hundreds of pounds.

'Tossed in the harbour, you say?'

'They were, sir, down to the last tub of nails and length of cable.'

CHAPTER EIGHT

The very idea of going aboard HMS *Victory* was not one John Pearce had ever liked. On the maindeck, having given in his name, he joined what seemed like a whole crowd of folk seeking an interview with Lord Hood. There were British and French officers of several different ranks and services, men who looked to be local traders who would be seeking contracts to supply the fleet, as well as civilians recently forced to become émigrés in the Toulon evacuation, who no doubt wanted to know how they were going to get from this Italian port to some other part of Europe more congenial.

In his previous dealings with Hood, John Pearce had often bypassed the endemic queues his office attracted, but on those occasions the admiral had urgent need of his services. Now he did not, the task he was being asked to perform was not pressing, so he knew he was in for a long haul, yet hang around he must, and it had nothing to do with Hood's private correspondence. He needed passage home for his friends, and the only man who could give the Pelicans permission to sail on some returning naval vessel, in company with him, was the commander-in-chief.

He sought to remain unobserved, not easy on an open deck: he had been found waiting once before and that always led to an invitation to the *Victory*'s wardroom. Though the occupants were kind, they were avid warriors who would oblige him to tell his tales of action even if he had done so before: repetition of exploits never troubled the naval mind, they were the staple of conversation.

Added to that, they would be bound to enquire as to the purpose of his calling and he was in no mood to explain to a group of committed naval officers – who thought him a heroic fellow for the actions in which he had taken part, albeit leavened with a touch of jealousy for the luck he had enjoyed – why he was seeking to get out of a service they held in high regard and a theatre of operations presenting such glittering opportunity.

The day dragged on, new bodies joined the queue and one of Hood's lower clerks, a scrub-wigged tub of lard sitting at a desk before the great cabin doors, called out the relevant names. Someone entered and remained there for as long as it took to transact their business, and as they exited the next name was called, obviously from some kind of list, with Pearce having no idea of the relative importance of the interviewees or where he stood in relation to them. Occasionally the pipes would sing out at the entry port, the marines would gather and someone of a superior sort would arrive to be ushered through the throng and, as soon as the cabin was vacated, sent straight in to meet with the admiral.

For the fourth time in as many hours, Pearce approached the desk to seek some information on how long he would have to wait, finding himself standing before a fellow who could barely contain a sneer when he replied to such a request from a mere lieutenant. He was of the sort John Pearce had met many times in his life, more often than not in the company of his late father, and the man did not know how close he came to having his ears boxed, being saved by the two marines standing guard outside the great cabin: it was their presence and the fact he would probably have to fight them too which saved the neck of this unctuous little toad.

'His Lordship has a list of who is seeking an interview and he decides who he shall see and in what order.'

'I do not ask to jump the list, merely to know whereabouts I am upon it.'

'That I cannot tell you.'

'Cannot, or will not?' Pearce demanded.

Getting no reply, and thinking a trick might work, he asked for use of the clerk's pen and paper; judging by the look that received it was as if he had asked for permission to sleep with his mother.

'I am not at liberty—'

Pearce leant over the desk, speaking quietly, but with passion. 'If you do not do that, or find out from within that cabin how long I will have to wait, I will inform everyone on this deck of something the admiral would not want them to hear, and for that he will blame you.'

'Such as?' the clerk scoffed.

Pearce pulled Hood's letter from his pocket and shoved it under the fellow's nose. 'Do you recognise that seal, even broken?' A nod. 'Then if you do not wish me to make public the contents of what is a private and embarrassing communication, go through that door and tell Lord Hood I will not wait another bell. And I assure you, if you do not do as I have asked, the price to me will be nil, while the price to you will probably be the loss of your position.'

The eye contact was an attempt by the clerk to discern if this lieutenant was bluffing. Perhaps it was the steadiness of the gaze or the sheer fury that suffused the face that persuaded him to rise slowly and enter the great cabin. He was gone for half a minute and when he returned he tried, by adopting a superior tone, to retrieve his position.

'I have told Lord Hood you are waiting, Lieutenant, and he has said he will see you shortly.'

Given Lord Hood was seeking his services, any hope that his welcome might be couched in polite terms was immediately dashed. They had never been good in each other's company but there was some grudging respect for an older man who declined to play the hypocrite.

'God, it's the bad penny, Parker. I prayed the last time we met I'd seen the back of you, Pearce.'

'While I would have been content never to lay eyes upon you at any angle, milord, and since I have spent several hours standing outside your cabin and I am here at your express request, I rather think something to eat and drink might be in order instead of insults for a greeting.'

'We're not a coffee house, damn you.'

'I think you have forgotten, milord, that you have requested something of me.'

'I have not forgotten, Pearce, but given the favours I have done you I think I deserve some repayment in kind, like a modicum of courtesy.'

'Favours? All I can ever recall is your putting me in mortal danger.'

John Pearce could see Admiral Parker looking at the deck beams above his head, this while he tried to recall a time when he and Hood had ever exchanged a pleasantry. As for those previous favours, they had reeked more of blackmail than anything else and had, in truth, seen him nearly killed in the execution of one of them. Hood was accustomed to deference; the snag with the man before him was his congenital inability to defer to anyone, however elevated their rank.

'Mortal danger is not uncommon for naval officers.'

'You want me to deliver some letters?'

'Of course I do,' Hood barked. 'I would not have written to you had I not.'

'Then you must provide me not only with them but with the means to get myself and my companions back to England.'

'I must?' the older man demanded, that before he realised Pearce was speaking nothing but the truth. His tone did not modify much, but it did a little, becoming affirmative in place of angered. 'I must.'

Parker intervened. 'You can take passage on the next ship returning home.'

'And when will that be?'

'It will be when I say it will be,' Hood insisted.

Parker stopped another objection from their visitor, acting, as he always seemed to do, as Lord Hood's more emollient half. 'When His Lordship decides on the next course of action we will be sending despatches back to England. There are several ships in the fleet in need of repair and since, without Toulon, we lack a dockyard, they will have to take turns to return home to be refitted.'

'We held Toulon for several months.'

'We held it under siege. You do not put vessels into dock if you might have to abandon them there.'

'Sit down, Pearce,' Hood growled, which had John Pearce looking at him defiantly. 'Damn it, man, can you not even respond to a civility?'

'I don't recall receiving one.'

The next words were softer, if not more respectful.

'Sit down, damn you, and Parker, ring for my steward and get this rascal some provender.'

'Milord, we have a list of people waiting to see you.'

Hood sounded weary as he responded to that. 'Are you going to argue with me as well?'

'No, milord.'

Sat at the table opposite Hood and thus closer to him than hitherto, Pearce saw that the lines in the older man's face were etched more deeply than he had realised. It was with some insight, and one he had not previously truly considered, that he realised the weight this septuagenarian carried. He was far from London and was required to make instant decisions that might or might not be approved by his masters back home, the burden carried by every commanding officer on foreign service.

It was almost as if Hood read that thought, for he referred to the very thing when he spoke and, when he did, it was in a weary voice that reflected his age. 'I doubt you can even begin to comprehend, Pearce, what I have to deal with.'

'You forget I have seen the number of supplicants outside your door.'

That produced a soft and humourless laugh. 'They, boy, are not the half of it, are they, Parker?'

'No, milord,' his junior admiral replied, as he too sat down.

'I have a far from perfect fleet in which every vessel is short of its complement of hands. I must find and hold a base in the Mediterranean, and given we have lost Toulon and elements of the French fleet are still intact, the closer to that port it is the better, but it will not, under any circumstances, have a dockyard.'

Parker cut in. 'If you knew the state of repair of some of our ships, Mr Pearce, it would make your hair stand on end.'

'I have to deal with my enemies and my allies,' Hood continued, 'one of the latter knowing they very likely deliberately frustrated my aims when we evacuated Toulon. You went to Tunis, so you know I have to keep the ruler there neutral. I must deal with the Austrians, our present hosts, who, if they had sent the five thousand men they promised, might have allowed me to hold on at Toulon until enough troops arrived from England. Then there are the Italian states, Genoa and Naples, the Ottomans and half a dozen other powers who must not be driven into the arms of the French, and I find every decision I make questioned by a man, Sir William Hotham, who has the task of supporting me and signally fails to do so.'

'Milord,' Parker said.

'Help yourself to wine, Pearce,' Hood said, as his steward placed a decanter and some fruit on the table. As the man departed, he added. 'I am going to take you into my confidence.'

'Milord.'

'Parker, do stop saying that.'

'I feel you are being incautious.'

'Odd, is it not, Pearce?' Hood said. 'You are such an

argumentative sod I actually think I can trust you.'

'I don't seek your trust,' Pearce replied quietly.

'No, and it might turn out to be a burden, but I fear the letters I will give you might not convey the true import of what I want to say, letters never do. I want Hotham removed and I want it done with despatch, for I cannot continue in command with him as my leading subordinate. You know, we both know, he set up Barclay's court martial to fail…'

'Which may bring him down, milord.'

'You have more faith in politics and the law than I, young fella. What I want you to do is to back up what I have written.'

'In what way?'

'You do not see that Hotham will go out of his way to bring you harm?'

'You're sure he will do that?' Pearce asked.

'He has, to mollify Barclay, put you in mortal danger more than once, and if you can think of another reason why he delayed my orders for HMS *Hinslip* to evacuate the St Mandrier hospital I cannot. He knew you were there.'

'So was Captain Barclay. Would he abandon him too?'

'I doubt he knew that he was even wounded, let alone where he was, but does it occur to you that Barclay himself may have become a threat to Hotham?' Parker gave a hearty cough. 'My captain of the fleet thinks I speculate too far but believe me, Pearce, if he knew what you were planning to do regarding Barclay he would seek to stop you and I think he would go to any lengths. I cannot say

127

that in my despatches, nor can I be that open in a letter, which could very well be read by others, but you can say it in private. You can drive home just how pernicious is his influence and help Billy Pitt to make up his mind.'

Suddenly Hood stood up. 'Find yourself some accommodation ashore, send word to my clerk where you are, and as soon as we know which vessel will be going home to refit we will put you and those fellows you have fought so hard to free aboard her.'

'Thank you, milord, and the letter I came to collect?'

Hood growled, showing something of his former mood. 'I think it best if I hold on to my correspondence, don't you, given the way you just used my seal. Can't have you carrying them around, can we, never knowing who you might threaten.'

Sir William Hotham was writing a personal letter of his own, not to William Pitt but to his own political patron, the Duke of Portland, leader of the faction of Whigs who voted under his banner and supported the Tory government in its pursuit of the war with France. Highly unpopular in many quarters, the war was most vehemently opposed by the main section of the Whigs under Charles James Fox. He was supported, more for personal advantage than from any deep conviction, by the Prince of Wales. Like most heirs to a throne, Prinny was at loggerheads with his father, King George, and, conscious of the state of the parental health, sought a Regency.

This not being the first letter he had composed

questioning Samuel Hood's dispositions as C-in-C of the Mediterranean fleet, he nevertheless felt it necessary for the sake of clarity to reiterate some of his previous objections to the way the present campaign had been run, not least in the way Lord Hood had made accommodation with the French Royalist naval officers over the occupation of Toulon. It was to his advantage that not all of their capital ships had been destroyed in the recent evacuation, though in his letter, as opposed to Hood's despatches, there would be no mention of the Spanish reluctance to see Britannia too dominant.

Even though it was months since he and Hood had fallen out over that subject, the mere recollection was enough to make Hotham flush angrily: his sound advice had been overruled and ignored. Toulon had been at their mercy, but his commanding officer, instead of sending them an ultimatum, surrender or be destroyed, had sent them an offer of accommodation, allowing them to become allies of the pan-European anti-revolutionary cause. They should have taken Toulon by force, destroyed every ship they could not man and every facility in sight, then withdrawn, leaving the place to the Jacobins to do with what they wished.

It was, as all his previous letters had been, a critique of the way things were being run by a man well past his prime, the obvious concomitant being that matters would have progressed better under his own hand. At no time did he mention the strained personal relations between himself and Hood, nor his manifest attempts to modify his clearly stated orders: this was a more-in-sorrow-than-anger type of letter. Sanded and sealed, he held it in his hand for a moment, before calling for his steward to order up his barge.

'I am going to call upon poor Captain Barclay, who is, I believe, bound for the shore hospital. Send for Mr Burns to accompany me.'

Poor Captain Barclay was seething and in pain; the man before him, Lieutenant Glaister, already lambasted for his manifest failures, sat stony faced and, in his case, it made him look barely alive. Glaister would, by a kindly observer, be called fine-boned; the less well disposed would describe him as skeletal, with his pronounced cheekbones, high forehead, delicate, if pronounced, nose, none of which was well defined by his pallid skin, wispy fair hair and pale eyebrows. He even spoke like a corpse, in his slow Highland way. Behind Glaister stood Cornelius Gherson, relieved that it was now the Scotsman getting it in the neck, not, as previously, him.

'I might remind you,' Barclay spat, doing just that, given he was repeating himself, 'that we are in the very place where such as we gained from the Toulon arsenal might have been usefully disposed of.'

Slowly, Glaister looked at the bulkhead separating the convalescent space from the rest of Captain Sidey's cabin, a silent plea for Barclay to lower his tone. Not a wealthy man – most of his pay was remitted to his father and his worthless Highland estate – he knew to nearly the penny the value of that which he had seen tossed into the harbour at Toulon, but he also knew the penalty for discovery. What he had become engaged in was illegal and criminal but it stood a chance of turning a profit, and while his captain had command of the ship and all the responsibility, he was all for it.

But with Barclay wounded and him in temporary command of HMS *Brilliant*, he had become exposed. What if a new captain was appointed? It was a situation in which he would bear the brunt of any opprobrium and he was half sure that Barclay, personally threatened, would deny all knowledge of what the bulging holds of the frigate contained: stores stolen from the French warehouses with the contrivance of the fellows who worked there, payment being a promise to evacuate them in case Toulon was abandoned, not an undertaking ultimately fulfilled.

'We would have had every privateer captain in Leghorn begging us for those supplies,' Barclay whispered, at least taking cognisance of the dangers of being overheard, then wincing as he moved his arm. 'A mint of money, Glaister, and all in hard coin.'

'Have you heard yet what is to happen to the command of HMS *Brilliant*, sir?'

'No.'

That was another cause for concern to the wounded man: Hotham had hinted at Ralph Barclay shifting to a ship-of-the-line, a seventy-four, but that had gone from being a promise to a possibility, the whole notion now complicated by his aching wound. There would be no new command till he was fully recovered.

'I wondered if we would be seeing a new commanding officer aboard,' Glaister added.

Ralph Barclay tried hard not to sneer, but he failed. 'You don't hope for elevation yourself, Mr Glaister?'

'I would not presume, sir, and besides it would require a strong recommendation.'

That induced silence: the most telling recommendation should come from Ralph Barclay and he knew he was being asked if he would put it forward. 'I doubt my opinion would count for much, Mr Glaister.'

There was truth in that: Sir William Hotham might propose, but it was Samuel Hood who disposed, and a word from Ralph Barclay in that quarter was more likely to hinder any chance of a promotion for Glaister than aid it.

'I could ask that, as of this moment, my command be maintained.'

'But your wound, sir.'

'It is the very devil at the moment, sir, but it will heal in time.'

'Something we all hope for,' said Gherson, with what he assumed was a sincere smile.

The whistling of bosun's pipes and marine stamping made them all cock an ear: they knew the sound of the arrival of someone important, and it was only moments before the door burst open and Mr Ault, his face bright red, told them breathlessly that Admiral Sir William Hotham was coming aboard.

'Out, both of you,' Barclay insisted.

They were gone before Hotham was shown in, Toby Burns at his heels, looking more like a faithful dog than a human. Ralph Barclay wondered at the bandage on his head, held in place by his hat: the last time he had seen the little scoundrel had been on the assault in which he had been wounded – or, to be more accurate, he had not seen him, for Burns had disappeared between the British position and the French.

'Captain Barclay,' Hotham said, with a sympathetic frown, 'I was of the opinion you were in the hospital and I am of the belief that is where you should be.'

'I am reasonably comfortable here, sir, and Captain Sidey—'

'Has duties to perform and we must get his ship away from the quay before half the crew desert to those damned privateers. I have arranged transport for you and it will be here shortly.'

'Most kind, sir,' Barclay lied.

'Your wife is toiling away there, saint that she is.' Hotham half turned. 'I brought your nephew along to visit you both.'

'I am sure Mrs Barclay greeted him most affectionately, sir.'

Toby Burns had to look at the deck then and the reply threw Hotham slightly: it had been impossible not to observe that the youngster's aunt had been less than fulsome in her welcome.

'Wish your uncle well, boy, then leave us.'

133

'Aye, aye, sir,' Burns replied. 'I hope you are soon recovered, Uncle.'

There was no choice, given the company, but to accept that with seeming grace, but it was hard.

'Well, Barclay,' Hotham said, as Toby Burns exited, 'you will be going home, and though the reason is a damned shame, you will at least see England.'

'Home, sir? Can I not recover here?'

'Captain Barclay, who knows what will happen here, with the French on the rampage? No, safer to go back to England, to fully recover your strength, then seek employment when you are fully fit.'

Ralph Barclay looked hard at Hotham then, wondering if he could change his mind, and guessing from the look of insincere concern he could not. 'In which I hope I can count on your good offices, sir.'

That had to be said, even if, inside, Ralph Barclay was both seething and miserable.

Hotham laid a hand on Ralph Barclay's good arm. 'Of course, and to aid you I wish you to do me a service that cannot but enhance your prospects.' Hotham pulled an oilskin pouch from his pocket, dropping his voice at the same time. 'I have here a private letter for the Duke of Portland and I am charging you with its delivery. I need hardly say that the chance to introduce yourself to such a personage, and in the circumstances show him that you have my complete trust, will ensure that when you reapply for an appointment, given you will have his support, it will be to something of a plum.'

CHAPTER NINE

If the celebration of Christmas was muted for the other faiths, it was done by the papists of Livorno in a way to please Michael O'Hagan – who somehow found a priest with enough English to confess him – with a high mass at the Duomo, then a procession through the streets, the Catholic faithful, singing lustily, trailing their mitred and gloriously clad archbishop as he blessed all who knelt to him at the side of each thoroughfare he traversed. Then the divine took to a highly decorated barge, which conveyed him around the canals of the city, each quay crowded with worshippers, finally returning to his splendid palace.

Aboard each ship a more prosaic ceremony was the norm, indeed many of those celebrating the occasion would have disapproved mightily of what was taking place ashore. To the officers and men of the Mediterranean fleet – all, apart from those of non-commissioned Irish stock, strong adherents of the Thirty-Nine Articles of their Protestant faith – the shore celebrations were superstitious nonsense and they would have laughed at the crowds of peasants prepared to abase themselves before their puffed-up prelate.

At the hospital, an Anglican divine, who had a church serving the British community of privateers, some of whom were as pious as they were bloodthirsty, came to say a special service for the wounded, and that was attended by the Barclays and Heinrich Lutyens, as well as a cynical Charlie Taverner – who would take salvation if it was going – and a more believing Rufus Dommet, who was, in truth, a simpler soul.

The whole thing left John Pearce at a stand, for if he was not vehement in his disbelief, nor was he prepared to put it aside for the sake of appearances: he would neither attend the colourful Catholic ceremonies or those of what was High Anglican, meaning that when it came to the signing, there was not a lot between them. He had to, in this, ignore Michael O'Hagan's worries for his soul, normally expressed in shakes of the head and a crossing, but more vocal in the face of the most important day in the Christian calendar. He had even managed to disappoint Horatio Nelson by declining his invitation to join him aboard HMS *Agamemnon*: the price of a fine dinner was too high.

But that was only for one day: King George's Navy loved to entertain, and so close to shore and a supply of food that was, if high priced, fresh and available, with wine plentiful and cheap, they took advantage of it. On every vessel in the fleet, over the festive week, every captain vied to throw a memorable feast, where they drank heartily, that before having themselves boated ashore to enjoy the delights of the port city, and it had to be said their behaviour was often questionable. The midshipmen were the worst, forever getting into scrapes with the locals, with indigenous knives produced to face visiting dirks, until Hood, fearing murder, confined them to their ships, but the officers, enjoying the taverns and the entertainments they provided, were not much better.

John Pearce, unlike a high percentage of his fellow lieutenants and a fair number of captains, was not a man for whores, though he knew the difference between that estate and a courtesan of the kind he had come across in Paris: if their morality was not much dissimilar, their refinement and conversation was markedly dissimilar, the transaction being a cut above the merely carnal. But he took some amusement in observation, in seeing how the charming Italians fleeced with smiles their only too willing victims.

On one occasion, leaving behind his uniform and wearing borrowed civilian clothes, he went out with his true friends to the part of the port occupied by the privateers, noting that the taverns they frequented were more like the Pelican in the way the visiting mariners had turned them into little pieces of their homeland: if the serving wenches had olive skin, they had the same shape as the Rosies of this world; the men who teased and bedded them liked their women buxom, this to go with ale specially brewed by the locals to keep their customers content.

Michael and Charlie drank copiously and, in eyeing the people around them, picked out those few they might trust, as against the many they would not, responding to the suspicious stares they received from some true ruffians with an air of impertinence. They also took the opportunity to buy some female company with alacrity. Rufus, alternately blushing and boasting, sat with John Pearce for an age until he was persuaded to an upstairs room by one of the girls, not knowing that it was Pearce who had prompted her to act. On rejoining them, he was the subject of much ribbing about 'losing his cherry', an accusation he vehemently denied, claiming, as all youth does, sexual conquests that were imagined.

Also available were the official entertainments, balls and masques arranged by the grand duke's satraps for the visiting officers of an allied fleet, topped by performances at the opera and that strange activity, to most of the British officers, of ballet. If they found the highly formalised dance slightly bewildering, there was no shortage of lieutenants waiting for the female performers at the stage door, lithe girls who were happy to be escorted to whatever gathering had been arranged for the evening, these at more respectable venues where food, wine and music were the staples; any other activity was kept discreet.

John Pearce had engaged with some of those dancers in stilted conversation, only to find that, outside the occupation they pursued, they had little or no conversation, something he had noted of the fraternity in Paris: dancers talked of dancing, singers chattered about the operas in which they performed, actors – in which this city was lacking – at least told witty tales against themselves or revelled in the humorous misfortunes of their peers. Livorno was not the centre of the grand ducal court, that being Florence, leaving him to despair of ever finding women of sophistication.

The grandest of the entertainments, thrown by an archbishop, was to prove him wrong. He was a man of secular tastes and he quite obviously and openly supported a mistress. It was at the end of Christmas week when he threw his masked ball, this to see in the new year of 1794, and he was wealthy enough to outdo the local magnates in splendour. His palace was illuminated outside by hundreds of lanterns, inside by a thousand candles, and it was clear the cream of Tuscan society found this a ball to attend. Hood and Hotham were both present – though never physically close – and, like the rest of their officers, in their best bib and tucker, but in the main they looked out of place, not in their dress but in their rather stiff manner: they did not intermingle.

Not for the first time as naval officer, John Pearce

found his facility in French his greatest advantage. The Gallic officers present were more at home in grand surroundings than their British counterparts, more inclined to engage with their Italian counterparts, so he sought out one he knew well, the Baron D'Imbert, and through him he was introduced to many of the leading citizens of Livorno, all of whom also spoke the international language of the world. And he met their companions, one of whom was the striking Contessa di Montenero.

He had spotted her a lot earlier and had noticed that her beauty, unlike most of her contemporaries, was unforced: high cheekbones, little powder to mask her luminous skin, smooth black eyebrows on a remarkably beautiful face and, even from a distance, a ready and entrancing smile that often turned to an appealing laugh. Her clothing had about it a simplicity many lacked, merely because she had no need to seek to exaggerate in her dress and head decoration what was natural. There were no plumes and no colourful turban, leaving her countenance and manner as the things that conveyed her personality to the room.

Naturally, with those attributes she had been surrounded by gallants, but Pearce knew how to be patient, as well as how, by an amused stare, to convey his interest from afar. She had turned more than once, having noticed that gaze, to see if it was still upon her, giving a slow swish of her fan that somehow conveyed no displeasure. He had waited until the Baron d'Imbert, circulating the room and conversing, came into her orbit, before moving to join him.

Introduced and close he was pleased to see her skin was flawless and that her eyes danced when she was in receipt of a compliment. The hardest part following on from that was to get her away from the babbling suitors who surrounded her and that took a very deliberate showing of his back to them, done with such determination she laughed, displaying lovely teeth.

'And how, Lieutenant, do you come to know the baron so well?'

'I had to negotiate with him for the surrender of Toulon.' Those black eyebrows went up a fraction and she could not help looking at his blue coat, with its lack of adornment denoting a lowly rank. 'I have certain skills not vouchsafed to my superior officers.'

There were ways of saying those words and he was pleased to see she took them in the way he intended: not boasting, yet leaving in the air the question as to what those skills might be.

'An accomplished emissary, then?'

'I like to think, Contessa, that my talents extend beyond mere negotiation.'

'You have talent, monsieur, for being very forward.'

'I have found that little is gained by being overly cautious.'

'Sometimes all is lost by being too bold.'

'If I had any knowledge of what I might forfeit I would know whether prudence was a course to follow.'

'Pearce.'

He knew the voice, it was unmistakable, and he cursed Horatio Nelson, because the look in the *contessa*'s eyes as he made that last remark, if they did not promise, hinted at a distinct possibility of pleasure. John Pearce sensed the mores of this part of the world were the same as those he had known in Paris: this woman might be married, and no doubt her husband was in the same ballroom, but he would very likely be about his own affairs leaving her to her own. Much as he wanted to ignore Nelson, and to keep holding the gaze of the woman before him, he was obliged to turn.

'Allow me to name to you Madame Carlatti, from the opera,' Nelson boomed, before dropping his voice into what was supposed to be a manly exchange, hinting at something salacious and underlining that while he was not drunk, he was close. 'She has the most remarkable voice, which, sir, is not the least of her accomplishments.'

She also had the most remarkable bosom that would have been extraordinary had it not sat on a body that was in proportion. Madame Carlatti was in all respects a big woman, a head taller than her companion, with an overmade-up face, eyes outlined in kohl and thick red lips, the very antithesis of the well-proportioned *contessa*.

'Do introduce me to this charming creature,' Nelson added.

'The Contessa di Montenero.'

The little captain took the *contessa*'s hand and kissed

it, in a rather sloppy fashion, adding some compliments in barely comprehensible French. In leaning down, Pearce was presented with a trio of nervous lieutenants standing several feet back, who were watching Horatio Nelson with concern.

'I see you travel with some of your officers,' Pearce said, hoping that he would go to join them.

'Ah, my guardian angels,' Nelson joked. 'They worry for my soul, but I have told them more than once, a man is a bachelor east of Gibraltar.'

This amused Pearce, given Nelson, with his young face, blue eyes and bright blond hair looked so virtuous, almost angelic. 'You are not concerned that Madame Carlatti will discover you are a married man?'

'Doesn't speak a word of English, you know, Pearce, which, while it has its advantages, can be damned awkward in a clinch. She speaks French, though, and since I have orders for Corsica I am thinking of asking her if she wants to come along.'

Pearce laughed out loud, which had the Italian opera singer looking at him suspiciously; the hint that he should pose the offer was too obvious. There was also the image of this pair having congress, this huge woman and Nelson.

'Would Lord Hood approve?'

'Shan't tell him.'

The band, which had been silent for an hour, struck up again with a lively rondo. Nelson's eyes lit up and he swung round to his painted paramour and made all the signs requesting that they dance, which allowed Pearce to turn back to the contessa, only to find her once more surrounded by eager suitors.

'Forgive me, sir.' He turned back to face another lieutenant, one of those Nelson had called his guardian angels. 'I know you to be Mr Pearce, and I wonder if I could count on your good offices?'

'And you are?'

'Lieutenant Hinton, sir, at your service, premier of HMS *Agamemnon*.'

'Looking out for your captain?'

'Trying to. He seems to esteem you, and we must get Captain Nelson away from here before he commits a public indiscretion. '

Pearce had dined with Nelson once, in company, off Tunis, and noted he was light-headed in the article of drink. 'From what I have seen you need to keep him away from the punch bowl.'

'I need to get him back to the ship.'

'And his opera singer?'

'What happens in his private quarters is his affair. What happens in public view could become the object of gossip.'

'In letters home?'

'The King's Navy is a small world, Mr Pearce, and there are certain places where tales of misbehaviour would not play to his advantage.'

Especially with his wife, Pearce thought. 'He wants to take her to Corsica, Mr Hinton.'

The eyebrows shot up. 'Were it not a court martial offence I would sandbag him and set sail while he was still unconscious.'

'Tell me, Mr Hinton, is this association with Madame Carlatti an aberration?'

'It is not his first adventure, sir.'

'And how do they end?'

'With much remorse.'

'Then I fear you will be wasting your time, sir: a man who displays remorse then goes on to commit the same sin is a lost cause.'

Pearce looked over to where the *contessa* stood, still surrounded, but she glanced in his direction at the same time and smiled, making him determined to end this conversation: the doings of Horatio Nelson and the effect it would have on his marriage were none of his affair, he had better fish to fry and he was sure that little persuasion would be required for him to make this a memorable night.

'Perhaps my original advice was mistaken. The best thing you can do is get him so drunk he must depart this place. Either that, or get Lord Hood to order him back to his ship.'

It was an irony too far that in the letters home to England from Italy in January of 1794, the incident that most amused or scandalised the correspondents was not the antics of Captain Horatio Nelson and an Italian opera singer, but the tale of a certain Lieutenant John Pearce being caught in flagrante with a Tuscan *contessa* in her bedchamber, not by her husband but by her present, irate lover. This fellow, a minor nobleman of tender years, besotted with the lady, took the precaution of turning up with a trio of his retainers, brutes bearing clubs, forcing an unarmed Pearce to leap from a first-floor window with his breeches in one hand, leaving behind his blue uniform coat and hat.

Needless to say, his arrival back at the hospital *sans* clothing required some explanation, a tale he told of robbery, which was quite blown when the truth was the talk of Livorno the following day, given the *contessa*'s young lover, distantly related it seemed to the grand duke, wanted it known that he intended, once the culprit had been identified, to challenge him to a duel.

'You will do nothing of the sort,' said Lord Hood, when Pearce intimated his desire to accept. 'The last things we need are strained relations with the locals, which we will most certainly have if you skewer some callow love-struck youth who has imperial blood in his veins.'

'He might do that to me, milord.'

'Don't get me excited by the prospect,' the older man hooted. 'The letter, Parker.'

'HMS *Grampus* is bound for home and you are to sail on her,' Parker said, handing him an oilskin pouch. 'I suggest it would be best if you repair aboard her at once.'

'And stay there until she weighs,' Hood added.

* * *

HMS *Grampus*, a two-decker of fifty guns, looked perfectly fine from a distance, but in coming close, John Pearce could see the thickness of the paintwork and the places where it had peeled, which argued that her scantlings were not as sound as they first appeared. In his newly acquired broadcloth coat pocket – the property of an officer who had expired fighting at Toulon – he had the communications handed to him by Admiral Parker, on his head was a replacement hat and his feet rested by his sea chest, while looking at him and trying to conceal their smiles were Michael, Charlie and Rufus Dommet.

He soon discovered that Lord Hood had stripped the vessel of every seaman she could spare, leaving her perilously short of hands should she be required to both work the sails and fight the guns; but his whole fleet was like that, with the men the admiral had originally fetched out from England, as well as suffering from the normal rate of losses, having suffered casualties at Toulon. What remained had to be spread through the captured vessels taken from the French.

The ship did not weigh immediately, leading to a frustrating few days, which saw HMS *Agamemnon* raise her anchor and depart, with Pearce wondering if Madame Carlatti was aboard. Somehow he doubted it: freed from the illusions brought on by too much wine, surely Nelson would see such an idea as what it was, madness. Pearce was not competent to inspect the ship, but even he knew by the smell of rot that she was in a poor state, and in a conversation with the carpenter he was made well aware of her manifest problems: scantlings that worked enough to let in water in any kind of sea, futtocks so rotten that the man could poke a finger into the wood fibres, masts that were far from proper in their seating, while he was in despair about her hanging knees.

'She will get us home, I hope?'

The carpenter shrugged, showing that fatalism which was necessary in a wooden ship at sea, the attitude that said any man's fate was in the lap of the Gods. 'Got us here, your honour, and she weren't fit for it when we weighed from the Nore. Barkies like this'un float better than most folk think. Long as we don't get a true hurricano, I'd say she'll get us home, even with only half our true complement of hands.'

'And then?'

'State she's in they'll break her up, I reckon, an' I shall be on the hunt for a new berth. Wi' luck I will get a warrant on a seventy-four.'

The sight of Ralph and Mrs Barclay coming aboard, with Devenow and Cornelius Gherson in tow, was not one to cheer John Pearce much, yet there was nothing he could do about it: to protest to Lord Hood would only expose him to ridicule, and besides, when would there be another ship heading home? Heinrich Lutyens came aboard too, having volunteered to replace the surgeon of HMS *Grampus*, who was unwell, causing Michael

O'Hagan to opine, and not entirely without a degree of wicked pleasure, that it was just like old times.

The fact that Barclay glared at him when he espied him did not bother John Pearce, except that the prospect of spending several weeks in close proximity did not appeal; that, and the fact soon made plain that Barclay and Captain Daws of the *Grampus* were old shipmates, boded ill. But Emily Barclay would not catch his eye and that was wounding; clearly she had heard of his nocturnal, carnal exploits and she was no doubt shocked by his behaviour. The crew were not, and neither were his Pelicans. It was obvious everyone had heard the tale: Pearce could not walk the deck without the men nudging each other and grinning.

The morning came when their number was raised at the masthead of HMS *Victory* and the signal gun spoke out to ensure the order was observed. Under a sky as grey as that with which he had arrived in Livorno, HMS *Grampus* weighed anchor with all the usual stamping on the capstan, as it was used to haul in the great anchor cable, the nippers running hard to attach lines as the wet slimy rope was taken to the bitts, to be laid end on end.

Pearce was on deck when the anchor, with *Grampus* running over it, was plucked free to be fished in and catted, watching, with interest, the topmen letting go of the sails as ordered by the ship's master, seeing them sheeted home by the men on deck. It all went very smoothly, as it should under the eye of several admirals, a whole host of foreigners looking out from the shore, and on a ship which, having been in service for months, was well worked up.

Ominously there was another sound: that of the pumps already fully operational to keep the bilges clear of water even before they had cleared inshore waters.

CHAPTER TEN

The Mediterranean could be trouble at any time of year, surrounded as it was by the various land masses that produced hot, cold and disturbed air leading to violent storms as bad as anything that could be produced by the Atlantic Ocean, and HMS *Grampus* sailed straight into one. Fortunately, in both Captain Daws and the master, Mr Ludon, they had experienced seamen who knew the beast in which they were about to be caught.

The first intimation of the approach for John Pearce was the way the ship was being prepared: hatches battened down, oiled canvas covers being spread over the companionways, the deck coops being struck below along with anything movable, such as the cabin and wardroom furniture, while extra lashings were put upon the ship's cannon and the boats sitting above the waist. Instructions had also been sent from the deck to secure the cots of the wounded and transfer to hammocks those who could rest in them.

On deck, although the sky was a brassy hue, there was little to see. The water was certainly choppy, a vicious cross sea which made the ship shudder and groan, but it had been like that since the previous day and when he approached Captain Daws it was to find a man anxiously searching the horizon, the master behind doing likewise. They had spoken little previously, he not seeming the sociable type, but Pearce had taken the precaution of telling him, once Barclay came aboard, that there was bad blood between them and should he be tempted to bring them together it would be best to avoid that.

He did not interrupt a discussion about the amount of sea room the ship had, listening as the two men discussed the various options, depending on the direction of wind, the strength of the tempest, the distance between their present position and Corsica, as well as some outcrop called Gorgona that was, apparently, a speck of an island, the tip of an extinct volcano, that stuck up out of the ocean in the deep part of the Gulf of Genoa.

'You anticipate a blow, sir?' he asked as the master disappeared into his hutch and his charts.

'I do, Mr Pearce, and I would advise you it will be an unpleasant one. Look at the sky and feel the heaviness in the air.'

'From where will it come?'

'Too early to tell: the wind, you will have noticed, though slight, keeps shifting.'

It was in conversations like these that John Pearce felt most acutely his lack of knowledge: people like the naval officer had been at sea for more than three decades and had seen all there was to see, as well as benefiting from the shared knowledge of the profession. The navy was its own academy in which education was part experience and part instruction, and that was an institution in which he was an outsider; for all that, Pearce was a naturally curious fellow and not one to ignore the acquisition of free knowledge.

'Whatever, Mr Pearce, when it comes I suspect it will do so suddenly and be upon us with some speed.'

'Hence the preparations?'

'Yes, and before you ask if I might be wrong, that possibility does exist, but it is not wise, as I'm sure you agree, to tempt providence.'

As if ordered, the sky to the north was suddenly suffused with lightning, no forks, just a flash of brighter light that raced across the clouded sky. Pearce noticed Daws counting off the seconds on his fingers, waiting for the rumble of thunder, which came, deep and long, after about twenty of those.

'Now, Mr Pearce, we at least know from where we are threatened and we await the next sign.' On deck, all activity had ceased: the captain was not the only one wishing to measure the speed of the approaching tempest and they did not have long to wait. The next flash of lightning was mush brighter and the thunder came in half the time, which had the master moving forward, speaking trumpet in hand.

'I would advise, sir, we go down to close reefed topsails immediately.'

'Make it so, Mr Ludon, and I would suggest that you, like me, send for your oilskins.'

The sky to the north-east, where it met the sea, was turning from brassy grey to black and for the first time the lighting forked into the sea, a bright flash that made Pearce blink. Like most people, weather fascinated him and he had seen many storms in his time, from the shore, from the top of hills, and had them come upon him when far from any shelter. Even he knew this one was exceptional.

'Can I be of any service, sir?'

'I would imagine, Mr Pearce, that the pumps will require every available pair of hands. If you do not mind supervising that, I would be grateful, as my officers, I think, will likely be otherwise engaged.'

'Sir, I shall shed my coat and pump myself.'

That shocked Daws, who was putting on his foul-weather gear. 'I would hope, sir, you would remember your dignity as an officer.'

There was no point in saying he had none of that. He moved out of the way as the topmen were called aloft to take in the courses and double-reef the topsails. Other men were rigging extra lines, manropes along the bulwarks, hawsers to the masts, fore and backstays to take the strain that was bound to be put on them, and he was vaguely aware that the ship was turning slowly away from the oncoming storm: when it struck, Daws clearly intended to run before it.

He went below, calling on his friends as well as Devenow, leading them to where the pumps were already manned; they never ceased to work on this vessel as the timbers moved and leaked, but they would have to be employed at a harder rate if they were going to ship water over the deck: no amount of precautions could keep a goodly amount of that from making its way down through the decks to the bilges where, if it became too deep, it would affect the ability of the ship to manoeuvre, given it would sit lower in the water than hitherto.

A carpenter's mate was already there, measuring the water in the well, which as time passed would tell them if their efforts were holding it steady or, more worryingly, whether the depth of the bilge was rising, while on both sides of the dome pump casing men were working the crank handles in a desultory fashion, something which Pearce wanted changed right away on the very sound principle it was better to be ahead of the game than merely level.

'You don't want to go too hard at it,' said the carpenter's mate. 'There be all manner of muck down there and if the pump picks it up and gets jammed it will not do us no good. We's at three feet in the well now, and that we can live with.' Here he was again, faced with superior knowledge and being told something he should have known. 'Time to start goin' hard at it, your honour, is when it begins to rise an' not afore.'

'You have ridden out heavy seas and storms already, yes?'

'We have, sir.'

'How bad has it been before?'

'Bad,' the man replied. 'You'd best get teams of men ready, 'cause if this is like what is bein' said there will be hands expiring from effort.'

The crack of thunder was loud enough to penetrate the overhead deck planking, and above their heads Captain Daws was watching the bolts of lighting strike the sea all around the ship, none of which was visible to Pearce, given the gun ports were tightly shut and secured. But he did notice the timbers were creaking more noisily and felt the increased motion of the ship as the stern lifted higher than hitherto, causing Heinrich Lutyens, who had been walking towards them, carrying the case with his surgical instruments, to break into a sudden scurry that John Pearce halted with an outstretched hand. Behind him, Emily Barclay, dressed in an apron, was hanging on to an upright.

'The captain has said we must set up in the cockpit to treat injuries,' Lutyens said.

'It will be splints you'll need, Heinrich, for broken bones,' Pearce said, moving towards Emily Barclay, where, upon reaching her, he held out his hand. 'Let me assist you.'

'No, thank you, I would rather manage on my own.'

It was more the face and the way it was slightly turned away from him, nose in the air, that told John Pearce why she was being aloof: clearly she had heard of his nocturnal escapades – who had not? – and was offended to be offered aid from such a tainted source. If he had known how her husband had exploited that to make her feel uncomfortable, he would have been made angry instead of amused: on more than one occasion she had stood up to him on behalf of John Pearce and now that was being thrown back in her face at every opportunity.

'You may take it, Mrs Barclay, that I am cleansed of my adventures.'

'I do not know, sir, how anyone can merely wash away such disgrace.'

'What you term disgrace, madam, I would name as pleasure.' In receipt of a loud sniff, Pearce added, 'You should not allow the fact that such a thing has been denied to you to cloud your opinions.'

The look that got, aimed at him as she staggered on to follow Lutyens, was icy indeed, something Michael O'Hagan, working without too much effort at the crank handle of the pump, could not fail to notice, and since he was close enough to talk softly, in any event the creaking of the ship covering his words, he did so in a friendly voice.

'There you go now, John-boy, upsetting yet another lady.'

Pearce grinned. 'What makes you think I upset the *contessa*, Michael?'

'Sure, you'll be telling me next you left her smiling.'

'Laughing, Michael, not smiling.'

'Jesus, were you that poor? Mind, if the sight of you leaping through a window in your smalls did not make a body laugh, they would be a miserable soul.'

The stern lifted even higher as a larger wave swept under the counter. 'A bit more effort on the pumps, Michael.'

That got him a huge grin. 'I could say the same to you, John-boy, an' if you'd be after some instruction I would be willing to show you—'

That was not finished, because the ship suddenly lifted and listed as it was hit by a screaming wind, sending anyone not with a secure hold tumbling. Pearce only stayed upright because Michael took one hand off the crank to grab him, his arm fully extended before he was brought to a halt. Then the water started to pour down the companionways – not the full amount, that was held back by the covers, but enough to be visible – more squeezing its way, driven by the wind, through the gap where the gun ports sat against the hull.

From then on it was like slowly riding a bucking horse, and one that was capable of moving in surprising directions to catch the unwary off guard. HMS *Grampus* lifted, dropped, swayed, listed for an age before righting itself, and all the while the amount of seawater she was making increased, and this with the pumps now working flat out, the carpenter's mate, when he could steady himself enough to take a reading, letting Pearce know the water in the well was rising by the foot.

On deck the captain and the master, peering through spume-blasted eyes, gave shouted instructions to the quartermaster and his mates who were lashed to the wheel, seeking to keep the bowsprit, which kept trying to sweep right or left, pointing dead away from the screaming wind, a task made harder as the rudder was being continually lifted free of the water. There was no sky above their heads, just pounding rain sheeting forward to meet the sea shipping over the bulwarks, as *Grampus* was driven under by the head, and by now they were propelled by nothing but a main storm staysail, with men aloft seeking to gather in the reefed topsails and lash them tight to the yards.

The storm was still raging as night fell – not that they had enjoyed much daylight while the sun was still above the heavy clouds – and darkness was added to the nightmare of an existence confined to less than the hand in front of your face. Below there were now ten men working the pumps, Pearce amongst them, while another party of the same number sought to recover from their exertions before being called back to duty on the crank handles, and still the water rose in the well, which, if it endangered them long-term, acted as a form of extra ballast to steady the ship, making it lower in the water.

If the wind eventually moderated the sea did not, a scudding swell that tossed HMS *Grampus* around like a sodden cork. Men, including one of Daws' youngest midshipmen, had been washed overboard into a sea from which rescue was impossible: if they could be heard screaming it was not for long and they could not be seen. In the cockpit Heinrich Lutyens and Emily Barclay treated a steady stream of deep cuts and bruises, as well as broken bones caused by falls and men being thrown against hard wood despite their best efforts to hang on to ropes or netting.

Pearce, working flat out, was vaguely aware of the seams opening up in the main deck planking, before closing again, and a peculiar deep groan as the ship sailed atop a wave before plunging back down again, the whole weight of the vessel thrown on to the central section of the hull, leaving both bow and stern in the air as deadweight. Daws was aware of it too, but in no position to do anything about it. Ships had fallen apart at sea before, he was sure; in some cases there had been survivors to tell the tale of a broken-backed hull. If his command were going to do that it would not cease for his silent prayers.

The night was hell: endless darkness, movement, noise and toil, till it felt as though the attempt to stay afloat and whole could founder on sheer exhaustion. John Pearce, struggling to keep up, could only admire Michael O'Hagan and Devenow, the two most stalwart men on those crank handles, keeping going while others fell into a state of collapse around them, needing to be dragged clear so another, still trying to recover from his last bout, was drawn in as a replacement. Rufus Dommet was lying in a crumpled heap, utterly done, while Charlie tried gamely to take his turn, proving that whatever else he had gained from being pressed, he was a stronger creature now than he had been on the banks of the Thames.

Ralph Barclay lay in his cot, hanging from triangular ropes from the overhead beam, still while the ship swung around him, listening, for that was all he could do, to the sounds around him – the timbers creaking then cracking as the strain became too great – and that included the panic-stricken cries of his clerk, which, over time, had changed to low moaning. There was nothing to be done: if it was time to meet his maker, so be it.

Mid morning saw a clearer sky, but off the larboard quarter lay land and, quite soon, the sight of heavy seas breaking on rocks. It was that damned outcrop of Gorgona, the peak of the tree-covered island rising over seven hundred feet in the air, doubly dangerous as a lee shore for having high cliffs and deep water all around, with few places where dropping an anchor would find holding ground. Tired as the men on board were, they had to be summoned on deck, the topmen to go aloft and get some more way on the ship, for to keep just running before the wind was to founder by being driven on to the faces of those cliffs.

That took men off the pumps, meaning those

remaining had to work harder, and if the alternative had not been to drown, John Pearce was unsure he could have continued. But he must, and now it was necessary to try to keep the level of water in the well, now near to flooding the lower deck, at bay, for a ship sluggish to steer was a danger, not an asset. The course Daws needed to steer did not need to alter by much to avoid an island a mile and a half wide. Still it was touch and go, for to hoist more sail was to strain masts he knew to be far from secure, and if one of them went by the board the ship would be doomed.

If anything, it was the precautions he had taken which made possible the change of course: those extra hawsers attached to the fore and mainmast which held them, creaking and protesting as well as moving alarmingly, as the wind pressed on the loosened topsails, now sheeted home and taut. They passed so close to Gorgona they could hear the waves breaking, but once clear of that, and with ample sea room, Daws could ease the strain and let the ship run on the swell.

Finally, even that subsided enough to make pumping the most strenuous and necessary task, with every man on board taking his turn as those who had laboured through the night lay either asleep or wondering how muscles could ache so much: arms, thighs and backs. Pearce dragged himself back on deck, to find a quarterdeck full of men with red-rimmed eyes and strained faces who looked in need of much rest, but as yet could not risk it. But the time came when things eased enough to allow some respite and HMS *Grampus*, still dipping and swaying on the falling swell, could begin to put to rights all that had gone wrong and call a muster to find out who was missing.

The ship was a sorry sight, with various loose ropes and blocks swinging in the wind, including some of those hawsers rigged as extra preventer stays, sails that had blown out, one of the yards having parted from its slings, and in many places cleats that had been ripped off the shrouds. John Pearce was reminded of two things: that if a wooden sailing ship was a construct of shaped timbers, much of it only functioned because it was held together or operated by ropes, many of which he as yet did not the know the names of, or, if he did, struggled with the complexity of recalling which was which.

'Mr Pearce, I would be grateful if you would take charge of the party on the bowsprit and spiritsail yards,' shouted Captain Daws. 'You will not be aware, but two of my lieutenants are among the injured. Mr Lutyens is attending to one collarbone and my premier has a badly broken ankle.'

There was no option but to say yes, but it was an operation very much undertaken using the knowledge of the hands he had under his command, the men aboard rated able: rigging had to be cut away and replaced, and that meant intricate knots and rope work that was way beyond his competence. What was not parted had to be checked for damage that might weaken it in the future and that included the myriad lines of the running rigging which ran back to various points on the foremast, the hull and the knightheads. For men already weary it was hard going, but there was no room for complaint, every man jack aboard *Grampus* was suffering likewise.

Sails had been taken out of the locker and were being prepared for hoisting aloft as replacements for those damaged, and that meant work on the capstan to get the heavy canvas raised and toil for the worn-out topmen on the yards – men who had already had to replace slings and rigging – this while the ship dipped and swayed on the swell.

But more cheerful was the fact that the cook had got his coppers lit and there was not only hot water for the surgeon but men employed bringing up the casks of pork and beef that would provide a hot meal for officers and men alike. Then one watch could go to their hammocks and sleep, that followed by the next. Within twenty-four hours it was, if you could forgive the even noisier creaks of the working timbers, as though the storm through which they had just laboured was no more than a bad dream.

CHAPTER ELEVEN

If the Mediterranean could be cruel, it could also delightfully surprise, on a mid-January day, with sunshine aided by a warm southerly breeze coming off the North African coast that made for a pleasant interlude. Pearce was on the deck, pacing back and forth, having attended Divine Service, really just a homily produced by the ship's captain. Several of the recovering wounded, now including those who had suffered in the recent storm, had either come or been brought up to enjoy the air and, given they were sailing easy on that breeze, the crew were occupied in making, mending and prettying themselves for a hoped-for run ashore in Gibraltar.

Michael, Rufus and Charlie were with some of the *Hinslip*'s crew, jawing away while they tended to each others' pigtails, the sight of which, even if they had become familiar on the heads of his fellow Pelicans, made

Pearce stop and think. He could not recall their growing to the length they had: these standard accoutrements of the British tar had just seemed to appear naturally, but it did force upon him an unwanted thought – what in the name of the devil were they all going to do once they got back to England?

Michael could go back to his old life of digging ditches and foundations for the spate of speculative building which afflicted the capital city. What about Rufus and Charlie, who would certainly still have warrants out for their arrest? They would not have lapsed, though their absence might have seen others replace them in the minds of the tipstaffs, whose job it was to apprehend felons, and the kind of low culls looking for a bounty. Yet looking at them now, they were every inch the sailor; and him, what had he become?

While still fully aware of the level of his ignorance he also knew that in merely being aboard a ship he had absorbed a great deal: from barely knowing the bow from the stern of a naval vessel he was now conversant with many aspects of the way a ship was built, rigged and how it was run. He had also to admit that he had found leadership in tight situations something to savour, and Michael O'Hagan had more than once referred to his seeming love of danger. Was he just a thrill-seeker or did he actually enjoy combat?

There were also the things he did not enjoy: deference to authority, the loss of freedom inherent in a hierarchical service. Yet that same service had fed his need for independence as often as it had obliged him to act on the instructions of others, and had given him an insight into his own character, not always a view that presented unmitigated pleasure. Could he return to a life without adventure? Could he, with the few obvious skills he had, find an occupation that would afford him that which he had experienced since being pressed?

Sustained, as he had been, by the need to fulfil a promise to his friends, they were now on their way to liberty, the freedom to decide for themselves what they would do and where they would go, and it was very possible that, gifted that, they would each proceed in their own direction never to meet again; there would be no more Pelicans.

Certainly he had to deliver Hood's letters and then seek to bring a case against Ralph Barclay, something which may take years, but he also had to live, and without some kind of paid occupation that would be difficult. Looking at his companions again, he so much wanted to just go up and ask them if they had a plan, but that was not possible. Much as he saw them as his friends, there was a gulf between them now caused by his rank, a thing they might ignore privately, but also something they must publicly acknowledge. To ask them now would be to discomfit them.

Turning away he was presented with the sight of Barclay coming on deck, the ever-faithful Devenow at his heels, one hand always ready to steady his captain, though the man was becoming more accustomed now to not having his left arm. He was not cured, that would take a lot more time, months not weeks, but his face looked more settled, less lined with pain, evidence that the thing was on the mend. The eyes moved in his direction, but just as swiftly Barclay looked away again, this as Cornelius Gherson came on deck as well, he too taking care to avoid any eye contact.

It was not just he and Barclay who avoided meeting his eye: in the last weeks Emily Barclay continued to avoid him and that was less easy to accept. Though he knew her parochial upbringing was to blame for her being standoffish he was far from suffering any feelings of guilt, and besides, anyone who had agreed to marry a scrub like Ralph Barclay, albeit she was young and naive, showed a startling want of judgement.

Though there was not much in years between them he knew he was very different, and nothing underlined that more than his attitude to dalliance. Ever since he had come to manhood, John Pearce had been forward with women, too much so, probably, for English mores, but then he had come into the bloom of ardent youth as a tall, fine-looking youth in Paris, and at a time when the famous laxity of the French towards fidelity had eased even more thanks to the overthrow of absolute monarchical power. He had been seduced by women of experience, then gone on to enjoy the favours of a beautiful mistress without in any way troubling her wealthy husband: he too had his liaisons.

That had been a golden time, when the whole city

had seemed permanently *en fête*, the time before the purists, opportunists and demagogues of the Revolution had turned it into the bloodbath it had become, when the leaders of the National Assembly had been men of wit and intelligence, instead of purveyors of dogma and spite. His reputation having preceded him, his polemics against monarchy and privilege translated from the English, Adam Pearce had been welcomed like a long-lost brother, lauded for his views, his stand and his imprisonment. That changed when the power shifted to men who were no more prepared to be termed as wrong-headed than any crowned king.

He had known for a long time that his upbringing had fitted him for nothing and he certainly had no desire to follow in his father's footsteps: much as he loved him, much as there had been a time when he quite naturally agreed with everything Adam Pearce believed, such blind faith had not survived his coming of age. Long before the flight to Paris he had begun to question the tenets by which he had been raised, and his experiences there had done much to increase his doubts.

A short stay in Fleet Prison had exposed him to the dregs of humanity as well as society's victims, that in itself enough to cause any scales to fall from his eyes. In Paris he had seen a rampaging mob, egged on by firebrand orators of the likes of Marat, hack to death people whose only crime was to have been born into privilege; the question of whether they were good people or bad was not posed. And finally, he had visited the Conciergerie, where his ailing father was a prisoner, had seen how those who had once had much were reduced to beggary by a vindictive Revolution, had witnessed his own father die at the hands of that same body of odious extremists.

John Pearce shook his head sharply then: these were not thoughts on which he wished to dwell and he sought instead to take pleasure from the bright sky and blue sea. His promenading had brought him near to the quarterdeck, so to keep his mind free of memories, and seeing Captain Daws had come on deck, a man with whom, given he was messing in the wardroom, he had exchanged few words since coming aboard, he moved closer to attempt some naval conversation.

'Do you think, sir, this wind will be enough to get us into Gibraltar?' The response was a cold look, as if to address him so was extreme temerity. 'I ask only out of curiosity, sir, given I know, with the strong tidal flow from the Atlantic, it is not an easy approach from the east.'

'Time will tell.' No courtesy, no 'Mr Pearce' or 'sir' and in essence no answer, which was damned rude and not something John Pearce was inclined to accept.

'I'm sorry if my enquiry offends you, sir.'

'Offends? I wonder if you know the meaning of the word. I had the pleasure of Captain Barclay's company at dinner last night, given he is now well enough to be a guest, and he was most informative regarding your background.'

'There are, sir, two sides to every tale.'

'Are you suggesting I mistrust the word of a man I have known for years and, indeed, shared a wardroom with in the early years of the American War, not to mention an officer who has given an arm for his country? Where I once saw your escapade in Livorno as amusing I now know it is indicative of your character.'

'I am sure his arm will heal in time,' Pearce said, guessing at the nature of the conversation. 'I doubt, however, his malice will.'

'Might I remind you that you are talking about a superior officer.'

'If not a superior person, Captain Daws!' Pearce snapped. 'Might I ask, was his wife with him?'

The reply was equally sharp. 'I don't see that as any of your affair, sir.'

'Then I take it she was not, though I also do not doubt you invited her. Perhaps when Captain Barclay is maligning me the next time you should have her present and see if his story is altered.'

'You presume to tell me who I should have at my table?'

'I presume to tell you, Captain Daws, once more, that there are two sides to every tale…' Pearce had to stop himself then: to blurt out about the notion of perjury would be unwise. Besides, given the look on the face of the ship's captain it would not have altered his opinion one iota.

'You will not presume on my quarterdeck, which you will oblige me by vacating.'

'I will do so willingly, since I am beginning to think that being elevated to post rank deprives a man of judgement when it ought to aid him.'

Daws actually sneered. 'The kind of judgement that sees a fellow running through the streets in his flapping shirt, perhaps?'

'Better that, sir, than take the common route to naval gratification which is through the whorehouse or the mids' berth.'

Daws puffed up to blast him, but Pearce was already gone, making for the waist, running into Heinrich Lutyens, who had been close enough to overhear the conversation, as had half the people on the ship, given it had started normally but moved on to become noisily acrimonious.

'Such a talent for making enemies, John, I have never seen or heard the like.'

'When one is surrounded by fools—'

'You are angry that Captain Barclay has damned you to a stranger?'

'I care nothing for what he says of me.'

'Which flies in the face of what you have just done, brother. You care deeply and so you should, but neither should you be surprised.'

'Just let me get to London with the evidence I have and we will see Ralph Barclay in no position to blacken anyone, me included, lest it be the gaoler who holds the key to the perjuring bastard's cell.'

It was only because Cornelius Gherson stopped that

John Pearce spotted him: the deck was, after all, quite busy with people moving about and it was clear by the look on his face he had overheard the words just used, a stare that was part a question as to what was meant. Then he looked away and walked past Pearce and Lutyens before disappearing down a companionway with Lutyens' eyes on his back.

'I take it you mean your intention to see Captain Barclay arraigned for perjury?'

'Yes.'

'Then I would advise you not to speak of it, even to me. I have never known a place like a ship where it is so difficult to keep a secret.'

Going below to the wardroom, Pearce knew as soon as he entered that the atmosphere had changed: not one of those present would look at him, which included the lieutenant with his arm in a sling, and the premier, whose bandaged and splinted leg was resting on a chair. Hitherto things had been easy, he had been ribbed about his exploits in the bedchamber, not without a hint of jealousy for his good fortune, and it had, in all respects, been like any other wardroom where, even if there was dislike, it was well hidden by good manners.

Not now, obviously, and such a change could only have come from the captain. What had Barclay said about him? Was it just the truth of his distaste, supported by malevolence, or had he invented some tale to further blacken his name? The one thing which was certain was that he could not enquire, but he was damned if he was going to be discomfited by these fellows, so supine in their attitude to their superior that they eschewed any independence of mind.

'I am looking forward to Gibraltar, as I am sure you are too,' he said gaily. 'We must all take a run ashore together, we being such boon companions.'

The response was a series of coughs and splutters.

Cornelius Gherson was sitting on a sea chest, in a screened-off cabin, lit only by a tallow wad guttering in a lantern, wondering at the import of what he had overheard. Having been a witness at Ralph Barclay's court martial, as well as partaking in the discussions that had preceded it, he knew very well what a charade it had been, nothing more than a pretence set up and designed to exonerate him. Of all the witnesses who had spoken he had told the fewest lies, or if he had mouthed untruths, they had been of a nature difficult to challenge, either then or in the future, being impressions or recollections of one-to-one conversations.

But he knew to what degree others had perjured themselves. Barclay himself had been wise enough to decline to say anything other than to accept his responsibilities as the captain of HMS *Brilliant*: whatever others had done, mistakenly or not, his commission meant the blame lay with him. It had been a telling defence, more likely prompted by the fear that his wife, being present, might blurt out that he was a liar, though there was some risk in his acceptance that the testimony of others had been truthful.

The real danger to Barclay's position did not lie with either of them but with the other witnesses, yet the only one journeying back to England with them was Devenow and he would cut out his tongue rather than let down a man he seemed to venerate. Toby Burns, the true weak spot, the one who could sink them all, and would do so were he ever put in a witness box, was still in Leghorn, as was the only other witness, a rat-faced one-time bosun's mate called Kemp.

Yet Pearce had spoken with confidence and that had to have some basis. Mulling over the possibilities, he would have said from his experience that to bring a case against the captain was not only foolhardy, it would be expensive and futile, unless...did Pearce have something apart from his companions, his stupidly named Pelicans, to support an accusation? They were hardly a threat: a known felon, a stripling of a boy run from his apprenticeship and a fellow of large frame and limited intelligence, an Irishman, not a race to be given too much credence in an English court.

Self-centred in the extreme, though he would not have admitted it, Cornelius Gherson's underlying concern was not for Ralph Barclay but for himself. He had attached himself to the man because being a clerk, a position for which he was admirably fitted, was a damn sight better than serving on the lower deck. If John Pearce had railed against being pressed into the navy he had not been more vociferous in his objections than the man now contemplating his own future. Gherson hated the smells, the filth, the ignorance of those he was obliged to mess with, and being ordered about by blue-coated fools as much as anyone.

He was a man who had enjoyed comfort and yearned for nothing more than to return to that: to warm fires in good houses, with simple and compliant young wives wedded to older, busy men who required an assiduous clerk to oversee their personal affairs, too occupied to see that some of their hard-earned money was being siphoned off to their willing bookkeeper. That had been his life: he had had the benefit of good clothes, a full purse, usually wise enough to move on before matters reached the crisis of discovery. Only he had been caught out and that had led him to this place.

He rarely thought about being chucked off London Bridge, it being such an unpleasant recollection, but he did so now. He could see the faces of the grinning toughs employed by Alderman Denby Carruthers, feel their hands as they first stripped him of his good clothes before lifting him bodily over the parapet, the sickening feeling in the pit of his belly as he fell, and the icy-cold shock of landing in the waters of the River Thames. He harboured no gratitude for the hand of the man in the boat, HMS *Brilliant*'s master-at-arms, who had grabbed his collar and saved his life.

Taken aboard the frigate he was pressed like the others, low-life types whom he would have spat on in his previous life. His protests that he was a gentleman and thus outside the scope of the press gang had foundered on the fact that he was dressed in nothing but a shirt; indeed, his contention had provoked laughter, leaving him humiliated. Somehow, in his convoluted thinking, he managed to drag an image of John Pearce into that, so that all the hate he felt was fixed upon him. He and Pearce had clashed quickly, the man being an unctuous prig who saw himself as superior in every way, when he was nought but a jumped-up nobody, and that dislike had done nothing but deepen with the passing of time and acquaintance.

'He must know he cannot bring a case without evidence,' he said softly to himself. 'Ergo, he must, as he so plainly said, have evidence.'

Ralph Barclay would get another ship, probably one a great deal larger than HMS *Brilliant*. The opportunities for peculation were high in the King's Navy and one asset Barclay had was his lack of any false morality. He was as prepared to pilfer as any man should be, this as long as it was carefully done, and in Cornelius Gherson he had a man of some expertise. It was Gherson who had set up the removal of goods from the Toulon stores; he who had dealt with the various French officials, trading valuable commodities for a promise of evacuation.

Yet it would have been pointless without Ralph Barclay: only he could sanction and cover the use of the ship's holds to store the purloined goods. If that enterprise had ultimately failed to produce a profit he was sure there would be others. That was why he had stuck with the man: he did not like him much, but that mattered less than his prospects. He was in the top third of the captain's list during a war that could last for years. Commanding a ship he could line both their pockets, and should time allow him to advance to the rank of commodore or admiral, the sky was the limit. As for life in the navy, if it had its unpleasant side Gherson could live with that, given he had no idea if life ashore was still dangerous: if the man he had robbed and cuckolded found out he had survived, he might seek to dispose of him a second time.

He had to force his mind away from pleasant speculations of future wealth onto the present problem: how to confound John Pearce, if indeed he needed to be confounded. He needed to know what he had, or indeed if he had anything at all, and there was no point in asking the principal. What he needed was a weak link: Charlie Taverner and he shared the mutual loathing of two peas from the same pod, while nothing would be gained by seeking information from that brute O'Hagan.

But Rufus Dommet was young and something of an idiot. He might reveal things supposed to be secret and not even know he was doing so. One other thing Gherson had to do must be acted upon right away: he must apprise Ralph Barclay of the possibility of the threat.

Heinrich Lutyens was amused by the way Emily Barclay had repeatedly described John Pearce's behaviour in

Livorno as reprehensible; not endlessly, but somehow the subject had been alluded to more often than it should, given there was no connection between them other than social contact. Odd that all her troubles with her husband, though they had been deepened by his behaviour, had begun with her defence of the very same fellow; perhaps that was why she felt she could refer to him in such a proprietary way.

Whatever excuse Ralph Barclay had come up with to flog John Pearce it had been more to do with the familiar way the man addressed his wife than for any offence listed in the Articles of War, and Emily had made her displeasure at his actions as plain to him as had the crew of the frigate: the whole affair had hurt Barclay much more than his supposed victim. But it was really the court martial, which she had attended even though she had been forbidden to do so, which had ripped a seemingly irreparable tear in their marriage.

Cunningly it had been arranged to take place when several witnesses who would have damned Ralph Barclay were away on another duty, courtesy of Admiral Hotham, the verdict coming as a shock on Pearce's return, especially when he discovered that none of the written depositions he and the Pelicans had dictated to one of Hotham's clerks had been introduced as testimony.

'You may say what you wish, Heinrich, about the lax morals of the Latins, but to me, the vision of a

British officer being required to flee the bedroom of a married woman is shocking.'

'I fear you would find the behaviour of most British naval officers shocking, my dear.'

Working as she was on her embroidery, the needle moved more speedily as an indication of her discomfort: if he had not mentioned the whorehouses of Livorno he was alluding to them. 'Then I hope you will forbear to enlighten me.'

'There was one tale I heard that is amusing.' Seeing her lift both head and eyebrows, he continued. 'Do you know the name Hervey?'

'Is that not the name of the earls of Bristol?'

'Indeed, coming from Somerset I thought you would know it. A family of bishops and politicians to boot, though it is one of their number who was a post captain, a certain Augustus Hervey, who generated this tale. Seemingly he was based in Leghorn during the Seven Years' conflict and was such a Lothario, and so enamoured of those loose Latin morals you so deplore, he managed to father some fifty bastards.'

'Why are you telling me this?'

'Perhaps to put in some context the behaviour of John Pearce, whom you seem eager to condemn. Compared to Hervey he is a novice.'

'Two wrongs do not make a right.'

'Nor do fifty, my dear, and nor does your continuing refusal to share the quarters of your husband.'

That stopped the needle but she still looked at the

threaded pattern. 'I thought you, of all people, Heinrich, would not seek to chastise me for that.'

'I do not seek to chastise you, my dear, merely to point out to you that none of us are perfect. I would also point out, and I do this out of regard for you, that tongues are wagging aboard this ship as they were in Toulon. It was a mistake to decline to join your husband for dinner with Captain Daws. That will be remarked upon.'

'I cannot help it. The thought of sitting in pretence, of behaving as if all is well, appals me.'

'Perhaps it does, but I think you must turn your mind to how you are going to behave once we are back in England. Such an attitude will not serve.'

'Do you think I have not thought about it already?'

'And?'

Tears wetted her eyes and affected her voice as she replied. 'I am at a loss to know what to do.'

CHAPTER TWELVE

Getting into the Bay of Algeciras was difficult at any time, lying as it did on the western side of the Rock of Gibraltar. The tidal flow into the Mediterranean was strong and it needed a good wind from the east to weather Punta Europa; for two days the wind was, while not dead foul, far from helpful, so HMS *Grampus* was required to beat up, tack on tack, to make any headway. The delay gave Gherson time to seek to isolate Rufus Dommet, something he utterly failed to achieve.

Every time he got within ten feet of the youngster, Rufus sought out Charlie Taverner and a glare from that source was enough to stop Gherson in his tracks. Forced to seek an accommodation with Taverner, he was exposed to a stream of loud and foul abuse, as well as a question from Michael O'Hagan as to his ability to swim.

Frustrated, he sought out Devenow to seek his aid, well aware that the brute had reservations about him, jealousy of a man closer to his captain than he. The conversation was not one to produce a conclusion, but Devenow was vocal about one thing: the way the Pelicans were sure they were free men. In the end, it was Rufus who underlined that belief by boasting, within the hearing of another sailor, one Devenow was successfully able to bully, that the order for their release from the navy came from the mighty Sam Hood himself, a point Gherson made to his employer.

'Why, Captain Barclay, would Lord Hood do that if he had no reason?'

Ralph Barclay, mulling on that question, was aware he should have been more curious from the very beginning about the presence of Pearce and his friends on board HMS *Grampus*, though he did grant himself some leeway for the fact of his lost arm. The mere fact that they were travelling back to England should have alerted him to something, even if he knew not what.

'That alone makes me doubly suspicious,' Gherson added.

'Doubly?'

Gherson was good at extracting advantage from scanty knowledge, a necessary gift if you wanted to become someone on whom your principal relied; thus his hesitation and the adoption of the look which accompanied it, of deep thought mixed with an air of doubt, meant to convey that he was not sure he should speak at all. He had, unfortunately, forgotten the level of impatience innate to the man with whom he was dealing.

'Do not trifle with me, Gherson. If you have something to impart, do it and cut out the play-acting.'

The wish to protest died in the face of Ralph Barclay's glare, yet there was some pleasure to be obtained from being just a little brusque. 'I overheard John Pearce say he expects to see you in the dock, that followed by gaol, and he used an expression which implied the charge would be perjury.'

The word struck Ralph Barclay hard, so hard he had trouble in retaining an equable countenance, and at that moment his lost arm was a blessing, the act of easing it providing time to swallow the import of what had just been said.

'He is a man prone to bluster, Gherson,' he said eventually.

'He is, sir, as we both know, a man prone to many things. What we don't know is plain. Was he engaging in bluster, or speaking the truth?'

'How could he be?'

'If I may be allowed to quote him, sir, he said that with the evidence he had he would see you in the dock.'

Ralph Barclay was not looking at Gherson anymore, he was looking at his own knees, his mind set to racing by the word 'evidence'. As sharp to his own advantage as the man before him, it took only seconds to run through the various scenarios that would give some substance to those repeated words. Hotham was a treacherous sod, of that he was sure – all admirals were – but he could not drop him in the soup without being damaged himself, and he could discount Devenow or Kemp. For a fleeting moment he wondered if Gherson was playing a double game, before dismissing that too.

In his mind's eye he was back in that cabin-cum-courtroom, with the faces of the men who had judged him prominent. They would stand by their verdict or risk looking foolish, but there were two people present who could damage him and it gave him no pleasure to think one of them was his own wife. Yet she was barred from testifying against him by that very relationship, which left only her nephew Toby Burns. Had that little cowardly toad given something to Pearce that could hurt him, and if he had, what could it be?

'You will, I suspect, sir, have arrived at the same conclusion as me?'

'Which is?'

'Mr Burns.'

'He is still aboard HMS *Britannia*.'

'Perhaps he made a deposition.'

'When?'

'We were in Leghorn for ten days.'

'No, Gherson, the boy hates Pearce as much as I do. If he saw the bastard he would run a mile. Besides, any deposition would have to be witnessed by some kind of notary...'

'Or perhaps another post captain.'

'Who was Pearce friendly with?'

'I believe he got on rather well with Captain Nelson, though there may be others we have no knowledge of.' Seeing the effect that had on his employer, the implication that he was unpopular in places of which he had no knowledge, Gherson continued quickly. 'I confess, sir, I am unsure if deposing an affidavit to a post captain would carry the necessary weight to imperil anyone.'

'Sorry, Gherson, it won't wash, not with Toby Burns.'

Cornelius Gherson knew that another name had come to Ralph Barclay's mind before he spoke, just by the look, a mixture of hate and alarm, which swept across his face. When he spat the name, it made perfect sense.

'Hood!'

'Did he not confirm the conclusion of the court, sir, as he was bound to do as commander-in-chief?'

'He would not have done it with any pleasure, given he has little regard for me.'

'Lack enough to admit his confirmation was a sham? Surely the one cancels out the other and leaves only malice as a motive, which would be easy to discredit with a good advocate.'

Ralph Barclay's eyes narrowed as he looked at his clerk. 'You seem to know a lot about the law, Gherson.'

'I know enough, sir, to be sure that the verdict in any case is never certain.' He nearly added 'except your court martial', but thought better of it. 'And that applies to both the plaintiff and the accused.'

'Say Pearce has something, whatever it is must be aboard with him.'

'And he is berthed in the wardroom, to which we do not have access.'

From looking pensive, Ralph Barclay suddenly brightened up. 'We're making for Gibraltar, Gherson, and I know it to be a place where every officer, marines included, excepting the poor fellow left on watch, will go ashore. With the watch officer on deck that means the wardroom will be unoccupied.'

The look Ralph Barclay was giving Gherson made his stomach turn over: there was no way a one-armed post captain still convalescent could go skulking about a ship, even if it was at anchor. His employer was telling him, when it came to going through the belongings of John Pearce, it was a job for him.

'There will still be the wardroom servants,' he replied, trying to keep a note of panic out of his voice: he was not averse to theft, it was getting caught which bothered him.

'With their charges ashore they will stay snug in their quarters, or mix with the rest of the crew.'

'The marine guard?'

'I know Daws to be lax in the article of women at anchor. With the wardroom empty all the lobsters will be occupied making sure the whores don't bring illicit drink aboard.'

'Still, sir—'

'Gherson, I cannot do it and you know why. If you are to have a future with me this is a deed that must be done, otherwise I might as well call upon Captain Daws and tell him he has a new hand for the lower deck.'

Cornelius Gherson, while thinking he had no choice, was also thinking that one day he would make Ralph Barclay pay for that threat.

'Devenow will help you, by keeping watch, and if you wish, I will walk the main deck and seek to engage the wardroom servants in conversation should they show themselves.'

In the end the boats had to be used to warp HMS *Grampus* into Algeciras Bay, the great bight of water which housed Spanish warships on one side and a British squadron on the other, from where they had eyed each other, and occasionally fought each other, since the Treaty of Utrecht, which ceded the rock to the first King George, not surprising since his forces had possession of it and were not about to relinquish what was, after all, the key to the Mediterranean. Besieged several times, possession had often been hanging by a thread, but it was a central plank of British maritime policy, second only to command of the Channel, that it must be held whatever the cost.

Ninety plus years of occupation had turned it from a Spanish entity to a mixed one, for, while it had a strong garrison and many British officials, the place could not have functioned without the aid of the indigenes, happy to accept a steady wage and ignore whatever it was they owed to the Spanish Crown. The taverns looked, in all respects, as if they could have stood close to the hard of Portsmouth harbour, but the women who served the ale were as dark skinned as they were buxom. Every sort of vice was, of course, catered for and hardly had *Grampus* dropped her best bower anchor than the boats were in the water, to carry ashore those who desired to partake of the many pleasures Gibraltar had to offer.

That included trusted members of the crew, and given the Pelicans were not on the ship's muster, it was not surprising they too were intent on going ashore. But it was officers and warrants first, obliging them to wait for a boat, since they were unwilling to pay for their transport. The last person in the wardroom, Pearce, stood in his tiny cabin weighing in his hand the fair copy of Barclay's court martial report, a loose, bulky, sheaf of papers, wondering whether to take it ashore and deciding against it, yet being unsure if it was safe here. Lutyens he knew to be staying aboard, so he opted to leave it with him.

There was also Hood's letter, sealed and still in its oilskin pouch, something the surgeon knew nothing about and it would be best kept that way, so he left it behind, along with the order releasing his friends from the service. Padlocking the chest did not occur to him: the only things he feared to lose were in his hands and any money he had was in his purse. His last act was to open the lantern that lit his cabin and extinguish the flame.

Bumboats surrounded the ship, trading through the gun ports and since, as Ralph Barclay had said, Captain Daws was no prig, women had come aboard to turn the lower decks into a scene of music, singing, and a fair amount of indiscreet carnality. Every one had been searched by marines for illicit spirits, rum and gin, a lot of which, given the cunning of the carriers, the lobsters failed to find, meaning that a degree of drunkenness was added to the mix. Such activities confined Emily Barclay to the quarters she had taken up, next to those of Heinrich Lutyens. She could hear the noise of merriment but would shudder to walk through it, just as she could also hear, through a very thin partition, the request that the surgeon take care of a package Pearce did not want to leave unattended while he was off the ship.

'The transcript of the court martial, I presume?' the surgeon enquired.

Pearce's reply was soft, so low she had to struggle to hear it and was ashamed of herself for her eavesdropping, even more so for moving closer to do so more effectively.

'Heinrich, I have never mentioned aboard this ship that I have possession of these papers and I would be grateful if you would avoid mentioning it too. Ships are not places to discuss secrets, something you have already alluded to.'

'I am being admonished.'

'You know I trust you of all people, so silence on this is mere precaution. Only you and my friends know Lord Hood let me copy the transcript of Barclay's court martial and I would like it kept that way. If he knew of its existence, who knows what he might resort to in order to stop it reaching London.'

'I shall put it in the case with my bone saws. No one will lay a hand on those for a superstitious fear that to do so might see them lose a limb.'

'Thank you.'

'You are going to enjoy the fleshpots of Gibraltar, I take it.'

'I am going to share a drink with Michael, Charlie and Rufus, something I cannot do aboard ship. Fortunately Gibraltar is so awash with taverns we should have no trouble finding one where we will not be observed. I have some questions I need to put to them, questions to which I badly require answers.'

'For instance, what you and they are going to do when you reach England?'

'It is that obvious?'

'To anyone with half a brain.'

'A question, my friend, which applies equally to you.'

'Odd, is it not, John? We have a ship full of people who fear going home as much as they yearn for it.'

That hit Emily hard, making her recoil from listening, so the last exchanges were nought but a murmur, making her wonder if they were about her.

Devenow was not pleased at being denied the pleasures being enjoyed all around him, both women and drink, but if Captain Ralph Barclay commanded, he would obey. Loitering near the wardroom doors, now without a sentry, his broad back covered the ingress of Cornelius Gherson, who called softly to cover his entry as, carrying a shed lantern, he slipped through one of the double doors, lest there be someone who had remained behind. The pantry, where the servants might loiter, he had checked first.

The main cabin was empty, as Barclay had predicted, the octagonal table that dominated the centre of the room – really a panelled and painted cover to hide the head of the rudder – and the chairs set by it, showing evidence of the hurried departure of those who messed here: working coats and hats slung off, brushes and the like that had been used to clean their best uniforms, a smattering of powder over the places where a wig had been carelessly dressed, for the master, older than the others, still adhered to that old-fashioned habit. Given the disorder, it was obvious what Barclay had said about the servants was true.

'There are seven cabins,' Barclay had informed him. 'You can avoid the accommodation of the premier, his second lieutenant and the master, which are on the larboard side. There are four smaller cabins to starboard and Pearce will not be gifted anything approaching the best. The one you want will likely be that nearest to the quarter gallery that serves as the wardroom privy. I made sure Daws was aware of the poison he was carrying and I know that was a message he passed on to his officers. Pearce is lucky not to be bedded in the privy itself, but he will be close to the stink of the place, which serves him well.'

The space was tiny, painted white and barely big enough to sling the cot that filled it. The lantern, unshaded, revealed Pearce's sea chest, with his initials upon it, parked beneath. Lifting the lid, the first thing Gherson saw was the oilskin pouch and that went straight into his coat pocket. Rummaging around, all he could discover were spare shirts and stockings, plus an old battered tin which, when he prised it open, revealed compacted, dry earth, a bit of which fell to the floor and had to be hurriedly brushed into the planking.

Satisfied he might have what he was looking for, Gherson shaded the lantern again and made his way back out on to the main deck, nodding to Devenow to tell him that he could go and indulge himself with the rest of the crew. Then it was back to Ralph Barclay to open the pouch and see what it contained. The folded but unsealed order releasing the Pelicans, signed by Parker, was of interest, causing Barclay to curse both the captain of the fleet and the man he served.

It was also a strong indication that, despite Hood

confirming the verdict of his court martial, he harboured doubts about it, which made Barclay wonder what that might portend, though he was quick to dismiss any worry. The trio named were lowly seamen so any threat they might present would be minimal. The response was different when he examined the letter.

'The Right Honourable William Pitt MP,' Barclay said, in a hushed tone, when he examined the superscription. Then he turned it over to look at the seal, catching his breath as he examined it. 'Damn me, that's Hood's seal.'

'May I?' Gherson asked, holding out a hand, taking the letter and examining it when Barclay did as he was bid. 'I take it you would wish to know the contents, sir?'

That got Gherson a hard look. 'Am I right in thinking you can open this?'

'Not only open it, but reseal it so no one would know it has been tampered with.'

'I am forced to ask what it was you did to earn a crust prior to joining the navy, Gherson?'

That got a terse response. 'I think you of all people, sir, know I did not join, I was pressed.'

'That is all water under the bridge,' Barclay spat, before laughing as he saw the horrified look on Gherson's face. 'An inadvertent pun but, by the devil, a good one.'

'Let me take this to my berth.'

'No. Whatever you do must be done in my presence.'

'You do not trust me, sir?'

'Nonsense,' Barclay lied, 'of course I do, but I want to see how it is done.'

Unconvinced, Gherson gave him back the letter and exited, to return in a few minutes carrying a knife so thin the blade appeared too flexible to wound. He also had a shaker of wig powder and a square of cloth.

'Where did you get those?'

'In Toulon, sir, where else? Please be so good as to fetch over that lantern and open the door.'

That done, Gherson lifted a cushion off the stern locker and smoothed the cloth over the bare wood, then he laid the letter on that and very carefully sprinkled a little powder around the seal. He indicated to Barclay to put the lantern down, heating his thin knife blade over the tallow flame, turning it this way and that until it glowed, then took it off the flame and allowed it to cool.

'It must be hot, but not so that it will burn the paper on which the letter is written, which is fortunately of a very high quality.'

'That makes a difference?'

'Very much so, sir, given this would be much more difficult with paper of poor quality. That marks more readily.'

Kneeling down, Gherson spread his index finger and thumb and pressed down on the paper, peering close to slip the hot blade under the very edge of the seal, flattening it, then making a gentle sawing motion as he worked the wax loose.

'The powder takes the heat not the paper, so there is no burn mark.'

Barclay reached for the now open letter, only to have Gherson knock his hand away. 'You must wait till the wax has completely cooled.'

Ralph Barclay had to stop himself from swiping him with his one good hand: no one treated him with such contempt, but he was too curious about the contents of the letter to do so. Gherson closed the lantern door and, once he had unfolded the letter, he held it over the writing so that both Barclay and he could easily read it.

'By damn, he's trying to ditch Hotham, the old fraud.'

'I see no mention of you, sir, and that I think is more important.'

'Are you sure this was all you could find?'

'Yes,' Gherson snapped.

'Do not get above yourself, Gherson, I won't stand for it.'

'What do you want to do with this?'

'Can you reseal it?'

'Of course.'

Ralph Barclay had to restrain himself again: no one talked to him in such a manner, damn near to sneering, regardless of their nefarious skills.

'Then it needs to be copied, resealed and returned to Pearce's sea chest.'

'What?'

'Which, Gherson, means you best get about it.'

He had to take it back to his berth, carefully refolded and hidden inside his coat. There he quickly copied what Hood had written and took it back to Barclay's cabin, where, blowing off what powder remained, he reheated his knife and ran it over the exposed back of the seal, taking care to keep his other hand underneath the wax to ensure it did not drip. The act of resealing was carried out quickly, pressure applied to allow the melted wax to congeal. Having waited to make sure it was solid, Gherson slipped it back into the oilskin pouch.

'You will have to aid me, sir.'

'What!' Barclay exclaimed, lifting his head from Gherson's fair copy.

'Devenow went to join his kind. If he is not astride some whore he will be in drink and I would not trust him in that state to keep watch for me.'

'No, Gherson, I cannot be seen to be complicit. This is a task you must carry out alone.'

'What if I were to suggest, sir, that it need not be returned?'

'You're not shy are you, man?'

'No, sir, I am at risk, while you are not.'

'In a good cause, Gherson,' Barclay replied, trying and failing to suppress a yawn. 'Best, I think, you do what must be done quickly.'

The mutual eye contact was far from friendly, but both men knew that there was little choice in the matter.

'After all,' Barclay added, 'we would not want you caught in the wardroom once our stalwarts come back from their revels. It is not unknown for officers in drink to be free with their fists.'

Sat anxiously, with the book she had been trying to read in her lap, Emily Barclay prayed that Lutyens would leave his part of their shared berth, while also alternating between determination and apprehension. There was also the problem of justifying her intention, rationalised on the grounds that, with difficult decisions to make regarding her own future, she needed to know what Pearce's words portended for the man to whom she was married. Every time she tried to read, the words 'perjury' and 'court martial' played on her mind and it was with a panicked reaction she got the book up to her nose as the screen twitched before being hauled back.

'I must walk the deck and see what is going on,' Lutyens said.

'Hardly necessary, Heinrich,' Emily replied automatically, before cursing herself. 'You can hear enough to guess.'

'A picture paints a thousand words.'

'The picture of which you speak requires only one – disgraceful.'

That got her a wan smile. 'We must not be too quick to judge.'

Then he was gone and she strained to hear his receding footsteps before pulling back the curtain once more to ensure he had truly departed. Seeing no one, she slipped quickly into the other berth, kneeling before the chest in which he kept his instruments, many secured to the lid of his chest. The case with the bone saws she recognised immediately, having seen it too many times since her first experience of helping him treat the wounded.

The papers were not hidden, they lay instead on top, and a quick perusal of the first sheets told her precisely what they contained, though her heart skipped a beat to read the words, written in a fine sloping hand, which opened her husband's trial. Leafing through she came to the parts at which she had been present, the words, or to be more accurate the lies, familiar from memory. There was no time to read them all and no need: she knew what they were and that sufficed.

When Lutyens returned, looking in to say he had done so, she was still holding the book, but reading it, difficult before, had become impossible now.

CHAPTER THIRTEEN

With a great deal of shipping in Gibraltar, finding a quiet corner to talk was not easy, that made doubly difficult by the obvious desire of his trio of friends to visit the more interesting fleshpots. Rufus in particular, having dipped his wick in Leghorn, was afire to compare where they were now with what he had experienced there, and it took damn near an order from John Pearce to get them to allow him the time he thought he needed.

'Sure,' Michael O'Hagan said, 'the navy all comes down to where you are serving and who you are under, John-boy.' Then he grinned. 'And I'd add to that the number of heathens you have to mess with.'

'Dogs lead a better life,' said Charlie, leaving Rufus, who had been nodding at Michael's opinion, half shaking his head at the same time.

'Like the one you led when we met?' asked Pearce.

'I was my own master, John,' Charlie insisted, before looking around, he being sat on the very edge of the booth they were occupying, to ensure he had not been overheard.

'Holy Mary, Mother of God,' Michael swore, crossing himself out of habit. 'You as a master of anything makes a soul shudder.'

Pearce looked at him hard. 'You were damn near starving, Charlie, and I recall your tankard was empty and I had to fill it.'

'I had my mates,' he replied, suddenly looking wistful. 'Old Abel, God rest his soul, was a good friend, and Ben.'

'I wonder whether he is still in the land of the living,' said Rufus, his gaze on John Pearce.

'Don't look at me like that, Rufus. There was nothing I could do that would not get us all killed.'

That had them drinking silently and thinking about Ben Walker, who, for reasons of his own, had declined to leave HMS *Brilliant* and the command of Ralph Barclay, off the coast of Brittany, when given the chance. Pearce knew that to be a better vision of him than the last time he had clapped eyes on him, toiling as an emaciated slave, burdened by grain sacks and being whipped to move faster by a pitiless overseer on the Barbary shore. Ben had recognised John Pearce, blue coat and all, which had led to a confrontation with the whip-bearing overseer, and a noisy one at that, only to find himself surrounded by the quick arrival of armed men.

Forced to go back aboard ship, as much by his own superiors as any threat of weaponry, Pearce had set out to mount a rescue, thwarted by the man who commanded the ship on which he was serving. The fact that such an intervention was fitting did not make the memory of having to leave Ben to his fate any more palatable. Looking over the taffrail at Tunis sinking into the horizon had been hard, reckoning, as he did, that he was leaving a friend to die.

'Can't understand why he didn't want to come with us,' Charlie said, shaking his head. 'You had words with him, John – do you know?'

'I think he'd found a place, Charlie, and maybe some peace. He never told you why he was in the Liberties, did he, what he was running from? The rest of you were open, he was not.'

It was Rufus who articulated the agreement. 'No, he kept that to hisself: close was Ben.'

'Then I reckon it was something he could not happily live with,' Pearce responded. 'Somehow he saw the navy as a break with whatever it was.'

'Bad, then?' Rufus asked.

'We'll never know, will we?'

At that moment, hundreds of miles to the east, Ben Walker, well fed and healthy, was continuing in his efforts to learn Arabic, without which he could not go on to be instructed in the Mussulman's holy book, the Koran. His teacher, appointed by the Bey of Tunis in an act of caprice that hinted at salvation, was a grey beard with soft brown eyes that mirrored a gentle manner. To Ben it was barely believable: by reputation the pirates of the Barbary Coast, and the Bey was certainly that, were the stuff of nightmares, inclined to sell into concubinage any women they captured; men were either killed or made slaves.

Ben had enjoyed a brief moment of hope when he espied John Pearce, only to see that disappear as the local power forced him to retreat, the whole played out on his defenceless back by the man who whipped him doubly hard for his disobedience. He had then been dragged off by force, this pointing to only one fate, and Ben had no idea what had saved him from summery execution. He only knew that, being interrogated by one of the Bey's courtiers, for the first time since he killed the girl he deeply loved and the man who had seduced her, he had told another human the story and allowed the tears he should have shed years ago to flow.

Instead of the beheading he anticipated – no doubt after a decent bout of cruel torture for both his crime and his Christianity – he had been treated with gentility: first bathed and allowed new clothes, then taken to the comfortable cell he still occupied, fed so that from being a near skeleton he had been brought back to full, rude health. The price of his deliverance was this instruction; he had no idea of the why and wherefores, he only knew that life was better than death and that he had gratitude for whatever God of whatever religion had intervened to let him live.

Alone at night he often wondered about the men with whom he had been pressed from the Pelican Tavern – given his solitary life, more than they thought about him – men he had come to know through shared misfortune, and even more closely through shared adventure. When they had left to go back to England he had declined to join them, knowing he would be returning to a life he had not enjoyed one bit, a life where his past deeds weighed heavily on his conscience.

Often he envisaged that separation, those last farewell gestures from the deck of the merchantman they were taking home, a quartet of figures in their ducks and short jackets. Given that image he had struggled with another. What in the name of eternity had John Pearce been doing in an officer's blue coat and behaving as though he was entitled to the wearing of it? Had the others been with him, Charlie, Rufus and that giant O'Hagan? The thing he thought about most, though, was obvious: his own eventual fate.

For what had he been spared, perhaps so he would make a more convincing victim? Those were the thoughts of the dark nights: during the day, as he was allowed to wander, with an escort, the courtyards and hallways of the Bey's palace, allowed to dip his finger in the many cool fountains, and even occasionally be taken outside the palace walls and into the bazaar,

Ben Walker wondered if he had been blessed in some way. But more than that he wondered if he had been forgiven.

'To Ben and Abel, may God bless and keep them,' said Michael, lifting his tankard and, as the others joined with him, emptying it in honour of their dead comrades.

That made John Pearce more reflective than the others: Abel Scrivens, crushed between barrels in the deep hold of HMS *Brilliant*, had died in place of him, the real target of the malice of Martin Dent. Odd that he thought of the boy in a kindly way now; how strange life was. So many things had been resolved when they had all been stranded on the Breton shore, not least that Martin had behaved with enough bravery and application to impress him, even more so when the boy asked him for forgiveness. He knew, for a fact, that he had come into his own then, had shown that he could think clearly in a crisis, lead and, more importantly, command both loyalty and obedience; that was until he thought of Toby Burns, who had not only proved to be lily-livered, but deeply treacherous to boot. The mention of his name darkened Michael's demeanour.

'Sure,' he growled, 'I am not a man to wish ill on anybody, but if the good Lord could see fit to take off that boy's head with a cannonball I would be content.'

'A lying little shite that Toby Burns, Michael,' added Charlie.

'Now don't you go givin' shite a bad name.'

'Refills,' said Pearce.

Toby Burns was on deck, sharing the watch with Mr Beddows, trying to look as martial as possible, with HMS *Britannia* ploughing her way towards Corsica and more battle. The bandage he had been required to abandon, but he had taken to combing his hair forward over his brow when not wearing his hat, and if those he messed with wondered if there was a scar to show, they were too polite to ask: after all, their fellow midshipman was much cosseted by Admiral Hotham and no one wanted to offend him.

In a ship of few secrets – there was no ship in the fleet adept at keeping those – the proposed destination towards which they were heading was common knowledge. The town at the base of the Bay of San Fiorenzo was to be the first place on the island that Lord Hood intended to subdue. It was even known how many arguments he had undertaken with his army generals, who were adverse to any kind of action until they had more troops to command, acquiescing in the attack only when not to do so would smack of being shy.

Naturally, being bullocks, they had to be got ashore before they could fight anyone. Toby Burns had learned that he, under the command of Beddows, had been given a place on the first draft of boats that would land them on the hostile shore. At dinner, after orders had been issued, those others who would have the same sort of duty had been eager to talk of how quickly they, too, could get ashore and take part in the action. They at least were honest if foolish, in contrast to the hypocritical senior of the mids' berth, who would be remaining aboard: he had somehow escaped the proposed landing.

'Burns, you of all people must be afire to add more lustre to your reputation. I am envious in the extreme.'

Looking at a man near thirty years of age, a shallow thinker whom he knew would never make lieutenant, the fellow having already failed the examination twice, he wondered on how unfair life was, while at the same time enthusiastically acceding to the expressed sentiment. The older fellow only kept his place as a mid so he could be fed and watered at the king's expense: with no pay and no private means he would have been reduced to beggary ashore. His seniority in the berth came from his years not his ability. Why was it that such a useless creature was spared risk when he was so regularly exposed?

Toasting the coming attack with wine that was almost undrinkable, he thought back to the last time he had taken a boat into a proposed attack. God, he hoped the man who would command him off that round tower was cleverer than the old bugger who had run them aground in Brittany: he had nearly drowned in a maelstrom of rocks and spume-filled water for want of the man's ability to steer the right course, and then he had been stranded with that swine Pearce and the others, who had acted as if he should solve their problem. He would have done if left to his own devices, surrender being better than stupid sacrifice, but no, clever clogs Pearce had had them all risking their necks in the most stupid fashion and for, to his mind, a dubious purpose.

'By God, Burns,' the senior cried from the top of the table, his face flushed from over-consumption, his voice laced with drunken hyperbole. 'You have about you the face of wrath itself. God help Johnny Crapaud when he feels your steel.'

'Hear him, hear him,' called the rest of the berth, all red-faced, all taken with drink, as they slammed their pewter mugs on the table in support of the senior.

'The question still stands, friends. What are you going to do?'

Greeted with shrugs, Pearce carried on, enumerating the thoughts on which he had already ruminated, Michael, surprisingly, looking less than pleased at the prospect of going back to his shovel.

'You don't get it, John-boy, it's a short life, and as sure as there is a God in heaven, it is a hard one. The men who employ we Irish don't care much if we live or die, and enough do when a trench falls in or a shored-up wall of earth gives way.'

'The pay is good,' Rufus said, with a melancholy air: as an indentured apprentice he had not seen much in the way of that commodity.

'It needs to be, Rufus,' Michael replied, 'for the work is endless. You would not know near despair till you have dug out a lake for some great lord, with teeming rain on your back, or sunk a shaft for a new mine, up to your knees in water.'

'You drank every penny you earned,' chuckled Charlie.

'With what I was doing by day, drink by night was what kept me going. I won't say sailing a ship is easy, nor will I say it is not without risk, but by Jesus it has the legs on ditch digging.'

'Do you want to go back to the Liberties, Charlie?'

'You know I don't, John, just as you know I might not have a choice.'

'You could go back to Lichfield, Rufus, you would surely be safe there.'

Looking at Pearce, Rufus shook his head. 'What do you think my master would have done when I ran? He will have demanded back from my pa what he paid to indenture me. The only thing I would get back in Lichfield is the back of his hand, and more'n once before bein' tied once more to a bench.'

'Warrants might have expired,' Charlie said, but not with a look of any hope.

'And you, John-boy, what are you going to do?'

'You mean after I see Barclay locked up in the Fleet, Michael?' He looked at them all in turn. 'Put your hands on the table, palms up.'

Slowly they obliged, showing skin near black, so ingrained was it with the tar from rope work. There was no need to say what he was implying but he did so anyway.

'Even if you can dodge the tipstaffs, you'll be had up by every crimp in creation and the first thing they will do is ask to see those same hands.' Then he looked at their heads. 'Pigtails don't help much either. You'll be tagged as sailors right off, and unless I can get you protections, you'll be back aboard a king's ship in days, and it's not unknown for them to be ripped up in your face.'

'There will be broken bones and blood spilt, John-boy, if a body tries that.'

'Yours, Michael. The crimps will take one look at the size of you and resort to clubs; Charlie and Rufus they will just nab by force of numbers.'

That induced another bout of silence: what John Pearce was saying was true. To press them would be as illegal as the first and second times it had happened, but once you were on board a ship and out of sight of land that counted for little.

'There are ways to avoid the press, John,' said Rufus, 'as every man aboard will tell you.'

'Not in a port, Rufus, you would need to go inland to be really safe and I don't need to say what risks you run then, even the Liberties have already proved not to be that – safe, I mean.'

211

'But you can get us protections?' asked Charlie.

John Pearce knew what he was driving at. The men who wanted to execute the warrant on Charlie Taverner, who stood on the exits to the Liberties of the Savoy looking for anyone foolish enough to step outside the safe boundary, would have eyes for a fellow quite different to the man sitting opposite Pearce now. Charlie had kept his hair short before, now he had a pigtail; he had walked like any other soul, now he could not help but sway like a sailor; and his tarred hands might be a shield against arrest: the warrant was issued for a landsman.

'I think I can, but I would say to you stay aboard *Grampus* until I put them in your hand. But let's go back to the question Michael first posed. The truth is I have no occupation and little in the way of coin, so I have to find some way of living while the case goes through the lawyers, and I think that will take time, a lot of time if the Admiralty defends Barclay.'

'So?' asked Michael.

'My first job on going ashore is to take a private letter from Lord Hood to the king's first minister. It was he who got me out to the Mediterranean to rescue you in the first place, and I have good grounds to believe if I ask him for a favour he might grant it.'

'That favour bein' what?'

'Maybe I can get the warrants on Charlie and Rufus lifted or, failing that, find us a berth that will keep us in body and soul and keep us together.'

'A naval one?' asked Rufus.

'Probably.'

'With pay?'

'Of course.'

'You're forgetting, John,' said Charlie, grinning, 'that the first thing we want is to see your back.'

'The only time you want to see my back, Charlie, is when I am ordering more ale.'

'For which,' Charlie replied, waving his tankard, 'you seem a bit slow to get a'movin' on, which I seem to recall is your way. You needed a nudge the night we met.'

Emily Barclay had given up trying to read: those papers she had found under Lutyens' bone saws impinged too much on her thinking and the ramifications of what they would mean were endless. For her husband they would possibly mean a life in hard labour or transportation and, much as she had come to see him in an unflattering way – even if she knew the case to be correct – she yet did not want to see that wished upon him. If he was incarcerated what would become of her? Was it a selfish thought to imagine a life in the shadow of that disgrace, certainly one in which she would have no income, for his pay would cease with conviction, but also one in which she would be left in the limbo of a grass widowhood?

How would she live? No one would take her in as a governess, the only occupation for which she could lay any claim to be qualified, with that stain of association to her name, leaving her with a vision of a life spent in penury, perhaps as a washerwoman or a seamstress. Then there was her family, what would become of them? The house they occupied, indeed the reason they had been so keen on her marriage, was entailed to Ralph Barclay through a line of obscure cousinage to her mother's family: had she refused his offer he might have turfed them out. What would happen to his property if he was a convicted felon? Would it be forfeit, would they be rendered homeless?

Raised to be respectable, to never do anything to bring the family name in disrepute, how could her family walk the streets of Frome with this hanging about their heads? If she knew it to be a bit of a backwater, Emily also knew that it encompassed their whole life, and had hers until she came to sea. Many times it had been a duty to visit and give succour to those unfortunates forced into the workhouse. It was all too easy to imagine that was where her parents would be forced to reside, given they had between them only the most meagre of stipends upon which to support themselves, certainly too constrained to allow for the cost of renting a decent house.

The noise of merriment had abated somewhat, what with both coin and bodies exhausted, even those on the fiddle and the flutes sending out weary sounds. The greater noise was of those coming back on board from their exertions in Gibraltar, with much shouting of a drunken nature, fortunately too indistinct to tell her, as they were telling their shipmates, what they had been about. No one would be allowed to sleep ashore, for if Captain Daws was lax in the article of what happened in his absence, he was not about to allow others a privilege denied to him: no captain could spend their night outside their ship without express permission and he had made that a condition of anyone going ashore this night.

The Pelicans came back aboard as merry as anyone, for their quiet conversation had given away to a move to noisier and more entertaining places. Rufus was grinning from ear to ear, content to be ribbed by Michael and Charlie. John Pearce was inebriated, but still, in his mind, he knew that nothing had truly been resolved. Matters would have to wait until they dropped anchor in whatever harbour for which HMS *Grampus* was headed.

He had no inkling that anyone had been in his cabin until the next morning, when, with a clearer eye and seeking a clean shirt, he saw traces of dirt in the gaps between the planking and places where the caulking had, like almost all of it aboard this ship, moved. Touching, it, smelling it, he then reached into his chest and brought out the tin of earth. Taken from a Parisian graveyard in which he had buried his father, it was to him a talisman, for he had sworn that one day he would return to that spot, exhume the remains of Adam Pearce, and take him home to Edinburgh for burial.

It only took a pinch of that, matched to what he had observed on the floor, to tell him his sea chest had been searched, it also took no imagination whatsoever to guess who might have been the culprit. An examination of Hood's letter, taken into the cabin and to the stern casements for better light, showed it to be intact, that at least had not been interfered with. But he had to thank his luck that he had left the really important papers with Lutyens...unless?

He was reassured as soon as he enquired: Lutyens looked and they were still where they had been left. 'Would you do me a service, Heinrich, and keep them there?'

'You do not see your own cabin as secure?' the surgeon enquired, his pointy nose in the air, denoting his surprise.

'Here is safer, brother.'

'So be it.' Looking past John Pearce, he said happily, 'Emily, my dear.'

Pearce turned to look at her, smiling; she had come to ask Lutyens about those papers, but the words died on her lips and she turned and left quickly, leaving John Pearce to grimace to his friend.

CHAPTER FOURTEEN

Dawn brought on a sore head, not much helped by unexplained excitement, running feet on the deck rather than the accustomed and soporific sound of holystoning, causing John Pearce to go on deck, there to find HMS *Grampus*, seemingly with half the ships anchored in the bay, being made ready to weigh, which was strange given he could feel the wind was gusting uncertainly with no fixed direction. Not on friendly terms with his fellow officers, he was not able to ask any of them why they were so cheerful; in the end it was the master, an older man and less constrained by the captain, who enlightened him to the presence of a levanter, which if it increased in strength would be the perfect wind to get them through the strong east-running current that came in from the Atlantic.

'See that cloud above the rock, Mr Pearce, the way it

seems to be blowing off the peak towards the west like a triangle? That is a sure sign, and if the wind increases it is even better.'

'You will know?'

'For sure, given that there cloud will break away and disperse. Then we will have a right proper wind of strength enough to make getting out as easy as kissing my hand. We shall weather Tarifa with no trouble at all, instead of being obliged to creep along the coast.'

And so it proved, for the wind strengthened to make taut the whole top hamper, the ship heeling over from the pressure, as she cleared Algeciras Bay, to be driven through a choppy sea and out and away from the southern Spanish coast. To the south rose the high mountains of Morocco and, as the master had said, they weathered Punta Tarifa at the extreme range of the fortress thereon. Pearce was reminded of what he had been previously told: that when at war with Spain, Gibraltar was a damn difficult place to get in and out of unscathed.

Ralph Barclay had come on deck and for once Pearce did not avoid his basilisk stare, yet he was taken by something else in that look, almost a gleam of triumph. Devenow and Gherson were behind him, with Pearce wondering which of them had rifled his sea chest, for he had no notion it had been one of the wardroom servants – had they been so inclined they would not have lasted in what was an undemanding position. It seemed to him that he had been at war with Barclay from the first night he had encountered him and was wont to wonder if that had produced in him an effect that was untoward. Had he become obsessed?

Once clear of the Straits the course was set to cross the Bay of Cádiz – again one which would not have been taken in a time of conflict, Cádiz being the main base for the Spanish fleet – the destination, once they had weathered Cape St Vincent, being Lisbon. Some subterfuge had to be used in the ship's logs to justify such an act but it was a time-honoured diversion for naval officers, frowned on in public and ignored in private, the Portuguese capital being the place where the mercantile City of London looked for its supplies of gold and silver.

Brought in from South America to both Spain and Portugal, Lisbon was the preferred trading port for British merchants, that nation being an old and trusted ally. Naturally everyone in Europe knew that such precious metals were the lifeblood of British commerce; they also knew that the destination for that specie lay at the end of the English Channel, and quite specifically in the Port of London itself. It was thus no surprise that every enemy privateer's dream was to take a vessel carrying such large sums of an easily tradable commodity. It was also no surprise that the agents of those London merchants and bankers were disinclined to ship their money in vulnerable vessels.

Thus a trade had evolved in which King George's warships, frequently passing in wartime between the

Mediterranean or the East Indies en route home, would call in at Lisbon to pick up cargos of gold and silver. To utterly avoid risk in trafficking such money was impossible, but a well-armed Royal Navy vessel was better than any poorly armed and manned merchantman, and it was well worth the bullion traders' while to pay naval captains one per cent of the value of what they carried: a tempting reward which had, over time, come to be seen as almost a right.

John Pearce was no stranger to the avarice of naval officers: if there was one topic to excite a conversation in even the dullest wardroom it was the possibility that the men there might be lucky enough to partake in the capture of a Spanish Plate ship, deeply laden with precious metals and jewels, coming from the Caribbean to Cádiz. The blockade of that port was one of the greatest plums in the gift of the Admiralty, especially for those frigate captains tasked to set a screen out at sea to alert their heavier counterparts to incoming vessels.

The sight of a fleet of Spanish galleons, at a time when the two nations were at war, was the dream of every naval officer. They might talk of glory in battle with enthusiasm, of forcing an enemy combatant to strike and receiving the thanks of the nation, but deep down the prospect of limitless wealth was the greater draw, the kind of prize taken that would set up even a lieutenant for life and make a ship's captain not just a fellow of independent means, but a person of real substance.

If the dream fulfilled was a rarity, a fee of one per cent of several thousand pounds was not to be sniffed at. So HMS *Grampus* was soon at anchor off the city of Lisbon, with Captain Daws having himself rowed ashore, this time with strict instructions that neither women, traders or entertainers should be allowed aboard, given the time it always took to clear any vessel of their presence. Indeed, there was one other boat making for the shore, carrying, despite their protests, several women who had come aboard at Gibraltar and managed to conceal themselves from the master-at-arms, his mates and the marines whose task it was to clear the ship. The excuses for stopping at Lisbon were varied and well worn, but delay was anathema to the men who ran the navy.

Daws came back aboard in a patently obvious fury and, as always, the reason for his anger spread through the ship with remarkable speed. A frigate, HMS *Fury*, on her way back from Calcutta, sailing alone instead of escorting a convoy, had been in the week before and scooped the pool. She had weighed for home with near half a million in bullion tucked safe in her captain's cabin, and since no more specie had come in from South America, Daws was obliged to depart Lisbon empty-handed. That there was no sympathy for him was natural and that extended from the meanest swabber to the premier: captains were not obliged to share their one per cent and thus rarely did so.

So it was back to deep water and a course set

north, and with no land in sight the ship settled into the familiar routine: the decks were cleaned, swabbed and flogged dry every morning before the hands were sent to breakfast; following that meal, the various tasks detailed by the premier were carried out on sails and rigging, interrupted by slight adjustments to the sail plan. Then came the piping of the hands to dinner, at which point he was obliged, as he too ate in the wardroom, to endure the way conversation flowed around, but did not include, him – something he accepted with annoying equanimity, though occasionally he was tempted to speak when one of their number mouthed some patent absurdity. As soon as he had consumed his food he made his way to the deck, thus relieving them of his presence and his own ears of their dull conversation.

The days the guns were run in and out in dumbshow to exercise the crews were worth attention, each action timed and commented on by a watch-holding Captain Daws, poor results getting the lieutenants in charge a roasting, the next attempt expected to show visible improvement, for here was the seat of British naval superiority, the ability to load and fire their cannon faster than any enemy and to sail their ship with greater skill of manoeuvre. There was boarding practice to follow, as well as the concomitant need to rehearse how to repel the reverse act, which had the deck full of men supposed to be fighting in dumbshow, but using it to entertain themselves or settle scores, which gave work to Surgeon Lutyens.

Pearce also took great interest in the fencing practice carried out by the lieutenants and midshipmen, and since no one barred him from instruction he took to aiding the younger mids in their swordplay: valuable instruction, given he had been taught in Paris by a master of the art. Odd how his competence produced on the faces of his wardroom companions looks of malevolence: they did not care for the notion that this upstart had any ability at all.

Each noon the midshipmen gathered with their sextants to shoot the sun at its zenith, thus marking the beginning and end of the naval day, and he had to admit some of these boys did that task with an aplomb he would struggle to match. Then it was back to the schoolroom for those not on watch, to attend their lessons in mathematics and navigation, that followed by a certain amount of skylarking in the rigging.

Given the master was not ill-disposed towards him, Pearce talked to him often, asking about the sail plan and why various strips of canvas were being employed and not others, discussing the state of the sea and currents, learning by absorption those things which stood as the accumulated knowledge of generations of seamen, acutely aware that he was lacking in the deep learning that made for better than competent sailors.

They encountered no ships going north but many passed them heading south, including one massive convoy which included East Indiamen of the same size and displacement of the ship on which Pearce stood, each deeply laden with goods that, all told, must have run into millions, and even he could see they had suffered some recent storm damage and were undergoing floating repairs.

Two days later they came across further evidence of a heavy storm, when the lookout aloft warned of a hazard in the water dead ahead, which, when they hove to alongside, looked to be the top half of a mainmast, and included a tangle of rigging and ripped canvas. Prepared to let it drift by, one sharp eye spotted something in amongst the labyrinth of ropes, wood and sailcloth, so a boat was put over the side to find what was a dead body, bloated by immersion, but unmistakably a Lascar.

'Could be off any ship, Mr Pearce,' said the master, 'but given we just missed that frigate from the Bay of Bengal, it would not shock me to find he's from her.'

'It must have been a hell of a storm.'

'And thank God we missed it, sir, for we have had enough foul weather for one cruise.'

'We might have more.'

'True,' Mr Ludon replied, looking grim, 'so let us hope the timbers of old Granny *Grampus* are not too injured by what we have endured up till now.'

There was discussion about what kind of ceremony should attend the interment of a man from the Far East, but, in the end, he was sewn in canvas with a shot at his feet and slipped into the ocean by use of the Anglican rite. For all it was sad, John Pearce saw it as relieving the boredom, and almost wished he had duties to perform to keep him occupied. With Michael, Charlie and Rufus he could exchange only a few brief words: naval convention discouraged chats between the lower deck and officers and there were precious few places on a ship that were not under observation by someone.

Nor, without permission, could he go aloft, for that required a nod from the quarterdeck and he would not ask for it. And like a leitmotif, day in, day out, and at night as well, came the clanking sound of the pumps, as the endless battle to keep at bay the level of the water in the well went on.

'I know you are feeling better, husband, just by the colour of your cheeks. There is blood where so recently there was pallor.'

'I still feel great pain, Mrs Barclay, and, as you know, I still require the surgeon to treat me with tincture of laudanum.'

'I should have a care not to rely on it too heavily. Mr Lutyens tells me he has known of cases where patients, once they have formed the habit, cannot rid themselves of it.'

'I hope you know me well enough to discern that I am of a stronger character than that.'

Emily had watched the fencing practice on the foredeck as much as anyone and she could see the similarity to what was taking place now: verbal thrust, conversational parry and no intimacy whatsoever. They were not in the least comfortable in one another's presence and she lacked either the will or the inclination to alter that state of affairs, while underlying everything was the knowledge she had acquired so surreptitiously while the ship lay at anchor.

The notion of telling her husband had occurred to her: forewarned he might be able to evade some of that coming in his direction, yet she could no more talk of it to him than she could to John Pearce, and the longer that went on the harder it became. Several times, seeing him on deck, and knowing he was well disposed towards her, she had thought to plead that he drop the matter for the sake of her and her family, but the words would no more come than they would now, and this to the man she should tell. Whatever else, they were bound together by the tight bonds of holy matrimony.

'My dear, we cannot continue like this.' That he had spoken shocked her into paying attention. 'I am aware that I have in some way offended you, but I am forced to counter that you have likewise distressed me.'

Tempted to say, 'by pointing out your failings,' she remained silent.

'I have some hope that time will heal the rift between us, and I also know that continued propinquity will not serve that aim. I refer, of course, to you accompanying me to sea to share my cabin.' He moved his stump. 'This will heal in time and I have high hopes of another command – perhaps something of the nature of *Grampus* might be seen as my due.'

Suddenly he smiled, but it was more of a rictus grin than truly anything warm: he was so obviously thinking of his own future happiness, not theirs.

'Then I can only wish you joy of it, sir,' Emily replied.

'Naturally, when we land in England I will require a period of convalescence and that will have to be taken at home, though the waters in Bath will not be out of the question, given they are efficacious, but...'

She knew she had to pick up on his silence. 'You are concerned, sir, that my behaviour may embarrass you.'

'I know, Mrs Barclay, if it continues in this vein, it is bound to.'

'I am not well versed in subterfuge.'

'That,' he said in a sharper tone, 'is mere dissimulation. You know of what I speak. I have my sisters and you have your family. We cannot act like this before them without drawing them into some concern for the state of our marriage and, I might add, I have no wish to be the subject of gossip for every tongue in Frome.'

'And what, Captain Barclay, would you say is the state of our marriage? Have you forgotten how cruelly you last used me?'

'I exercised my rights as a husband, madam, and while I would have you willing I will have you when I must.'

He was struggling to contain himself and Emily could

see it was getting harder. He would have been happier if she had shouted at him or wept with the shame of her near rape, the way he had taken her brutally and without consent while in drink, the very act which had caused her to move to the St Mandrier hospital. The calm tone of each response was doing nothing to cool his ire: he was finding that increasingly irritating. Memory of that assault was working on her temper too, so that she had to struggle to stay composed.

'Then I have to tell you, sir, that as of this moment, I fear you will have to employ such methods should you wish to exercise them again.'

'Are you saying you will not perform your wifely duty, madam?'

Ralph Barclay could not shout, there were too many ears on a ship, not least Daws in his main part of the cabin, but he wanted to, just as he wanted to do to his wife what he had done in the cabin of HMS *Brilliant*. If she would not give him his conjugal rights willingly, then he had the right in law to take them. But the proximity of others was not the only constraint on such an act: with one arm, and that as yet to fully heal, he was only too well aware he could not manage it.

'Then I must tell you,' he hissed, 'that I will have you adhere to your marriage vows, and I would warn you, madam, that I have shots in my locker which will make life unpleasant for more than me. Do not force me to act in a manner that will bring about harm to others and I know that is a subject on which I do not need to elaborate.'

Nor did he: Emily knew only too well that her family kept the house in which she had been born only on her husband's generosity: the property was entailed and he, having inherited that, could throw them out of it at will.

'Captain Barclay, I promise this and no more: to be polite, to show, in public, acquiescence, to always treat you with respect. But in private I will be what I am.'

'Then your first act will be to move from the sick bay to take up your quarters here. You will also take your meals with Captain Daws and myself.'

Emily stood up. 'You have about you, sir, a tone that is reprehensible, one you no doubt employ on those poor unfortunates obliged to serve under you. I do not and will not respond as they are constrained to do, and as to your request that I share this cabin, all I will say is that I will consider it.'

With that she swept out, to pass Cornelius Gherson sitting in a small cabin to the side, the look on his absurdly handsome face, his knowing smile, designed to let her know he had heard every word.

Devenow was up to his old tricks, though discreetly, since he had been warned by some of the harder bargains on the *Grampus* 'to mind himself'. But in any ship's company there were those who could be terrorised into passing over their grog and made to do so in a manner that ensured they did not pass onto others what was happening. The consumption of it also had to be carried out with prudence, so it was necessary to find a quiet spot where he could sit unobserved and consume what he saw as his good fortune.

While happy onshore to get drunk with friends, he nevertheless did not find companionship was required, being quite content with his own company and the grog he had accumulated. Sat in the sail locker, sure with the ship sailing easy on the big Atlantic swell nothing would blow out and need replacement, he was alone with his own thoughts, which turned to talk as the drink took hold.

Happiness, as most men understood it, was not a concept Devenow would have been able to comprehend: he was a bully who used his fists to get his way and only ever gave ground to superior force.

That was what Ralph Barclay had, his rank and the power it gave him. Some men saw him as a hard horse, Devenow saw him as fair. Labouring on a farm when news came that a war was in the offing, he had gathered up his belongings and made his way to where he could find out who was getting what in the article of a ship, and he never doubted that Ralph Barclay would be in line. Was he not a fine seaman and a fighter? HMS *Brilliant* was a tad smaller than he had anticipated but a berth was a berth; if he noticed, when he came aboard as a volunteer, the greeting was not entirely wholehearted from his hero, it did nothing to dent his pleasure in once more serving a man he admired.

Of course he got flogged, as he had been on previous commissions, and by damn he deserved it, for if he had gathered enough he was a bad bastard who might start to imbibe in secret, but would want to let the world know his thoughts when the drink took effect. For Devenow the navy was home – in truth, the only one he had ever truly had, having been raised in a workhouse in which he had learnt that punishment went with offence and the level of both that and the wrongdoing was to be decided by others; that was the way of the world and not to be gainsaid by the likes of him.

Steadily he drank, feeling the warmth spread through his body as fast as the thoughts raced through his mind. The singing started softly enough, a reprisal of all the old ditties he knew, those he had learnt as ship's boy, crude songs that when sung ashore had passing womenfolk covering their ears. Slowly but surely the memory went from happy recollection and started to cloud with anger: the remembrance of how he had grown to take his vengeance on those who had mistreated him when he was nothing but a skinny nipper with his ribs easy to see, running back and forth alongside the thick, slimy anchor cable, tying it to the messenger that led to the capstan, sliding, slithering and sometimes coming to a tumble on the soaking deck, which would earn him a backhander or a clout with a starter.

He had run cartridges for the gunner too, priding himself on being the fastest lad between the handling chamber and the guns he was tasked to serve. Not that he got away without blows then either, for however swift he was it was never fast enough. Some of those old sailors had treated him hard, the marines being worst, none of them taking a liking to his lip when berated, and many a swipe round the ear he had got for his cheek. But he had grown to make them suffer, drawing blood for every remembered blow.

'That's what I did, see,' he said, slurring to the lantern he had filched. 'They whacked me good an' proper when I were little but lived to regret it bad when I grew to a height.' Then he laughed. 'I made them buggers bleed and serves 'em right, I say.'

This recall was made even if it flew in the face of his own habit of clouting nippers if they annoyed him. In fact, Devenow would clout anyone who got his goat; right then he saw in the guttering tallow the face of Michael O'Hagan.

'That Irish bastard not excepted, an' all. He might think he bettered me bare-knuckle but he got lucky, that's all. Next time I'll knock that Paddy grin off the stupid papist bugger's face.'

O'Hagan's face was only an image and one distorted by rum, but the fist that swung broke it in half, and the fact that it went on to smash into the planking of the sail locker was not felt even if it broke the skin. Looking at his hand, Devenow saw it was bleeding at the knuckles, but to his addled mind that was Irish blood, not his. Pulling himself upright, though struggling to stop swaying, Devenow began to take apart an image of every man he had never bested in the one fight they had engaged in.

Devenow was no longer in the sail locker, he was in a dozen places where his fists had been employed: taverns, back alleys, 'tween decks where he had set out to punish. He had no memory of hitting the lantern or of it falling over so hard the door flew open and the tallow dropped out. Nor did he see or smell the flame begin to singe the bone-dry canvas. It might have been fine if the flame had not also got to some of the rum he had spilt, which flared up quickly, creating enough heat to allow the fire to spread. It was only when the smoke made him cough he realised what was happening, and all he did then was flee, leaving the fire to turn from a hazard, with the aid of the air from an open door, to an inferno.

CHAPTER FIFTEEN

John Pearce was in the wardroom, sitting on a locker, trying to read Voltaire in the French, not easy since his contemporaries seemed intent on annoying him with loud and distracting conversations. Heinrich Lutyens was writing too, copying into his large ledger the notes he had made of the mayhem of music and carnality he had witnessed as the ship lay off Gibraltar, while a few feet away, but out of sight, Emily Barclay was embroidering a sampler. Michael, Rufus and Charlie were jawing away at a mess table while Cornelius Gherson was with the purser, who was getting increasingly impatient with his enquiries as to the value of his stores, this while Ralph Barclay lay in his cot dozing, having just been dosed with his pain-relieving tincture.

Captain Daws was at his logs, bringing them up to date from the hastily made notes off which he and his officers would work, each one ensuring that they tallied, so that those nosy buggers at the Navy Office would not spot some anomaly to excite their interest, especially in the article of stopping at Lisbon, this put down to the need to examine the rudder – feeble, for sure, but enough to avert even the most remote chance of censure.

The master was in his hutch off the quarterdeck, plotting the ship's position with his charts, having taken a reading from the slate and employing his protractors, noting down the rate of sailing, making allowance for the currents acting on the deep hull and thinking that, given the state of the ship's timbers, her progress was as good as could be expected and that he was heartily glad they had missed the eye of that recent storm.

The carpenter and his mate were making their way, crouched down, for the passage was low, along the walk that ran round the hull of the ship, bearing tarred rope, bolsters and mallets, as well as a bucket of pitch to hammer into and seal off the seams that were opening excessively – he too, like the master, thanking his own God for having missed what must have been a typical tempest for the time of year, while at the same time worrying about the waters they were now sailing through, the notorious Bay of Biscay.

All heard the cry of 'Fire down below', the one most dreaded by all on a ship at sea. Daws was out of his cabin in a flash, in time to hear the orders being given by the officer of the watch to get out and rig the fire engine, one which was carried out quickly, the hose going over the side to suck up seawater while the engine was taken to the seat of the blaze which was right under the gunroom. All over the ship there were men running, some carrying messages of how bad it was, others, who were by nature pessimistic Jonahs, rushing to where their kit was stored to gather up any money left over from the recent debauches, this while the marine guard was doubled on the spirit room to make sure they did not break in and drink themselves senseless.

The terror of fire in a wooden ship was not hard to fathom, but there was a drill to deal with it, one that was practised as often as running the guns in and out and, had the blaze been caught quickly, it could have been contained. But it had been given time to take hold, and that on timbers seasoned by years of use. The lower holds might be damp, but that did not truly apply to the higher decks.

The gunner had rushed to his place of work, and had the ship's boys taking any filled cartridges to the upper deck, where, if the fire got out of hand they could be chucked into the sea. He knew that the order had gone out to stop pumping and indeed he wondered if the captain was already taking steps to scuttle the lower decks, which would flood the magazine and render harmless the stores of powder, a wise precaution to avoid them all being blown to perdition.

The fight was not going well: from the sail locker it had spread to the bread room, in reality dry, hard biscuit, but with enough oil or lard in its consistency to make it highly inflammable, and already it had come through the planking to fill the gunroom with such dense smoke as to make seeking to contain it from above impossible.

Above, the rest of the crew were working just as hard. As a precaution, while also being part of the well-rehearsed drill, the four ship's boats were being hauled off the battens on which they lay across the waist, while at the same time men were working below and on the deck to gather provisions of water and portable food, seen at this stage as a precaution. That took time: the boats were heavy and required hard work on the capstan to get them aloft then over the bulwarks so they could be lowered into the water, held in place long enough for what stores had been gathered to be loaded aboard, the whole slower than perfect with the ship being short-handed.

By the time they were in the water the upper deck had begun to burn, a clear indication that, below, it was out of control despite the hard work being done by the fire engine, backed up by what men could be mustered passing every bucket the ship carried. Several hands had suffered burns and were being attended to where they lay, by the surgeon. Captain Daws, also as part of his duties in a drill, but now beginning to appear a necessity, had gathered up the ship's papers, his logs and the book of recognition signals for British vessels on service.

He was enough of a gentleman to have alerted Emily Barclay early on to be prepared to depart the ship. One of the first things Emily had learnt at sea was the need to be tidy: with constant drills, added to the possibility, always, of sudden action, her clothing had to be kept in its chest, as did all her other belongings not in use, outdoor garments always to hand. So she was able to grab quickly her heavy, hooded cloak, a comforter of some length to wrap around her neck and enough of her possessions that she could decently carry with an emphasis on warmth, it being February in the Atlantic.

The midshipman who had told her to prepare had gone – he had other duties to perform – and Lutyens' cabin was empty, given he was occupied. At some point one of his assistants might come to remove his medical chest but that had not happened yet. It was so easy to enter, less so, for a person well brought up, to open his instrument chest and lift out those papers. Emily did hesitate, unsure why she wanted them, only aware that she did, while also conscious that what she was doing was morally wrong. She bit her lip hard as they went into the bag with those items she held dear.

Ralph Barclay, still light-headed and obviously nauseous from being so rudely awakened, was now being helped from his cot in a smoke-filled cabin by a less than steady Devenow, a man whose breath stank so much of drink that even the half-comatose captain recoiled from the blast. Gherson, irritated, if not near to panic, was helping too, his efforts, because of his agitated state, doing more harm than good. The arrival of the man's wife to supervise his care, as well as to oversee the gathering of what possessions he needed and could be carried, was seen by Gherson as hypocrisy and he made no secret of his disdain.

'Both of you, leave him be. He's in more pain with your handling—'

'Who are you to tell us what to do, Mrs Barclay?' Gherson spat, cutting right across her. 'The way you treated him.'

Emily responded with equal ferocity. 'His wife, and I will say it once: if you force him to choose between us, you will be swabbing the decks in an hour. Now let go of him.'

Bleary eyed, Devenow looked at her, swaying back and forth in a manner that had nothing to do with the motion of the now stationary ship. Then he touched his forehead and slurred, 'Savin' your presence, ma'am, it needs a strong hand to aid him.'

'It needs a steady one, get away from him.'

'My dear,' Barclay said, his eyes glazed.

'Don't speak, husband,' she said, with a gentility to which he had not been exposed for months, this while she got his cloak round his shoulders. 'Let us go, but slowly, there is as yet no need to panic.'

'Gherson, my papers.'

'I have them, Captain Barclay,' he replied rushing out the door.

The sound of retching had Emily concentrating on Devenow, who was now bent over, one hand on the bulkhead, no doubt affected by the smoke and voiding his gut, so she missed that exchange. Another look around established that Gherson had fled from a place in which it was now becoming painful to breathe. Slowly she helped Ralph Barclay to move forward, leaving Devenow to follow if he wished, vaguely aware that somehow the attitude of those they passed on their way to the deck had changed.

'Mrs Barclay, you must make your way to the entry port and get aboard the pinnace at once.'

'How are—?'

She never got to finish the question, for Daws' reply was too swift. 'Bad, Mrs Barclay, very bad.' Then he turned to a midshipman, a youngster trying and failing to look brave beside him. 'Give orders to scuttle the lower deck.'

It was clear from the way the men below, who included the Pelicans, were retreating from the flames, that the fire was winning the battle, not them. The heat was spreading the flames as much as any sparks, and any water thrown on them was immediately turned to scalding steam. Few could stand more than a minute or two at the face of the conflagration, some retiring of their own volition, others requiring to be hauled back as they fell from the effects of the ferocious temperature. Behind them Lutyens was on his knees, trying to ease burns with salve, while his assistants used some of the water in the buckets to douse clothing that was singed and smouldering.

To Pearce and those with him, officers, warrants and hands all toiling without distinction, the world had reduced to that before them: the red and orange inferno crackling as flames jumped forward to set alight timbers, barrels, cannon trunnions and the tools required to work the guns that had what little moisture they contained sucked out by the heat. They took turns on the handles of the fire engine, pumping up and down to keep flowing a jet that could only delay, not douse out, the flames, backing up time after time as the fire forced retreat.

The point of no return was not the smouldering deck planking, with some of the upper-deck caulking already burning: it was when flames licked out of the upper scantlings. The carpenter's walk, that narrow, low passage that ran right round the ship near the waterline, now slowly sinking under that, was, unknown to those fighting the fire amidships, acting like a funnel to progress it, taking it past them time and time again.

Eventually it set alight to those newly hammered-in pieces of pitch, and that acted on the scantlings, fire breaking through to the battens that held not only the shrouds, but also the blocks on which the falls were lashed. Then they caught the rigging, which began to burn quickly, the ropes being heavily impregnated with tar so that they went up like Roman candles, the flames snaking up towards the now flapping sails. The master, as soon as the alarm was sounded, had ordered the sheets let go, and brought HMS *Grampus* up into the wind to reduce a draught that was bound to feed the fire.

With the whole of the mid-to-stern area alight, the flames beginning to lick at those sails and the ship settling into the water as her lower deck was flooded, it was obvious HMS *Grampus* was in dire peril. The order to abandon did not come at that time: men, officers included, were sent to get what they could from a wardroom cleared by their servants, their sea chests now on the open deck. Especially needed was warm clothing, boat cloaks, and if they could manage it, foul-weather gear. Just as vital were the instruments by which they would navigate, the last thing of importance their personal possessions and logs. The captain's servants had moved steadily back and forth to the cutter throughout the past half hour, carrying the things their master deemed necessary to aid them to survive.

John Pearce, blackened, as was every man who had been fire fighting, found his own chest, thankful to whoever had retrieved it, and flung it open, grabbing Hood's letter, the order releasing his friends from the navy, as well as the tin of Parisian earth. Then, with his boat cloak bundled in his arms, he set off for the upper deck at a run, intent on trying to get to the other side of the fire and Lutyens' quarters.

He wondered if he was too late as soon as he emerged onto the upper deck, and was shocked by the speed at which the fire, no longer being fought, had spread, aided now by gun ports opened to allow men to exit to the boats;

flames were shooting up the nearest companionway, as well as billowing smoke, making his aim look impossible. But he tried anyway, glad to see that Michael, Charlie and Rufus had waited for him as he had asked. They inched along the walk that bordered the waist now empty of boats, with flames rising and licking at them, seemingly with a life of their own as they sought out flesh to burn.

The most forward companionway was clear of fire and so they moved down together, aware of the increasing heat, making for the next set of steps that would take them down to the Orlop deck. All around them men were running for safety and it was clear that, marine guards notwithstanding, some of them had got into the spirit store and purloined the contents: they were drinking as they ran. Suddenly a bolt of fire shot up from below; clearly the fire had touched something that acted like a torch.

'It's no good, John-boy,' Michael yelled.

'Barclay's court martial papers are down there,' Pearce shouted back, edging towards the companionway.

'So is Old Nick,' Charlie bawled.

'Leave it.'

'You go, Michael. Get into a boat.'

The hand that grabbed John Pearce's collar left no room for dispute: he was nearly lifted bodily off his feet and dragged backwards, far enough to hear over the roar of the flames the continually repeated cry of 'Abandon ship'.

Eyes streaming, they made their way back up the deck, to where the entry port was open and a crowd of men were jostling around it trying to get out. That was when Captain Daws took charge, his bellow enough to still panic in even the most fearful breast, insisting that there was enough room in the boats for all, and that they form an orderly line.

When the Pelicans, near to being backmarkers, got to see daylight, only the cutter, smallest of them all, was left with space to spare. The barge, launch and pinnace were all standing off, the latter with its mast stepped and already with some canvas rigged.

'Pearce, you will command the cutter,' said Daws. 'Thank God we are short-handed and can get everyone off.'

'Aye, aye, sir,' he replied, given there was no choice. 'And you, sir?'

Daws looked at him as if the mere posing of the question was tantamount to a hanging offence. 'What I am about is none of your concern. Once I am sure everyone is off the ship I will call the cutter in.'

It was a tale oft told, of captains going down with their ships, as if to lose one was more damning than life itself. The image of Daws, who was glaring at him, doing just that, was unmistakable, and this while above their heads they could hear the dislodged spars and blocks thudding into the deck as the fire detached them from the rigging.

'Do not be tempted to stay, sir, it is nought but romantic folly.'

'Do not presume, Mr Pearce, to tell me my duty,' Daws shouted. 'Now get aboard that damned cutter.'

There was no inclination to disobey. Michael, Rufus and Charlie had already lowered themselves down the manropes – not very far, as the ship was still settling – and were now looking up at him. Yet he was not going to leave this fool to his chosen fate, if indeed that was what he intended. He might well signal for the cutter to come and take him off, but then he might not. Suddenly Pearce spun round and the punch, one of which Michael O'Hagan would have been proud, took an unsuspecting Daws right on the jaw and he went down like a sack of dried peas.

'Below, catch the captain, he has inhaled too much smoke.'

There was no way to throw the man, he had to be dragged to the edge, and no way to avoid him rumbling down the battens that lined and protruded from the side of the ship. He would be a bruised and battered soul but at least, John Pearce reckoned, he would be alive. Daws was caught with no expertise, and throwing his own hastily gathered clothing first, Pearce lowered himself into the cutter, which immediately cast off.

By the time they got far enough off to rest the oars and look back HMS *Grampus* was alight from end to end. One of the hands had been using seawater to try and revive his captain, with some success, given his eyes began to open and he began to groan. The man who had administered to him was speaking softly, urging him to come round, which he did eventually, sitting up and nursing his head, that followed by gentle touching of the various parts of his anatomy which had met with those wood battens. That did not last: the head lifted and the eyes fixed on Pearce.

'I'll see you swing from the end of a yardarm for that.'

'What, sir?' asked Pearce, looking innocent.

'For laying hands –what am I saying? – for punching a superior officer, damn you!'

Pearce affected surprise. 'I fear the smoke must have harmed you more than I suspected, sir. You collapsed from inhalation and I was required to help you. I observe a certain amount of pain was caused by that, which I could not help and for which I apologise.'

'You punched me, Pearce.'

'Did I, sir?' Pearce replied, eyes open in surprise. Then he looked at the rows of eyes examining him in what was a crowded boat. 'Did anyone see me punch the captain?'

It was amusing to watch the reaction: sailors loved a guy and were much given to ribbing their mates. They could not openly shake their heads or nod, because Daws had turned to scrutinise their reactions. Did he see what Pearce saw in those blank looks: a substitute for mirth?

'Barky's goin', your honour,' said one fellow, nodding towards the ship.

Every eye fixed on *Grampus* then, as she slowly settled, hissing as the fire turned water to steam, not going down by bow or stern but as if she were lowering herself into her watery grave. She only tipped when water filled the hull, which tilted the burning upper works towards the cutter, but soon they sank too, in that continued stately fashion, until the last of the top part of the mainmast slid into the sea. Pearce looked at Daws then looked away, given the man had tears streaming down his face.

'Man the oars,' he croaked. 'Let us join with the other boats.'

The figures the master produced, forty-six degrees north by some nine degrees west, put the four crowded boats squarely in the middle of the Bay of Biscay, and if the numbers did not mean much to most of those who could overhear – Pearce was struggling with them and not alone in doing so – the location was enough to dishearten anyone, that along with the knowledge in the souls of the doubters that they might not be entirely accurate. The only bright spot was that HMS *Grampus* had been on course to weather Ushant on the Brittany coast, en route to the Lizard, and any ship heading home to England would sail the same line; there was some hope of being rescued.

Daws, who had transferred with some difficulty to the launch, leaving the cutter with twenty-eight souls aboard, had called for an inventory of stores and water and ensured the distribution was fair. He then fell into a discussion of the state of the weather and the way it might develop, the conclusion being that even if they were bobbing up and down through ten feet of swell it seemed clement for the time of year: the wind was stiff but not severe, certainly not at present dangerous enough to make it imperative to head for the French shore.

'It's getting dark,' Daws said finally, examining a glowering, cloud-filled sky that might threaten rain but would certainly produce no moonlight. 'We will raise sail on the launch and the pinnace, but we must each tie a cable with an oared boat overnight. In daylight they can keep pace rowing, but in the dark they will be in danger of becoming separated over several hours. At dawn we will spread out, but maintain sight of each other, and look out for a ship, hopefully one heading towards home, but I will not trouble to be taken back south.'

Pearce looked in the gathering gloom towards the pinnace just ahead of them, containing the Barclays and Lutyens, as well as Devenow and Gherson, this as the line was passed so they could progress in line ahead, the same arrangement taking place between the other two boats.

'Heinrich, did you manage to rescue your instrument chest?' he called.

'I'm afraid not, John. I lost everything.'

'A pity, my friend.'

It was no good cursing the fate that had seen him leave those papers with Lutyens for safety, and he reassured himself that he still had Hood's letter, so if he could get home, he would get to see William Pitt. Something might be possible, after all, and he could always write to Hood asking for another copy, not that he held out much hope there. Looking past Lutyens to Emily Barclay, he was half amused, half annoyed by the way she deliberately looked away. It seemed to him deeply ironic that here they were in a very steep tub indeed, and still she hung on to her foolish morality.

Complete darkness came slowly, preceded by a long period of low, grey and diminishing light. Pearce organised those aboard to sleep or man the oars, the only object to keep the cutter on course, then issued a cup of water to each man, plus a ship's biscuit and a morsel of cheese, thinking, as he compared that with which he started, set against that with which he was left, they had best be picked up quick.

Well wrapped up, he tried to sleep, which should have been easy now it was pitch dark. The only light was a small lantern on the top of the mast of the lead boat, and that was only there for a short while because it began to rain, the light being far enough off to be blotted out by the fall. Having issued instructions to drink as much of it as they could, and to gather more in anything they could, he rewrapped himself and fell into a fitful slumber.

It was hard to have a whispered conversation in the pinnace, so crowded was it; even harder for Cornelius Gherson, once he got to his captain on the opposite side to his wife, to persuade Ralph Barclay on the course of action, then to find a reason to get into the position he needed to carry out what had been agreed. Then he waited until sleep took over from concern. Unfamiliarity with ropes and knots – he had served on the lower deck but was useless – meant it took him time to loose the cable, but eventually, without disturbing his sleeping companions in misfortune, he got it free and lowered it into the water.

CHAPTER SIXTEEN

'It is my opinion,' said Admiral Hotham, in a voice loud enough to carry, he wanted to be overheard, 'that the attack is a waste of effort. The Bay of San Fiorenzo is too open to a northerly gale, and according to my reading of the charts, there is precious little deep water inshore and plenty of rocks on which to rip out the bottoms of our ships should they drag their anchors.'

The reply came from Mr Holloway, the captain of HMS *Britannia*; no one else on the quarterdeck would have dared voice an opinion and it was precarious for him: like most flagship captains he was not of vast seniority, admirals preferring to have running their ship a man they could easily overawe.

'Do the French not use it as an anchorage, sir?'

'Only for the odd frigate, Mr Holloway.' Hotham waved a lazy hand to where the French had scuttled the only ship stationed in the bay, to avoid it being taken. 'Like the fellow whose topmast we can just see sticking out of the water. I have no knowledge that they have ever used it for a fleet anchorage.'

Those in earshot, and there were many, were left to wonder at the truth of Hotham's remarks, given his relationship with the man who had ordered the attack was no secret. If Hood proposed, Hotham objected, not that such opposition changed anything: it was also common knowledge that in the counsels of the fleet he was generally ignored. It was, therefore, doubly galling that he had been given the task of carrying into the bay the troops necessary to take the town at its base.

Hotham raised his telescope and ran it along the shore of Mortella Point: dark green hills running down to broken-up grey rocks full of stunted bushes where it met the sea, with only the very odd patch of beach. Those rocks, boulders really, strewn along the shore, were enough to indicate that the northernmost point of the island of Corsica was subject to violent storms, which produced waves big enough and powerful enough to break them up and toss what remained into the confusion of boulders they could now observe.

'That's a damned odd-looking tower, is it not?' Hotham exclaimed, which had every other glass on the quarterdeck following the line of his own. Round, some forty-feet high and near the shape of a crown roast of lamb with its slightly wider crenellated top, it stood right on the shoreline and commanded the western entrance to the bay. On either side there was nothing but jumbled rocks, making any assault from the actual shore troublesome, though it was about to be attempted, this while the navy sought to subdue it from the sea.

'Genoese, sir, I believe, built when they had the island.' Hotham dropped his telescope and looked at his flag captain, the bright-blue eyes seeming to imply that being in possession of such knowledge was somehow unbecoming. 'I bespoke a fellow in Leghorn, sir, when our destination was first mooted,' Holloway replied quickly, making much effort to sound confident in order not to be diminished in front of his own officers. 'He told me of it and seemed to think it would cause us trouble.'

'A single tower?'

'Housing as its main armament the equivalent to a pair of our eighteen pounders, sir.'

'Hardly a match for thirty-two pounders, do you think?'

Hotham, as he said that, looked around the faces of the assembled officers, his half smile inviting, if not demanding, agreement. That such a gesture did not elevate Captain Holloway was inherent in the act and it was not singular: the admiral wanted everyone to know he was vastly more experienced than the younger man, to know that it was his judgement that mattered. The fact that it hit home was obvious by the stiff face Holloway adopted.

'I look forward to pounding it to dust, sir.'

'Which we must do, of course, before we can secure the bay.' No one reacted visibly to that piece of hypocrisy, Hotham having dismissed the tower as no threat in one breath to then term it a hazard with the next; admirals were like that. 'Let us get our bullocks ashore and see what Johnny Crapaud has to oppose us. Signal *Fortitude* and *Juno* to proceed to their stations.'

The lieutenant in charge of the flags had been standing by for this very order, so the various pennants were swiftly bent on and raised, a signal gun firing as soon as they broke out – quite unnecessary, for on the deck of those two vessels, as well as the troop transports close by them, every eye had been on the flagship waiting for such a command. Indeed, many of the soldiers destined to land were already in the boats, gathered from every ship in the fleet, so that the first body of troops could set off immediately.

Toby Burns was in one of those, leading a line of several more. He looked at the approaching shore, still some distance off, with trepidation: a beach of grey sand that looked dirty in the cold morning light with the dark green hills rising behind it, hemmed in at both ends with a jumble of boulders and scrub which look impassable; once they were on that beach they would advance or die – not, to the midshipman, a very enticing prospect.

Sat in the stern thwarts of *Britannia*'s launch he was facing the stony-faced bullocks who were under his charge, while his superior, Lieutenant Beddows, no doubt to underline his personal bravery, was stood in the bows, one foot on the prow, as if he was prepared to take in his chest the very first volley of musket fire from the French defenders. The great boom of cannon fire broke the stillness of the morning as the warships designated to support the attack opened fire to subdue any shore-based batteries.

The black balls flew over their heads to land in the trees which lined the rear of the beach, sending up great founts of sand, earth, wood and foliage. In between the lines of boats loaded with bullocks were armed cutters, each with an eighteen-pounder cannon in the bow and a crew to work it. They began a cannonade too, their shot, lower in trajectory and being grape, designed to sweep out of the defence any human component, in the hope of driving them away so the soldiers could land unopposed.

The counter-battery fire was not long in coming, the land-based guns firing from elevated batteries, both on the hillsides and the tower itself, and so able to project plunging fire. The sea around them was full of plumes of white water shooting up in the air, but one gunner got lucky and struck home just two lines to the left of where Toby Burns sat, crashing into another boat and causing it to fold like a piece of paper, bows and stern rising to meet each other as bloody bodies, redcoats and rowers were thrown into the water, that accompanied by loud screams of pain and distress.

His stomach already troubled, Toby Burns could feel it getting even more taut. He was vaguely aware that they were now in shallow water, pale instead of deep green so clear was it, and it was not long before the keel of the boat ground into the soft underwater sand. Beddows leapt forward immediately to land in no more than a few feet of water, just enough to cover his knees. As soon as his feet touched the bottom, the sea around him began to boil with spouts as a volley of grapeshot was let loose by the French. Any balls that went into the sea, given the angle of fire, lost all velocity immediately, but one, which must have just skimmed the surface, hit his upper leg and with a yelp Beddows went down, the cry of anguish followed by a shout.

'Mr Burns, take charge and get these fellows onto dry land.'

The youngster's mouth moved but no sound emerged and it was as well for him that the bullocks knew only too well that they, sitting with their backs to the shore, were prime targets. The man in charge, a sergeant of some years by the look of his greying locks, gave the order to disembark and, as one, the troopers went over both sides of the boat, in a very disciplined fashion that showed the act had been carried out before, for it kept the boat steady.

'Best look to the lieutenant,' cried one of the oarsmen, his gaze fixed on the still-rigid midshipman. It was only when all eyes were on him that Toby was shamed enough to move, jumping over the side, aware that balls were still arriving in quantity, either hissing into the sea or cracking as they passed his ear, and wondering, in his terror, if his bowels would hold. The cold water he barely noticed and he forced his way forward to where Beddows was still on his knees, his trunk surrounded by blood.

'You there, get Mr Beddows back into the launch. We must get him to a surgeon.'

'Your place is ashore, Mr Burns.'

'Don't speak, sir,' Toby gasped, as he tried to lift his superior, glad when more hands came to help.

'You must see if the soldiers need support with cannon and take back some assessment of their progress.'

Toby wanted to shout at Beddows that he was passing on the job he was supposed to undertake, the very one he had heard him volunteer them for, to tell him if he had not been so stupid and determined to show off he would have been able to carry it out, and what right did he have to put forward someone else without so much as a by your leave?

Now raised to his feet, although supported, the wound in his thigh was visible, bleeding but not pumping blood: nothing vital had been hit. 'Go, Mr Burns, the men can tourniquet my injury.'

There was no choice: loss of face, which would come with a refusal, was not an option. It was only as he surged forward he realised that along the beach men were landing, realised that with some already ashore and advancing on the line of low trees, the rate of musket fire and grapeshot was diminishing. Out of the water, the sand on which he stood was firm, and his progress to those trees he could carry out at a run; he hid behind one as soon as he reached them.

Toby Burns's chest was heaving, yet he knew it was not from much in the way of exertion, for the beach was not that deep nor the sand soft. Out of sight, he wondered what to do next: to follow the soldiers in the hills, now through the trees and out of sight, was one option; the other was to stay here.

'You all right, lad?'

The voice made him jump and he looked around in alarm to see a red-coated officer, senior by his rank badges, in his hand a walking stick, looking down at him.

'Just getting my breath, sir. I am supposed to see how the attack progresses and report back about the need for support.'

'I think we have that already, boy,' the redcoat said pointing out into the bay.

The seventy-four-gun ship-of-the-line, HMS *Fortitude*, accompanied by the frigate *Juno*, thirty-two, had got into position and were in the process of using springs on their anchors to swing their sides round to bombard the tower. The gunners in the fortress had not waited: already shot were peppering the sea around the warships.

'Don't take much puff to walk, boy, even uphill, so why don't you come with me?'

'Thank you, sir,' Toby lied, falling in behind the bullock as he strode off, dashing slightly to get close so that the man's body would shield him from danger, vaguely noticing as he passed them the abandoned French positions: dead artillery men and the odd dismounted cannon, though most, surrounded by various accoutrements, seemed to have just been abandoned. There was also a number of crumpled redcoats and they passed some wounded going in the opposite direction, en route to attention.

'A poor lot we have fought this day, don't ye know.'

The boy was thinking even a damn fool could get lucky. 'The attack seems to have been a success, sir.'

'It will be that, lad, when we have that tower.'

The sound of a broadside filled the air and, looking out to sea, although they could not espy the ships screened by the trees, they could see the billowing clouds of smoke rising into the air. Moving on, they were now passing mixed French and British wounded, mostly sat against trees, their heads lowered in despair. There was also the odd body, all in blue coats.

'Regular soldiers, boy,' the redcoat exclaimed before stopping suddenly and demanding of him, 'What is your damned name?'

'Burns, sir, Midshipman.'

A tree suddenly splintered by Toby Burns's shoulder as a musket ball hit it, making him jump sideways and cry out in alarm. His redcoat merely turned and glared at the now visible outline of the tower, sure that was where the shot had come from.

'Damned impertinence,' he cried, before looking back at Toby. 'Mustn't react, Mr Burns, it only encourages them. Coolness under fire, young sir, an absolute prerequisite.'

The only thing the youngster could think of was that the man who had fired was busy reloading for another attempt, so he was glad when his companion strode off in the direction from which that shot had come and he was quick to get his body between himself and possible harm. Still trending uphill, they finally came to clear ground and what had obviously been a defensive redoubt, to see French soldiers being taken prisoner. Another red-coated officer, seeing Toby's companion, rushed to meet them, stopping to raise his hat, his face alight with joy.

'We have the position, Colonel Moore. I have sent the men ahead to clear it right through but I reckon the resistance to be broken.'

'Their commander?'

'No sign of him, sir, he's taken to his heels and fallen back to the tower.'

They were above the tower now, though still too far off for muskets, and so were presented with a clear sight of the whole bay and the battle going on between ship and shore, and it was far from clear to Toby Burns who was winning. The round shot was not denting those outer walls, if anything it was bouncing off them to ricochet ineffectively into the surrounding rocks. Occasionally a huge cannonball would hit right on the face and that would chip at the stonework, but it did not in any way look as if it was creating a breach: stone flew but no cracks appeared. Also obvious was the brazier sitting in the tower top, right by the two long cannon: they were firing red-hot shot, which could be deadly to wooden ships.

The boy did not know the half of it and had he been aboard either vessel he would have known the true meaning of terror. That red-hot shot had hit the hull of HMS *Fortitude* on half a dozen occasions, lodging in the scantlings to start fires which must be extinguished by cutting the balls out of the hull, a task that was full of risk to those employed. Three of the ship's lower-deck thirty-two pounders had been dismounted, leaving six men killed, and some fifty were already wounded so that in the cockpit the ship's surgeon was hard at it with his saw, knives and a needle and thread.

Their fire was having practically no effect: the fortress being round meant the cannonballs could rarely strike with any consequence and, on a stationary vessel they were more at risk than the defenders. Broadside after broadside had ripped out to hit at those walls, some missing completely, for, even anchored, the ship was subject to the tide and the swell while enough returned shot had missed the hulls to either hiss into the sea or slice through the rigging, setting that alight so that the fire engine was in constant use.

Toby Burns saw the springs let go so that both frigate and ship-of-the-line swung on their single anchors, thus reducing the size of the target they presented. Soon those same anchors were being plucked from the water, this as sails were sheeted home to take the ships out of range, *Fortitude* trailing smoke from smouldering wood as she did so: the bombardment had failed. Aboard Hotham's flagship, Captain Holloway was required to work hard to keep off his face a smirk, certainly as long as his admiral was in plain view.

'A poor showing,' said Moore, 'but damned brave.'

'Quite, sir,' the other officer replied, though the look on his face implied he disagreed.

'I must report back to the shore, sir,' Toby cried, 'to say you have achieved your object.'

Colonel Moore let the tip of the walking stick touch his gold-edged, tricorn hat. 'Then, young sir, you'd best be off, but tell whoever you are to report to we overlook the tower. A pair of cannon up here and we could make their lives warm.'

If the defenders on the tower at Mortella Point were cheered by their success, and thought themselves impervious to either ground assault or bombardment from the sea, they reckoned without the Royal Navy or the ingenuity of Colonel John Moore. Toby Burns, given he knew the man in command and the route to the redcoats' camp, was employed as a messenger, running back and forth, convinced that every bush and boulder hid a Frenchman, but through his offices a plan was hatched.

Next day they saw a stream of boats coming inshore, as well as near to a hundred sailors, to rig uprights and pulleys onto which were winched cannons and their trunnions, those brought in on a hatch cover lashed to empty barrels. More triangular stanchions were erected ashore, with yet more lines and blocks, this while a path was cut through the trees by the soldiers, the wood being taken up to where Colonel Moore was waiting. He had been examining the tower for some time and a notion of how to subdue it had come to him.

'It seems a great pity to me, gentlemen,' he eventually said to the assembled officers, 'to waste all this firewood. It will make a bonny fire, I think.'

All day the sailors toiled, roving and rigging, hauling and lifting, creating a run of lifting gear that raised those two-ton lumps of metal up the steep hillsides , until finally they were ready to be put in the emplacements the bullocks had made ready. Also brought ashore, requested by Colonel Moore to the mystification of his naval contemporaries, was the equipment to heat shot, the long-handled carrier that could be lifted onto the fire and held there until the cannonball glowed.

Prior to heated shot, the range had been tried and established with round shot, but it was clear that, even plunging on to the fortress, the place was so sturdily built that little damage would be done, certainly not enough to entirely overcome defenders who could shelter inside. Any break in the bombardment brought them rushing out to fire cannon now elevated to the maximum, which posed great danger to the sailors manning the British cannon and the redcoats who were alongside them, though it also exposed them: it was seen a pair were not swift enough when the British fire recommenced, and they paid the price, being cut in half by a volley.

'Heated shot, sir?' asked the officer commanding the party of sailors who had provided the men to both haul and work the guns – Lord Hood's nephew, also called Samuel, captain of HMS *Juno*. 'Against stonework?'

Colonel Moore smiled and handed over his telescope. 'I bid you, sir, look upon the parapet of yonder tower and tell me what you see.'

Sam Hood took the glass and did as he was asked and it was clear that, whatever it was Moore had in mind, it was not immediately obvious.

'Our French friends,' the Colonel pointed out, 'have lined the outer and inner parapet with a material called bass junk, the object of which is to defray shot and stop stone from shattering, which would send debris flying in all directions to the detriment of the men manning the guns. I believe, if I were to employ a naval expression, it would be a sort of "gammoning" and it extends all the way down to the flooring.'

Sam Hood, still looking through the telescope, smiled. 'Would I be right in thinking this bass junk is flammable?'

'It will not burn, sir, but it smokes like the devil.'

'Then I look forward to seeing the effect of your heated shot, sir.'

Normal round shot was employed to clear the fortress gunners, who were through the trapdoor before the first ball landed, this so they would not see the heated shot. Loading that was a tricky affair, a task for men who knew their game, and not for the bullocks. Two sailors, each with a pair of handles, carried the red-hot shot to the cannon, not delaying, for that would obviate the purpose, but with care, given they were surrounded by powder in cartridges and barrels, which had only to be touched by those cannonballs to blow the whole encampment to perdition.

Loading had to be quick, any false tipping and the ball would miss the cannon muzzle, and it needed solid oak, slow to fire, to drive the ball home, with both the men tasked to load the ball and the man tasked to drive it down to its furthest seat getting well clear immediately their work was done, lest the heat conduct to the powder and set the whole thing off prematurely. The man on the flintlock did not hesitate either: the gun had been pre-aimed and he pulled the flintlock lanyard as soon as there was clear daylight before the muzzle.

The first ball flew over the top of the tower, leading Colonel Moore to speculate on the scientific possibility that the nature of the ball, allied to the amount of powder used, was affected by the heat. Range dropped, the process was repeated again, this time the ball dropping into the top of that crown roast to roll until stopped by the parapet.

'A few more, I think,' the redcoat colonel said, 'will do the trick.'

And it did: soon the whole top of the round tower was wreathed in smoke and it was obvious that the colder air of the interior was drawing in through the trapdoor that led to the next floor down, and in time, Moore had surmised, the whole building would be full of dense smoke making it impossible for those inside to breathe.

In the hope that his stratagem would work, the colonel had placed a company of his soldiers in the rocks leading to the base of the tower. The doorway, twenty feet in the air and unassailable even with ladders, was suddenly flung open and smoke began to billow out, followed by coughing and spluttering Frenchmen, the signal that the notion had worked sent to a ship, then passed on to those working the guns.

'I think we have our fortress, Captain Hood. You may tell Admiral Hotham the upper reaches of the Bay of San Fiorenzo are his.'

It wasn't over: there was a redoubt named Convention, of twenty-one heavy cannon, which was easy to see held the key to the town, one that to assault over open ground would be murderous in casualties. Again the navy did the impossible, transporting guns along paths meant for donkeys, sometimes wide enough for only one man, often with a drop of five hundred feet to one side, never once losing a tar or equipment as they manhandled tons of metal along on ropes and pulleys, using the very rocks as stationary points, to set up a battery that overlooked Convention from the one angle at which it was vulnerable. Once employed they destroyed it in two hours; the whole anchorage and the tiny port was now in British hands.

At a dinner to celebrate, Colonel John Moore, returning a toast from Sir William Hotham, named Captain Sam Hood and his men as heroes, and then he added that Midshipman Toby Burns had done sterling service as a runner and, if the admiral did not mind the temerity of a soldier suggesting a course of action to a sailor, the lad deserved a mention in whatever despatch was sent back to London.

CHAPTER SEVENTEEN

There was no way of knowing how much time had passed before the loss of the tow was discovered, only that the line which had attached them to the stern of the pinnace was slack enough to be hauled in. It looked as though the two men on the oars had, like John Pearce and every other soul in the boat, fallen into a troubled sleep, which not only allowed the cutter to drift but also meant they had failed to turn the sandglass and wake a relief. He also had cause to curse himself for failing to note the miscreants were a pair who had probably got into the spirit store, this established when dawn broke and not only their bleary eyes told a tale, but their rank breath as well.

Shouting proved pointless when, on the crest of several waves, no sign of a sail could be seen. Pearce felt even worse when presented with the end of a piece of rope which showed no signs of fraying: if anyone could tie a secure knot a sailor could, even the most useless sod. Yet he could not say what he suspected: that the knot might have been loosened, given the propensity of Jack Tar to see evil in any unexplained event.

Sailors were the most credulous folk he had ever met in his life: put the wrong foot on the ship first and it was doomed, any number of birds sighted promised perdition, so that sometimes it seemed there was a superstition for every waking hour, which on a ship at sea was twenty-four. There had been mutterings too, he suspected, about Emily Barclay. Every ship in King George's Navy had women aboard, even where captains were strict about their presence, some even going to the length of disguising themselves as males. It would be the status of a woman like Mrs Barclay that made her an object of nautical misgivings.

Looking at the faces in the crowded boat he surmised there were no natural navigators present, this allied to his own knowledge of his lack of ability in the subject: they were in the middle of the Bay of Biscay and they might as well be in the middle of the moon. Nor did he have the instruments necessary to even try for a course that would take them home; there was, in short, no choice but to set the prow towards the point at which the sun had risen, albeit that was partly guesswork given the dense overhead cloud.

'Which would be where?' asked Michael O'Hagan quietly, his head lowered to make sure the question did not carry.

Pearce, too, dropped his head. 'The coast of France.'

'Holy mother of God,' Michael hissed, 'do you so love the place you cannot stay away?'

'I have no choice. My sextant went down with the ship and even if I had thought to fetch it I am not sure I can remember all I need to know about fixing a course by starlight, as Mr McGann taught me.'

'Holy Christ, we need sight of that sainted man now. Are we not on the same line as he would sail to and from Gibraltar?'

There was brief flash of hope then: McGann's postal packet ran the route from England to the Straits on a regular basis. It was he who had taken John Pearce to the Mediterranean in the first place, carrying the letter to Lord Hood, which had occasioned him being entrusted with the reply he now had in his coat pocket. When Michael called him sainted he was not far wrong, for McGann was one of the kindest and wisest persons Pearce had ever met, that is till you got him ashore and near a tankard of ale, from whence he became a burden.

'Michael, we have been drifting all night. I have no idea where we are in line of longitude. All I could do is probably establish our latitude, which would not be much help if we are in the middle of the ocean with nothing but oars to propel us. We are not well supplied and drifting in the hope of the sight of a sail could see us all expire. We must make for land.'

'Where there are heathens waiting to lop off our heads.'

'Savin' your presence, Lieutenant, we would be obliged to be knowing what it is you and Paddy are a'whispering about.'

Pearce looked up into a sea of eyes, all on him, and they included Charlie and Rufus, though they, at least, were not full of suspicion. These men were part of the crew of HMS *Grampus*, on which he had been a supernumerary with no actual duties; they did not know him at all and therefore had no loyalty to anything other than his rank, which would be tenuous in the extreme if they thought he had no idea of what he was doing. The bargain between officers and hands was simple: blue coats got respect because of their knowledge, and sometimes from the fear of their power in the article of punishment, but it was a covenant easy to rupture when neither were present.

Odd that he should think of his father at that point, for here was the very notion over which they had disputed often, once Pearce junior had become old enough to form his own opinions. Adam Pearce maintained there was a basic good in people, not Christianity, in which he did not believe, but in their innate nature, the caveat being that a lack of the necessary means to exist in comfort – food, warmth and security – allied to a dearth of education, was what often rendered them little better than beasts.

His son had disputed the contention, on the very good grounds that there were men of high education and full bellies, surrounded by servants to see to their every comfort, well warmed by blazing fires and devoted families, who behaved like ravenous monsters. Incarcerated in Fleet Prison, they had found it necessary to take turns in sleeping to avoid being robbed of all they possessed, which stripped the scales from young John's eyes, and his thinking had not altered with their subsequent flight. In the latter stages of their gentle arguments John Pearce was wont to point out to old Adam that being in Paris, in the midst of revolution going from euphoria to bedlam, they were surrounded by events which supported his argument. What did he face here?

'We are crowded into an eighteen-foot cutter with supplies insufficient to keep us alive for very long. We have two choices, to drift around in the hope of rescue or to head east for land.'

'That bein' where?' asked the man who had first spoken, his question producing nods in the others: clearly they were happy to see him take on the role of spokesman. Pearce concentrated on him, searching his face to try to discern the kind of man he was. The nose was flat as if it had been hit often and hard, the eyes were brown and small under heavy black brows, they topped by a flat forehead. Yet the look was not one of threat, more of enquiry.

'France.' Beside him Pearce could feel Michael shifting sideways to get his right hand free, something that did not go unnoticed: those small brown eyes flicked slightly and the brows knitted a fraction, though it was impossible to tell if that was caused by the answer or the Irishman's movement. 'Might I enquire as to your name?'

'My mates call me Polly, and I can't say the word "France" makes me happy.'

That name, with the obvious hard look of the man, nearly made Pearce smile, but that would be, he knew, unwise. 'Then, Polly, if I may be permitted to call you that, I have to tell you that I do not feel competent to suggest any other course.'

'You not bein' a true lieutenant, like?'

'You know?'

The positive reply was accompanied by nods from the rest of the tars. 'It be a habit to find out about folk, Mr Pearce, an' you bein' you, that weren't hard, it being special, like, that you was the prankster of the fleet.'

'Leghorn?'

'An' the ladies thereof.'

'I'm curious to know if such a reputation flatters me or damns me?'

'Neither one nor t'other, but what happens to us here might have a bearing on that.'

'So if I ordered you to row east, I might not be obeyed?'

'Depends on if you is certain or not.'

Why do I think I like this man? Pearce thought. There is no passion in his speech, he is not trying to guy or overbear me, just asking the questions that

274

are in every one of his shipmates' minds.

'If you know about me at all, it will not surprise you if I say I am not the man to navigate you to safety and I am of the opinion, formed by standing on the deck of the ship and seeing nothing even on a busy route, that to hope to be picked up by a passing vessel is too risky to contemplate. I would therefore suggest, since I am in no position to command...' Pearce paused as Polly nodded: they both knew this cutter was a republic. 'My view is the only safe course is to seek the nearest land.'

'And I go with that,' said Michael.

'As will your two mates, Paddy, but I doubt Mr Pearce would mind if we stick in our ha'penny worth.'

'Not at all.'

Polly raised his voice. 'Seems right to me, lads, but it is up to you to speak your piece if'n you dispute it.' The murmuring was low, no man prepared to speak other than to his nearest neighbour, this while Pearce was fixed by those small and unblinking eyes. After half a minute, Polly spoke again. 'Seems, as is common, none of you have a voice, so I say we go with what the officer suggests.' Again no one spoke up, so Polly added another opinion. 'Then we'd best get our backs into it, mates, and say thank Christ that the way the sea is running is in our favour.'

Aboard the pinnace, there was certainly no republic: there might be a lieutenant and a midshipman aboard but there was also Ralph Barclay, and for all his infirmity and being in constant pain, he was still a senior post captain. With the cloud cover he decided on a direction of sailing by the location of the rising sun, as well as the north-east current which was common to this area, a good enough course until the sky cleared, hopefully at night, where the north star would help to guide them home.

If he was in pain it had no affect on his ability to command, and so ingrained were the habits of the service that no one, not even the most contentious lower-deck lawyer, of which there might well be a few aboard, was going to dispute with him, and that included the way he dealt with the loss of sight of the cutter and the suggestion from the lieutenant that they should instigate a search.

'It is unfortunate, I grant you, but we must trust to the competence of the people aboard to look to themselves.' Seeing his inferior about to protest he added sharp words. 'Do you see Captain Daws or any sign of the other boats?'

'No, sir.'

'And what, pray, does that tell you?' Faced with no reply it was easy to nail an end to any discussion, which he did with a firm tone. 'It tells me, sir, that the amount of drift we have all suffered is substantial. It tells me that the cutter and the men aboard her could be miles distant. If we were safe on a ship, with sharp eyes high on the masthead, your notion would be a good one, but we are not. We are able to see no further than the wave height allows us and at some risk to ourselves, therefore we are constrained by circumstances to look to our own needs.'

Overheard by all aboard, it was easy to see it as a base appeal to their collective self-interest, so Ralph Barclay saw the need to give a nod to a more Christian notion, knowing he was on safe ground.

'Your concern, Lieutenant, is commendable and is, I am sure, shared by all of us in this boat, as is fear for our own safety. But I am no tyrant, sir. If the sentiment lies with what you say I will abide by it.'

Another voice spoke, that of a man on the oars. 'Would we be allowed to ask what the odds are, your honour?'

The speaker received a glare in response: no common seaman should address an officer so, yet some allowance had to be made for circumstance. 'Fellow, if William Bligh can sail a boat over four and a half thousand miles to safety, I am sure I can get us all home and dry.'

That cheered all he faced and got them nodding; he would not look sideways to his right, where sat his wife. Then the man who had posed the question spoke again. 'Thank you, your honour, much obliged.'

'Lieutenant, I wish to take that man's name, for I propose that a loss of discipline will not be to our benefit. The matter can be left till we reach England, but dealt with it must be. For now, I wish you to supervise the distribution of the rations, then we must rearrange the way the boat is manned to get maximum advantage for our rate of sailing.'

'Aye, aye, sir.'

'You know who is in that cutter, do you not, husband?' Emily asked, her lips close to his ear.

His reply was made with his head down, and quietly. 'It makes no odds, my dear, it could be the devil himself or my bosom companion, my thinking would not differ. You do not comprehend that we are in grave danger, being as we are in an overcrowded boat in a bad place. Biscay is home to many a violent storm and I have to tell you if we face one we will not be likely to survive it, for we will be swamped. The wind is favourable and the sea benign for the time of year, we have a window of hope but no more, so it is imperative that we take advantage of our good fortune.'

'Yet you did not tell everyone that?'

'It is our spirit as well as our luck which will get us to safety. Now I must ask you to leave me be.' Then he raised his voice. 'Lieutenant, some men on the larboard gunnels; let us see what better rate of sailing we can achieve.'

The orders that followed saw the sail hauled round to take more of the wind, the weight of bodies on the larboard side used to compensate the extra pressure, with the midshipman now sat with Ralph Barclay, doing what he was told on the tiller. When it came time to tack, the sail and bodies shifted, and if it was not fast sailing of the kind Ralph Barclay had experienced as a younger man, for being overcrowded the boat was low in the water, the increase in speed was obvious by the way the bows were now creating white spray every time they hit a wave.

Rowing was hard work, requiring constant changes of oarsmen to prevent fatigue, but that same current which was aiding Ralph Barclay was even more kind to John Pearce. If he was less the experienced sailor than a man he saw as his enemy, he knew well the reputation of Biscay, for that same sainted Captain McGann had told him of its troublesome vagaries on their voyage south. He, too, knew that a storm would likely prove fatal, so the way the rowers were rotated had to be tempered by the need to achieve as much speed as possible.

He was glad that those aboard had allowed him the authority to decide, though he worried as the day wore on that he had no certainty he was holding to a true course. He had set the prow to where the sun had risen to tinge the horizon but that was a pretty nebulous thing to rely on, and while he might suspect the current ran towards the shore he had no way of knowing, or any deep learning, to say if that was true.

His darker thoughts were relieved by his taking his turn on an oar, an act which got him a nod from the fellow called Polly, who, it turned out, had the surname of Parrat, which was close enough to the bird, especially spoken, to explain why he was so named. Just as he was willing to share the burden of toil, he was also well able to take instruction from the men around him, who knew how to best employ their sticks in the rolling waves, gaining as much speed from crest to trough as they could, then fighting to maintain it as they rose to the next, always careful to rest when all their oars could make contact with was fresh air.

One man – again they took turns – was tasked to stand in the prow and look out for any sign of a sail, in his hands two pieces of rope tied to the boat to make sure he did not go overboard if the cutter jibbed suddenly, but all every man employed saw was miles of deserted ocean. The winter day might be short, but it had enough hours to exhaust the entire complement, which presented Pearce with another dilemma: should they seek to row on through the night or rest? In the end it was a best guess to keep some men rowing so the cutter had way enough not to be broached, but with the minimum effort, this as the others took turns to sleep.

The sky began to break up overnight, which was a good thing, since the stars began to show, the mass of the Milky Way affording enough light to allow faces to be seen, but against that came an increase in wind and from the wrong quarter, which Pearce suspected to be the north or north-east, which made rowing into it much harder, as well as altering the run on the surface water. That meant more men had to eschew sleep and row to keep way on the boat.

He knew enough to be sure the current would be unaffected, just as he knew that what applied in terms of pressure to a deep-hulled ship did not apply to a cutter. Examining the sky, he tried without feeling much in the way of success to identify those objects Captain McGann had sought to teach him: the seven celestial bodies the older man had called shooting stars, by which he had been able to establish his position and plot a course. Failure to identify them all mattered little for what he required: all he needed was Polaris to set the prow to what he was sure was due east.

Way to the north, having made good progress throughout the daylight hours, Ralph Barclay welcomed that same clearing sky and the sight of that same North Star; his prow was set right towards it and the English Channel.

A sip of water and a couple of ship's biscuits were not enough to provide sustenance for men working as hard as oarsmen, yet it was all they had and must be eked out. Nor was Pearce able to contemplate rest: if they tried to lie to, the wind, now strengthened, would drive them away from their hoped-for destination and that was another source of worry: Revolutionary France was not a happy place for which to aim and he knew that the coast where he hoped to make landfall was one of the most turbulent in that troubled country, even more so than Toulon.

The Vendée region had been in revolt against Paris for nearly a year, indeed he had heard himself of some of the horrors committed by both sides when he was off La

Rochelle the previous autumn. Was that revolt still alive? If it was, he and his companions might be lucky enough to land in territory controlled by the so-called Chouans, the local forces fighting the armies ordered to pacify the region. Or they might land amongst the revolutionary army, which would be dangerous in the extreme.

The whole western part of France, from La Rochelle to Brittany, was reportedly soaked with the blood of the inhabitants, regardless of age or sex, as well as those sent to defeat them. The locals, led by priests and their landlords, fought with equal barbarity, showing no mercy to anyone they defeated and captured: like all civil wars it was ruthless, and pitted brother against brother, fathers against sons.

They would need great good fortune, a thought which gained something from the rising of the sun, the orange ball turning to gold right ahead of them, and so seeming to offer a prospect of salvation. It gave more than that, for the night had been bitterly cold, so the little heat they received as it rose in the sky, evident even at this time of year, was welcome. Looking into the salt-encrusted faces and red-rimmed eyes of his companions Pearce knew he would appear the same, knew that to blink brought on a sting, that to lick his lips was to be avoided, given it would only increase his thirst as he sucked in salt. And all around them was the rolling sea, nothing but that within sight as they crested each wave, no seabirds to hint at land nearby, which in turn produced gloom.

'A sail, I saw a sail!'

'Where away?' Pearce shouted, before admonishing the men, who had turned, to keep rowing as they fell off the top of the wave. Making his way forward through the mass of bodies was difficult and he was aware that having risen again the lookout had not spotted what he believed he had seen previously: was it no more than a vision caused by wishful thinking?

'There again, I see it, the tip of a mast, no two.'

John Pearce was with him now, his arms locked around the lookout's body to steady himself, his sore eyes straining forward, his heart beating with hope. Then he saw it as well and he shouted back to confirm the sighting, to tell his rowers to pull like the devil, which he realised as soon as he spoke was the most unnecessary command he would ever issue.

Closing with that vessel took several exhausting hours, though it was quickly identified as a two-masted brigantine of small displacement. The opinion was that whoever was aboard her was no sailor, given the top hamper was all ahoo: the square-rigged foremast had nothing but half a main course drawing, and that was clewed up at one end. It was also obvious the cutter was making more progress in closing than the sailing ship, which given the favourable wind was ridiculous. It took all of the morning and half the afternoon to get within hailing distance, which did not produce much in the way of joy since John Pearce was told, in French, by a loud and angry individual who stayed out of sight, to stay away.

'Whoever had charge of this barky is no sailor, Mr Pearce, she's a'wallowing not sailing.'

Pearce nodded to Polly and hailed the ship again which produced another negative response, as well as a sort of argument. He suspected the men who were relying on him wondered what was being said in the shouted conversation being carried out in a language they could not understand, but he was in a poor position to enlighten them, given they were too low in the water to see on to the deck, even when the vessel was in a trough and they were on a crest. All he had to go by was that single, irate voice.

'I have asked them,' he said eventually, 'or whoever the person is doing the talking, to take us aboard and he has refused.'

'We's shipwrecked,' exclaimed one of the men on the oars. 'They's got to take us.'

'They say they won't. We are to stay away.'

'Then why,' Polly demanded, 'if they mean to leave us, don't they sheet home some sails proper and leave us behind? Even what they have, made taut, would be enough to show us a clean pair of heels.'

Pearce cupped his hands and shouted again, his tone harsh instead of the supplicant way he had called before, which had Polly asking him what he had said.

'I said we are coming aboard, whether they like it or not.'

CHAPTER EIGHTEEN

Pearce fully expected, as the prow of the cutter was aimed at the scantlings, to find the side suddenly filled with armed men, which, given they had few weapons with which to effect a boarding, served to underline how desperate was their situation. Yet not a soul appeared and the cutter clattered to the hull with little grace, the men of HMS *Grampus*, with the Pelicans at the fore, fatigued as they were, leaping for the bulwarks, rasping shouts coming from dry throats. What they saw on the deck stopped every man jack of them stone dead, most before they had both feet on the planking.

The priests and nuns, some thirty in number, knelt, heads bowed, and hands clasped together around rosaries, obviously praying, the low murmuring sound of their devotions like the buzz of a hive. Michael O'Hagan immediately crossed himself, this while Pearce held up a hand to still the exclamations coming from the men he led. Slowly they climbed down on to the deck and stood in a confused huddle, not knowing what to do, until Pearce spoke.

'Michael, how do we address folk at prayer?'

The shake of his friend's head left little choice but to advance towards the man leading the devotions, not that he was sure it was leadership, only that he was in front and separate from the rest. Stopping before the priest he took the time to look around a deck that was untidy in the extreme, with nothing shipshape: loose ropes hung down from the masts and bits of half-unfolded canvas lay here and there. Also he thought he saw, in a stain in the unclean deck, a black shapeless mark that could be blood.

Never comfortable in the company of priests, he was at a loss to know what to say. It was also true that those he had met, and with whom he could hold a conversation, were those of a more secular mien than this obviously devout fellow kneeling before him: exchanges of a political nature with the likes of Tallyrand, the ex-bishop of Autun, or the Abbé Sieyès, both anti-clerical politicians, in the salons of Paris, did not fit a man for a situation like this.

'Monsieur l'Abbé.'

One hand, palm open and facing him, came up, but the head stayed down, forcing him to turn and shrug, that before he realised that no one had moved, so he made frantic hand signals to tell them to search below, while also ensuring in a low voice that their cutter had been secured, a query that got him a look from men too long versed in their duties to have failed in such a task. Raising his head he looked at the half-set sail, seeing it had been let go two-thirds of the way along the yard but was still clewed up on the rest, while the lines to sheet it home were taut on the winged side and loose where it flapped.

He was still standing waiting when whispered words informed him the ship was carrying no cargo: though there were supplies of food, the holds were near empty as was everything else, including the main cabin, though it looked as though that had been used as a place of rest. Michael tapped his shoulder as the kneeling priest, his voice rising a fraction, made a blessing with the hand he had used to silence Pearce. Then he finished his quiet prayer and looked up showing a face full of sadness.

'We have made our peace with God. You may do now as you wish.'

Replying in French, Pearce asked him what he meant, which engendered a certain amount of confusion until he added that they were Englishmen and explained the circumstances by which they had come to be here. It was quite amazing the way the priest's eyes could open so wide, and the gabbling explanation he passed on to his companions had them all raising their hands to heaven and loudly, almost ecstatically, praising the Lord. Then the leader stood and kissed John Pearce, with some force, on both cheeks. Some of the nuns were now in tears, wringing their hands and still thanking their Creator.

'We were sure you were the apostates of Paris, sent to cut our throats.'

'You must explain.'

It was incoherent to Pearce and double Dutch to everyone else who had come on board with him, which may have been just as well, given it was such a bloody tale. They had fled from a monastery outside Nantes to escape the clutches of a ferocious Jacobin revolutionary representative called Jean-Baptiste Carrier and his assistants, taking refuge in the small estuary port of St Nazaire, from where they had heard of the fate they had escaped.

'He has overseen the murders of thousands of good people, some who died for their faith, others for their wealth and bloodline, but the beast Carrier reserved his bile most for the clergy and those who chose to be brides of Christ.'

It was a horrific tale, of nuns raped and priests decapitated, of both being loaded into barges to which they were tied, they then sunk in the waters of the Loire River, the occupants drowning with prayers for salvation on their lips and the braying yells of the mob in their ears. Even more was what the Abbé termed 'republican marriages', overseen by the Jacobin representative in person, of priests and nuns first made naked then bound tight, face to face, to be either run through with a single sword or to be thrown into the river to drown.

'We were fortunate, monsieur, for the captain of this ship, a good son of Mother Church and a Chouan, spirited us away before the beast could lay hands on us, though we saw our home, our abbey, burning as we fled. He got us aboard but his crew refused to put to sea for fear of what would become of their loved ones left behind, for the Jacobins were on our heels and they had no time to gather their families, leaving Captain Defrou with no choice but to ask us to aid him to raise the anchor; can you imagine it, monsieur, priests and nuns on that thing they call the capstan? The tide was falling and that took us out to sea. The crew took to the boats and went ashore.'

'And where is the captain now?'

The priest looked at that black stain Pearce had noticed earlier and crossed himself: there was no need to say more about the fate of the man but he did so nevertheless. 'He was no longer a young man and he told me that what he was about to do he had not been required to try for many years. I confess I did not beg him to avoid the risk, but then he made light of it and the fact that none of us could face the task of aiding him, from fear of the fate he suffered, may God rest his soul.'

John Pearce could imagine that fate: loosening a sail was a task for many hands not one, a job that was coordinated, not carried out piecemeal, and a flapping, half-released main course would be a threat to whoever was on the yard trying singly to release it. It was also a place for men who were young, nimble and fit.

'He fell when halfway along and smashed into the deck with the most frightening sound. I have heard a bone break but not many at one time and he was not a man of slender build so I fear his bulk did him harm. We carried him to his cabin and prayed for him, but it was to no avail.'

John Pearce bit his tongue then: the man was dead, so no good would come of saying a little physical ministration might have had more effect than religious entreaty.

'Where did he plan to take you?'

'Anywhere, monsieur, away from those Jacobin fiends.'

Pearce turned to Polly. 'Mr Parrat, oblige me by getting some men aloft to loose the rest of that mainsail, while I instruct our divines on how to sheet it home.'

Polly raised an eyebrow at being addressed as 'mister', but that was the least of his concerns. 'I'd be minded, and so would the lads, to hear this man's tale, as you have done.'

'Later. Let us get properly under way first, and second to that, let us calculate what stores are aboard. We will need to empty the sail locker and see what we have; also, we will need someone nimble at the masthead. We are in French waters and it would never do to be surprised.'

Polly nodded and shouted the requisite orders, then barked to see some of the men hesitate, for they were not topmen. Pearce turned back to the Abbé who was eager to know what was happening.

'You have the good fortune, monsieur, to have had come aboard a party of the best sailors on God's earth. Now I require you and your people to come with me while I show you which ropes to pull and when to pull them.'

'To what purpose, my son?'

'Why, to sail to safety, monsieur.'

'And where will that be?'

'England.'

The eyes opened in horror and the voice was full of doom. 'Is that not godless country?'

'No, monsieur l'Abbé, it is a country where you can practise your religion without fear for your life.' Pearce took his arm and led him to where the falls hung loose from the rigging. 'Now gather your charges and get them clasping hard on this rope, as if it would haul down to them salvation, when I say to pull.'

Ralph Barclay had got the lieutenant to make a knotted and weighted line by which they could make a rough calculation of their speed while he used a sandglass brought aboard to time their tacking and wearing: not dead reckoning but enough of a measure to keep them on a reasonable course, though he tended to lay longer to larboard than starboard with the knowledge that somewhere close by lay the iron shore of Brittany. Their course might raise one of the Norman Isles but he hoped to weather both Ushant, avoid them and make a landfall east of the Isles of Scilly, which would bring him to the shores of Cornwall or Devon.

They might be under sail but the work was having an effect on those aboard, for the eking out of the supplies meant they received little sustenance and less water, which left him with two conflicting hopes, cloud cover and rainfall, or clear skies that at night made navigation easy with that bright Pole Star, one degree off true north, to guide him home. Having steered by it throughout the night, all in all he was feeling fairly confident, certainly enough to allow himself to surrender charge of the boat and get some sleep at sunrise. That confidence faded when he awoke and it was pointed out to him that the sky to the west was showing signs of increasingly heavy cloud.

He did not need to be told the wind had swung yet again, nor what that increasing cloud portended, and it was not a happy thought that made the notion of that iron shore take on more meaning. If the wind came in at gale force from the west, which looked to be likely, it would be that much harder – in fact it might be impossible – to keep clear of it, even in a single-sailed fore-and-aft-rigged vessel.

In a time of peace, and seeing what was bubbling up on the horizon, Ralph Barclay would have immediately run for land and it was something he had to consider now, unpalatable as it was. Captivity might be unpleasant but it was preferable to death, for sitting as low as she was with overcrowding it would not take much of a cross sea to swamp them. The real question was how long he had to decide, given he was on a part of the ocean notorious for tempests: that Brittany shore, full of broken rocks, deep bays and high cliffs was testimony to the force they could generate.

'Husband, I require to relieve my bowels.'

Damn the woman, he thought: why could she not be like everyone else aboard and just void herself with having all aboard avert their gaze, and behind a screen at that? Impolite it might be, but they were in a dire situation where manners mattered little. Emily was thinking she had seen enough of the men aboard perched on the gunnels with their ducks around their ankles, or pissing into a bailing can before tossing the contents over the side, to last her a lifetime. She was also acutely aware of the approach of an awkward time of month and what needed to be done so she could avoid staining her clothing.

'One day I must introduce you to Portsmouth Cath,' Ralph Barclay said, maliciously. 'If you saw her antics you might be less worried about the eyes of the men upon you. She is wont to challenge your mids to a pissing contest, and even with her sex, she can outgun them every time, taking their bets as reward.'

'Spare me your anecdotes of the graceless whores of naval ports.'

'All I am trying to say to you, Mrs Barclay, is that these men before you have seen everything, and while you might suffer from embarrassment, they are more likely to react to the sight of you going about your occasions with indifference.'

'I have learnt much about life since I sailed with you, husband, but that I would like to be spared.'

'Then you will oblige me by waiting until we have established our latitude. Lieutenant, have your sextant at the ready, by the sight of the sun we are approaching the zenith.'

Having held on as long as she could, it was with some discomfort that Emily Barclay waited through the ritual of shooting the noonday sun, which not only gave them a time by which to set the sandglass but, by establishing the height of the orb relative to the horizon, a fairly accurate fix on where they were and how far they had yet to travel, and all the while she squirmed her husband was looking to the west with a wary eye.

Whatever else Ralph Barclay was, and opinions differed, he was a good seaman. He had been at sea since his thirteenth year, and if he had endured some awful maltreatment he had also been taught his trade in waters that ran from where they were now to the other side of the ocean. Each time they rose on a wave he saw that cloud thickening, but it was the darkening at the base which told him it portended real trouble.

'Devenow, the canvas screen for Mrs Barclay, and you men to avert your eyes.'

With that he went forward, handed from man to man, to consult with the lieutenant. Emily was left glaring at Gherson, who had on more than one occasion sought to peep round the screen Devenow held to get a look at her with her skirts raised; he was nothing but a slug, and that was underlined by the smile he gave her in response, which made her blush and made her furious for doing so.

'A little further round, Devenow, if you please,' she asked, cutting off his eyeline.

'Don't forget to hold on tight, Mrs Barclay,' Gherson said, a smirk on his face as it was cut out. 'It would never do to have to let fly the sail to fetch you out of the sea.'

'If it were you, sir, and I had charge, you could stay to drown.'

The voice that replied had no humour in it at all. 'People have tried to drown me afore, and, by damn, they have failed.'

'Mind your blaspheming, Gherson,' said Devenow. 'This be Captain Barclay's wife and not some common cull.'

Raising herself gently, Emily went about her business, careful to keep a good grip. It was the sound of a distant gun that nearly did for her, because the hand on the tiller, that of the midshipman, jerked slightly and, given the wind was reduced on the sail, so did the boat. Forced to wrench forward, she fell back into the boat still in a state of dishabille. Devenow, just as taken by the sound as everyone else, had dropped the canvas screen, leaving her exposed and very red in the face, this as her husband shouted.

'A signal gun, by damn, or I am a Dutchman's uncle.'

For all her blushes, no one was looking in Emily's direction, every eye being cast forward, which allowed her to rearrange her clothing. Then, and only then, did she realise the import of what was being said.

'We are somewhere off the Pointe du Raz, lads, and if that is a signal gun then it will be the inshore squadron blockading Brest.'

'It might be the Frenchies, your honour,' a voice cried.

'Take that damned man's name!'

They sighted the first of the sails mid afternoon, and, atop that, a long white pennant streaming forward to denote the rank of the commanding admiral – odd, given his nickname, if Ralph Barclay had the right of it, would be Black Dick Howe. Soon the three masts of the frigate were plainly visible, and they obviously had sharp eyes at the masthead, for almost as soon as they could make out the top strakes of her hull the sails were trimmed to bring her round to close, which produced a hoarse cheer.

'Belay that,' Ralph Barclay called, but without much rancour. 'Let them see we are true Englishmen. Hearing a cheer like that they might mistake us for Johnny Crapaud.'

'HMS *Nymphe*, if I'm not mistaken, sir,' the lieutenant called, joyfully, 'one of the finest frigates in the fleet.'

'By damn, sir, she could be the tub of Hades Hall for all I care.' That was when he caught the eye of his wife, who was frowning at his language.

The calls of recognition were exchanged as the frigate closed, changing course to present a lee side, with the midshipman on the tiller bringing the boat round, sweet as you like, to lay alongside with willing hands to help them. They came aboard a vessel as full of joy to see

296

them as they were to be safe on a deck, but there was no time for pleasantries, for as the captain, Edward Pellew, pointed out, there was a blow coming and he needed to get his ship into a fit state to confound it.

'In short, Captain Barclay, I must get some sea room, so please go to my cabin where my steward will make you right at home.'

'You have a surgeon aboard, sir?'

'I have.'

'Then I would be obliged if he too would come to your cabin and bring with him some tincture of laudanum.'

John Pearce would have admitted without a moment's complaint that he was far less a seaman than Ralph Barclay, but he had served long enough at sea to know trouble when he saw it. The darkening horizon along with the strengthening wind which had swung right round to the south-west had him in the captain's cabin studying the charts and looking for a place to shelter. He had been in a Biscay blow the previous year and the master of the vessel on which they had been sailing had got them into a safe haven; now, without an ounce of that man's knowledge, he had to do the same.

At first sight there were any number of places but the most obvious two were Belle Isle, to stay in the lee of that large island, or to make for the great hook which formed the outer protection of Quiberon Bay. Not trusting to his navigation – he might miss even a large island – he opted for Quiberon, putting up the helm of a vessel he now knew to be called *Guiscard* and sailing due north to get a sight of land.

The cry from the masthead had him on deck in an instant, and the news that there was a sail bearing due east took him up into the rigging, having grabbed one of the late captain's telescopes, to have a look. The red, white and blue flag streaming from the masthead told him the nationality of the vessel, while the fact of it coming out from the mouth of the Loire, albeit that river was way over the horizon, suggested it might be a warship hunting for the very vessel he was on. Or it might be another merchantman; it was too far off to tell.

He could not take a chance: he was on an unarmed ship and had a crew practically devoid of weapons barring a few cutlasses they had found in a rack. If it was an enemy warship he had no means of fighting them and that meant surrender, not a pleasant option given what he had been told about the activities of the Vendée Jacobins. If they were after the priests and nuns they would likely mete out to him and the others the same treatment used on them. Sliding down a backstay he gave the orders to alter course: if there was a blow coming they must head right into it, drawing on the pursuit, if it was that, in the hope that they, reckoning the game not worth the candle, would bear up for home.

'We'd best fetch out some storm canvas,' were the first words he uttered, 'and somebody go and find that Abbé. Tell him we need his prayers.'

CHAPTER NINETEEN

It was a common expression among sailors that the weather was a fickle beast and one wont to surprise a fellow rather than do as he anticipated; those clouds building on the horizon and the system they portended performed exactly to that maxim. The men had got the heavy storm canvas on deck and were bending most of it onto a topmast spar, not easy given their numbers and state of well-being, while another was being fetched up for the lateen sail of the mizzen, when the wind shifted once more, this time into the south-east, which meant the heavy thunderous threat ahead seemed to stay where it lay, neither closing in on them nor receding.

They had already been aloft, Pearce included, to get set as much sail as the brigantine *Guiscard* would carry, with the man in command racking his brain to recall everything he had ever been told about the task being performed, adding as much guesswork as knowledge, this while one of the crew who knew the duty cast the log to tell him if they were gaining any speed. At first they did, but it soon became apparent that the more sail they set, the less they gained, and Pearce had some taken in on the foremast, reckoning on something he had been told: that the head of the ship could be driven too hard into the sea with an excess of canvas aloft slowing the rate of sailing.

'Happen the father's prayers are working,' said Michael, seeing the weather still far off, this said with all the conviction of his religion.

'I would be inclined to agree with you if that fellow over our stern were not gaining on us.'

Taking a telescope once more, Pearce went back up the shrouds all the way to the mainmast top, there to hook a leg over the yard and settle himself so he could employ the thing. Time had taught him to use it properly: small movements of the tip were magnified, as much as was the observable object, so he quickly had the pursuit in plain view and the first thing he noticed, without in any way being sure of how to designate it in terms of a name, was that it was a three-masted warship, the deck carrying what were unmistakably cannon.

Keeping it in view, not easy as he swayed in an arc caused by the ploughing motion of the ship, he tried to work out a way to confound a vessel that was armed against that on which he sat, which was not; foul weather had been his only potential ally and an uncertain one at that, but to spin round and look over that dipping prow was to see that as a threat distant still. Nor could he really do what he had been told warships did in a stern case, lighten the ship: she carried no guns, no cargo, only bodies. Other questions intruded: would the chase be satisfied with the ship? If he took to the cutter again – not a happy prospect, given it had been overcrowded when he came upon the *Guiscard* and would be a damn sight more so with double the number aboard – would these pursuers let them go? Or were they after clerical blood to add to that already spilt? If they were, he and his men would not likely be spared a similar fate.

Nightfall might aid them, if they could stay far enough ahead, changing course as soon as darkness fell, yet the sky above was now a mixture of fluffy white clouds and clear sky that promised, if it stayed the same, long periods of starlight. With a waxing moon, that was damn near as good as daylight on the reflective ocean. Being an optimist by nature John Pearce was not yet in despair, but rack his brain as he might, he could see no way out of the dilemma. On the principle that several brains were better than one, he decided to put it to the men.

'If it be the holy mollies they are after, let's put them in the cutter with oars, I say.'

He had gathered the men he now led near the wheel, so that Charlie and Rufus, manning it, could be included, and he was pleased to see they looked shocked. Few on the now steeply canted deck nodded heartily at that suggestion, though it made many of them look thoughtful, while Michael O'Hagan wore an expression that indicated he wanted to clout the culprit. Much as it was distasteful, there was no denying it was a possible solution.

'No,' Pearce said, 'that is a course I cannot countenance.'

'Ain't up to you, mate,' replied Weary, the man who had made the suggestion.

The strangled cry as Michael picked him up by his shirt and lifted him four feet off the deck turned into a choking sound. 'Sir, not mate, you heathen.'

'Put him down, Michael.'

'Sure, I'd rather drop him over the side. Happen those chasing us will stop to pick him up and gain us time.'

'Can't blame him, Paddy.'

Michael looked at Polly Parrat with a frown. 'My given name is Michael, friend, and I'd be obliged if you would use it.'

'The name don't make no odds. We are in a pickle here without there bein' a clear way out. Mr Pearce here has told us what those Jacobin buggers got up to, and while I ain't no blind foe of a papist, I am no more minded to suffer as they are promised.'

Pearce looked at the sky and the way the sun, now hidden by a cloud, was well past its zenith and beginning to sink in the west, speaking his previous thought, trying to sound what he was not: confident.

'If we maintain our present rate of sailing he will not come up on us before night falls. We will change course and see if we can confound the fellow.'

'And if we don't?' Parrat asked.

'Let's see what dawn brings, Polly. Meanwhile, I will see if we can get the nuns to make us some dinner.'

The sailors had to fetch the wood from the store as well as the barrels of salt beef from the hold, this while others got the coppers lit. For once they could have as much as they liked, peas and hard cheese included. There was no biscuit but what they had brought aboard and that had to be shared with the clerics, but not before they had said grace in the Latin, which had some of the Jack tars fearing for their souls, having been raised all their lives to see Catholic priests as the servants of Old Nick.

There was cider instead of beer to drink, which occasioned the odd moan, so wedded were they to their small beer and, knowing the strength of that brew, Pearce put Michael in charge of its distribution and the storeroom where the barrels were kept. The last thing he needed was any of the few men he had getting drunk, which they would do readily if deep despondency took over from their limited hopes: he needed them alert.

Having eaten with them, drinking little, Pearce went aloft again to be alone with his thoughts, well aware that the discussion would continue without him and out of earshot of the likes of Michael. If they collectively decided they wanted to abandon those priests and nuns he was in no position to stop them. Certainly they would not respect his rank, which made him smile, given he had little of that commodity himself for his commission. Instead of dwelling on it he trained the telescope once more, to view a deck much more clearly defined now by the lower sun, so much so that he could see the figures moving about on it, as well as the men on the wheel. The figure that took his eye most, hanging onto one of the foremast shrouds and staring straight ahead, made him catch his breath.

He was dressed all in black from his tall hat, kept on his head by a scarf, through his coat, all the way down to his breeches and high boots, the only flash of colour the heavy tricolour sash he wore around his waist. He was too far off to be certain but that sinking sun was throwing a bright light from behind Pearce onto the enemy deck, and before it faded he had made out the face of a man who would most certainly kill him, and take pleasure in doing it slowly if he caught him, the one-time representative on mission from the Committee of Public Safety, Henri Rafin.

The last sight he recalled of him was the bastard floundering in the water off La Rochelle, he having chucked him into the sea, following on from a nip-and-tuck rescue in which he had been taken hostage. A man of outstanding arrogance, he was just the kind of turd that had floated to the surface thanks to the Revolution. And, if what he had heard of events in Nantes were true, he was, too, a perfect tool for vengeful pacification, a fellow who took pleasure in seeing others die, gloated in hearing the crowd bay as the blade of Madame Guillotine chopped off the heads of those whose only crime was dissent or having been born into the better classes.

Whatever his doubts before, whatever the conundrum, there was no way in creation he was going to give himself up into the hands of that man, and if there was no other way to avoid being taken he would steer the ship straight for Rafin and seek to take the bugger to the bottom with him, a notion which set his mind working long before he made his way back to the deck.

Night came slowly, as always in these climes, but not before they had experienced a glorious sunset, the heavy horizon clouds having broken up, the kind of golden light fading through orange to red which would have been inspiring for a less troubled soul, especially as it was accompanied by sweet singing from 'tween decks, where the holy passengers were celebrating mass. As soon as they were under cloud and in the dark, Pearce, having noted the position of Polaris before the star was blotted out, altered course to the north. If he was going to try to run that was the best direction with the wind coming in nicely over the starboard quarter: it was also the way home.

He had only held his previous course, sacrificing a certain amount of speed, to allow for this change, working on the principle that whoever commanded the chase, and it certainly was not Henri Rafin, would not know the *Guiscard* was manned by British sailors. He might, therefore, given a change of course had to be on the cards, suppose they would aim for a return to French soil. If they reversed their course while he held his new one, the gap might be opened enough to get them hull down and therefore hard to spot, even under a bright moon.

He was on the wheel himself now, calling for braces to be tightened, trying to feel through the spokes the best point of sailing and damn the course, his hopes dashed when the sky cleared and shafts of moonlight bathed the seascape to show that if they had made ground on their pursuers, they had held steadily to their original line, which was not enough to put them out of sight, this proved by an immediate change of course and a renewed chase.

'What now, Mr Pearce?' asked a voice in the pale light.

It was telling that he did not answer: there was nothing really to say.

The same condition having prevailed throughout the hours of darkness, there was a clear sense of foreboding when the sky began to lighten to the east, showing the chase to be no more than a couple of cables' lengths off their stern, so close that no telescope was needed now to see, when full daylight came, the details of the Frenchman. Soon they would be employing their bow chasers seeking to knock away something vital and bring matters to an even quicker conclusion than was inevitable.

'Gather round, all of you,' shouted Pearce, still manning the wheel. He waited till that request was obeyed, wondering about the words he would use to explain the thoughts he had formed aloft. 'Before we departed Toulon my companions and I were on a fireship and you know, having had to abandon your own vessel, how dangerous that is.'

'You planning to see us burnt off a barky a second time, Mr Pearce?'

Somehow Polly managed to say that without making it sound like an objection, which Pearce had been expecting, raising again his feeling of respect for the man. He was a natural leader: if he had decided to dispute his authority the men, Pelicans aside, would have backed him and it was plain he knew it. Yet he had not done so, nor, without any better suggestion to make, had he even set out to diminish the man to whom he had deferred.

'If we load the cutter with what she will bear in the article of stores, how long before we can get her back in the water, all hands on the task?'

'If we get her set right, minutes.'

'That's all you will have and that includes getting the bodies aboard as well.'

'The papists?' asked Weary, who had wanted to leave them behind. This time he had made sure he was not within reach of Michael O'Hagan. When

Pearce nodded, he insisted, 'They'll sink us.'

'No, we'll float – not in comfort – but the other thing we must do is step a mast on her. There are carpenter's tools below and we have spars which will serve. I am trusting there is one of you who can rig the tackle for a sail, and we do not lack canvas. That means we do not need room to row, so there is more room for people.'

'And then you are goin' to set this barky alight?' Polly asked.

'And ram her into the chase. If she's fired I doubt they will have much stomach to pursue us. They will be too busy saving themselves.'

'You're mad,' Weary said.

'If anyone has a better idea.'

The sound of the ball being fired arrived not long before the object itself, and looking aft Pearce saw the smoke being blown in their direction, thinking that even the wind was aiding them. The ball dropped short of the stern but not by much.

'An extra charge of powder will see the next one strike the hull. Time to decide.'

'Ben,' said Polly, 'you're handy with rope work. Sort out what we need for a sail while I get the right kind of spars for a mast and a gaff. Weary,' he continued, 'get them tools out and what you need to rig not only a mast, but places on the cutter for stays to hold it steady. The rest of you get that cutter turned over and the stores set by her that we need, more drink than food.'

He looked and nodded at Pearce, who then issued his own commands. 'Michael, Charlie, Rufus, I want anything flammable you can find placed right under the forward companionway as well as the means to get it ablaze.'

The crash of gunfire was louder as both bow chasers fired together: Pearce had predicted the powder charge would be increased, so the sound of tearing timber accompanying the arrival of the two cannonballs added to his standing.

'Michael, get the priests and nuns to help you. They will be safer further away from the stern and, if they are working, less inclined to panic.'

The chase crept closer over the next hour, firing steadily, reducing what had been the captain's cabin to a mess of glass and matchwood. Pearce was more concerned about the point at which the range decreased enough to allow those cannonballs to carry the taffrail: then he and everyone on deck would be at risk. Added to that, he dare not wait until they were within range to hit a mast, given he needed all the sails he had to manoeuvre.

Ahead of him the deck was alive with men working, some bringing stores up from below while the Pelicans were working out of sight: all was being done that could be, for what was a desperate throw. It was Polly, straightening his back from his labours, who froze, looking over the bowsprit. He waited for a moment before shouting.

'Ship over the bow, dead ahead, though Christ knows what it is.'

'Polly, take the wheel.'

Pearce raced aloft, glass tucked in his waistband once more, to sit on the crosstrees and aim it forward. What he saw was a ship all right, but nothing like one he had ever seen before. It had a decent hull, but stumps instead of masts and the most God-awful rig of sails in creation. Yet at the top of the fore stump flew a red pennant, indicating even to Pearce that it was under the command of a vice admiral of the Red Squadron and that told him the vessel was British. It was also the case that it was coming round to close, for Polly had seen the stern while he could see it broadside on. Even at a distance and taking into account his inexperience, he had never seen the like, so sluggish and ungainly was the manoeuvre.

That was when the taffrail was reduced to splinters and Pearce, looking down then, knew the next salvo, as carefully aimed as all the others had been, would come over that mess of timber and sweep along the deck. Yet there before him was a warship, a strange bugger for sure, but clearly armed. What to do, how quick were they closing?

'On deck, there, get below! Polly, lash off the wheel and do likewise and don't one of you dare dispute with me, that is a direct order.'

'I will hold my place, Mr Pearce,' Parrat replied, as everyone else rushed to obey. 'I got a bit of poop to mind my back.'

Pearce had his glass back on the chase, this time on the topmast. Did they have a man up there as a lookout? Had they seen what they were sailing towards and would they up their helm when they did? His answer came as the chase yawed round to present a broadside, every gun on its larboard deck, some seven in all, firing off as it bore, the balls smashing into the ship and taking lumps out of her bulwarks. If they hit anything vital, main, mizzen or wheel, maybe an important yard hard enough to dislodge a sail, they would take the ship, and it was no consolation being in possession of such knowledge when you could do nothing to prevent it. Yet some hope lay ahead, for the distance between that strange warship and *Guiscard* was now closing fast.

The chase had resumed its course, loading the bow chasers during that yaw so they spoke immediately. Pearce watched in fascination as the black balls arced through the air to land on the deck, one skipping by the foot of the mainmast to ram into the bulwarks, where it began to roll around. He had to just sit there, reckoning that another broadside was coming and it would be more dangerous than the last, for he was as safe up here as he was on the deck. That was until he recalled the Lascar they had buried from the deck of HMS *Grampus*, causing that feeling to evaporate.

The sound of more gunfire was not accompanied by smoke from the bow chasers, so he turned to see two great plumes of water a cable's length from the bowsprit. Who was the fellow aiming at? Pearce had no idea of the nationality of either ship before him, leaving him with the horrible possibility that he might be caught between two fires before anything was resolved. Then it occurred to him: the chase had no idea if the ship ahead was an enemy or a friend – the pennant he had recognised was stranger to them.

Time, if you discounted the now regular boom of those bow chasers and the more occasional broadside, stood still, as the three ships closed into an increasingly confined part of the ocean. Polly had used his brain and got everyone in the bows waving frantically to the ship ahead, which was all they could do in the absence of a flag, and it seemed to have some effect because when she fired her bow chasers again the shot was aimed well clear, clearly a warning to the chase, now so close he could see that there was a furious argument taking place on the quarterdeck, and it was the unmistakable sight of Rafin waving his arms that told him he was disputing with the captain about what to do.

That the man in command won was obvious: Pearce could see the hands on that pursuing deck lashing off their guns and rushing to the falls. Within minutes the sails had been let fly, the wheel was being spun and the bowsprit was spinning away. Ahead the captain of that warship had altered course to give him a clear shot of a ship flying a French revolutionary pennant and now it was his turn to yaw, albeit like a soaked log, and deliver a broadside.

The frigate, for Pearce now recognised the hull as

such, let fly with everything she had, and given they were bigger cannon and their range was greater, the slowly turning chase found itself surrounded by a mass of boiling seawater. If anything was enough to redouble their efforts then that broadside was it. Soon they were round, showing her stern lights, the sails were sheeted home again, with the yards braced right round as they needed to be to sail into the wind.

The shout came through a speaking trumpet, which obscured the face of the man doing the asking, a blue coat surrounded by many others, as well as a number in red.

'Ahoy there, who are you?'

For the first time in his life the reply, delivered through cupped hands, was one he was happy to give. 'Lieutenant Pearce, of His Britannic Majesty's Navy, in command of the French vessel *Guiscard*.'

'You have charge of a strange vessel, sir, is she a prize?'

This thought had not occurred to Pearce and it was a pleasing one. 'I have the makings of a strange tale, sir, which I will happily relate to you if I may come aboard.'

'By all means do so.'

'Might I also ask your name, sir?'

'Captain John Warren, of HMS *Fury*.'

'Let's get that cutter in the water, lads.'

There was also pleasure in hearing the man called Weary reply, 'Aye, aye, sir.'

Twenty minutes later Pearce was on the deck of HMS *Fury*, with its stumps in place of proper masts, shaking the hand of the captain and being introduced to his officers. That was followed by a salute to a Major General Sir David Rose, returning to England from having commanded the troops of the East India Company fighting the French around Pondicherry. The general, a rosy-cheeked, square-faced fellow, in contrast to the nut-brown naval officers, listened with interest to John Pearce's tale and added, before Warren could comment, 'Dammit, that demands a toast, if not several, the first to your surviving an inferno, the second to your timely finding of a ship and the third to such an amazing rescue.'

Looking into that face, somewhat too close in colour to his red coat, with the mischievous blue eyes and the smiling, slight overbite, Pearce wondered if the sentiment was celebratory or prompted by a love of the mere idea of a drink. It mattered not: he was in the mood to partake himself and just as happy, tankard in hand, to hear the fate of HMS *Fury*, a ship that had departed Lisbon days before HMS *Grampus*.

She had run into the storm of which they had seen evidence, losing first her foremast, then her main and mizzen, each having to be cut free with men still clinging to them, for fear they would drag down the ship; that Lascar they had buried was one, as were many of the crew, *Fury* having been in the east for several years.

'We were promised a refit by the Company in their

Calcutta dockyard, but delay followed delay and we were ordered home before it could be carried out.

'Slack folk, the Company wallahs,' said General Rose, then, seeing Pearce enquire he explained it as an Indian expression. 'More port, Mr Pearce?'

'Thank you no, sir, I have had enough.'

'Nonsense,' he barked, filling the tankards of himself and the others, without recourse to any servants. 'Don't do a man good to stint himself. Best thing in the world to keep the quacks at bay, what!'

'You have no idea what service in the east does to men and ships,' said Warren, leaving Pearce to wonder, by his expression, if he was including the general. 'But our timbers were worse than anything old Granny had to bear, and the seating on our masts, well, I reckon that poor man you had to bury tells you all you need to know.'

'It does occur to me, Captain Warren, that but for that hurricane, and the damage you sustained, you would not have been so slowed in your voyage as to be able to rescue us.'

'By damn,' boomed Rose, 'this young fella has the right of the matter. It's an ill wind which does no man any good.' The decanter was in his hand again, and Pearce's tankard was filled to the brim before he could say a word, as were all the others, the general standing for the toast, which forced them all to do likewise before emptying their drinking vessels.

'To an ill wind.'

CHAPTER TWENTY

It was ironic that Captain Daws and his party were the first to put their feet on English soil: Captain Edward Pellew and HMS *Nymphe*, along with their consorts of the Inshore Squadron, pleased at the turn the weather had taken, were required to resume their station off the Pointe du Raz to cover the approaches to the port of Brest, the main station of the French Atlantic fleet. Ralph Barclay was obliged to wait ten days, gnawing and irascible at the delay, waiting until the sloop carrying despatches came from Pellew's commander, Admiral Lord Howe.

That returned, carrying the squadron's logs as well as any intelligence, to Torbay where Howe's capital ships were anchored, ready to sail, given notice to do that for which their deployment was designed: to meet the French in the Channel and dominate that vital and strategic stretch of water. Ralph Barclay, along with Gherson and Devenow, was thus faced with an uncomfortable two-day journey from the West Country to London in a coach, which he swore was without a single working spring; thankfully he had secured enough laudanum to dull his constant pain.

Emily Barclay went straight back to Frome, a much shorter journey, ostensibly to prepare for his homecoming, in reality to be apart from the strain of being in his company; she, unlike her husband, had no reason to travel to London. Greeted first with joy, then with alarm at her adventures, most of her female relatives – her husband's sisters included – feeling it necessary to have a fit of the vapours when told the tales of battles, nursing the wounded, imprisonment and shipwreck.

HMS *Fury* limped up the Channel under her stumpy, jury-rigged masts, making slow progress, which was a situation that kept busy every officer on board, so hard was it to keep her on course. Captain Warren was grateful for the addition of those not required to sail the *Guiscard*: the notion that she should proceed independently had foundered on Warren's desire to have her in company in a dangerous stretch of water like the English Channel, just in case his frigate, wallowing, jibbing and taking in water, needed to be abandoned. But, and to John Pearce's relief, he had put one of his midshipmen in command of her and invited Pearce to share the frigate's wardroom, given what he had been through.

The slow progress frustrated John Pearce as much as his own delay had angered Barclay. He also had the added load, though in truth it was not a terribly onerous one, passed on by a captain too busy to undertake it himself, of keeping entertained General Sir David Rose, Knight of the Bath and a trencherman who, had his wine been poured into that large receptacle, would have drained it with pleasure, he being a man who appreciated his grub as much as he loved what was necessary to wash it down. Right now he was enjoying a dish of freshly netted sprats, fished for by his servants over the ship's side, alert enough to see them being pursued by a shoal of mackerel.

'God, I have missed these fish,' he exclaimed. 'They have nothing like them in the waters off India. There are some blessings to a vessel not sailing at speed.'

Surprisingly, the general, returning home with a nabob's fortune, turned out to be a man of radical opinions, who, while prepared to vehemently denounce the present barbarity of the French Revolution, was wholly in favour of the things which had brought it about. He also spoke kindly of Adam Pearce, whose writings he had read avidly in the Eighties, though he had never heard him speak. He was very like those people Pearce had met with his father and in whose houses they had stayed: folk who had all the benefits of a comfortable life but an acute awareness that it was tenuously held; in short, that all was not as well as it should be in the politics of the nation.

'You met Farmer George, you say, young fella?'

'I did, sir, it was he who granted me my commission with many a what, what.'

'Man's a fool, of course, as all royals are inclined to be. Ain't their fault, mind, they are surrounded by folk who tell them they are always right – kiss their bare arse given half the chance, the courtiers – though, I must say, the king's offspring show a stupidity remarkable even by the standards of the Hanoverians. It's a blessing monarchs have given up soldiering otherwise the lives of folk like me would be made a misery. Course, the Jack tars were burdened with that idiot William, who should never have been given charge of a bumboat, never mind a warship, the booby. Duke of Clarence, my foot, more like the damned Lord of Misrule. Burial in a butt of Malmsey, like his one-time namesake, would be a fitting reward.'

'You do not mind serving them, these Hanoverians?'

Rose laughed, swallowed a sprat and took a deep drink to wash it down. 'You won't catch me so easy, young 'un. I'm a soldier and an English one and, for all we has our faults as a nation, and for all things should be altered with rotten boroughs and the like, I know we are better off than many of Creation's other children. Remember, I have just come back from India. If you want to see injustice, sir, that is the place to go.'

'I was given to understand if a man wanted to become filthy rich, that is the place to go.'

'That, young man, borders on damn cheek,' Rose

replied, though he was grinning as he said it. 'While I have been told the way to riches is to be a naval officer and become not more than a licensed pirate. Have a sprat.'

'If you don't mind, sir, I'll decline. They are not a fish of which I have ever been very fond.'

'But they're delicious,' Rose exclaimed, biting into another, a look of deep pleasure on his ruddy face.

'General Rose, Mr Pearce, sirs,' said a midshipman, his head round the door. 'Captain's compliments, and we have raised the Needles.'

'Epic voyage, my foot,' Ralph Barclay exclaimed, flapping hard with a copy of the *Morning Post*, property of Brown's Hotel where he had taken up residence. It was full of praise for Captain Daws and the way he had brought home his two boats, as well as all his crew, to safety. 'It's not like Bligh in the Pacific, slung off his ship with short commons and thousands of miles to traverse. All Daws had to do was aim his prow at Polaris and wait till his keel touched bottom.'

'The nation needs heroes, sir,' said Cornelius Gherson, 'and Captain Daws will serve, when there is a lack of others more deserving of praise.'

'You read his letter?'

'I did.'

'And?'

'I see no purpose, sir, in you attending his court martial, quite apart from the fact that it is likely to be a formality. No captain can be in difficulty for a ship that caught fire, lest he can be shown to be personally liable. He was not and you have no knowledge of how the blaze began or what caused it.'

Devenow, standing a few feet away waiting for the coach that had been ordered, merely twitched his shoulders, grateful for the sight of the conveyance finally arriving, a chaise, which was to take them out of town to Hertfordshire and the county residence of the Duke of Portland. His memory of events was vague, yet that would not have fazed him: his ability to forgive himself for his transgressions outweighed any possibility of guilt or confession.

Ralph Barclay was helped into the chaise and covered with a blanket to ward off the chill, Gherson with him, while Devenow was obliged to take place on the postillion board at the back, pleased that he had armed himself with some gin to ward off the cold.

The captain's wife was sat in her marital home, listening to – in truth ignoring – the twittering voices of her husband's trio of silly sisters. To them, their brother was the finest man alive, a paragon of every proper virtue, a wit and a sage, who had, they would admit, made a fine marriage, though they were wont to wonder at some of their sister-in-law's more outré connections, hers being a branch of the family with members who raised questions in the article of indebtedness and being in trade: fortunately, in the main, the relationship was distant enough not to imply damaging consanguinity. To question their opinion of their brother would be fruitless and ongoing, so it was best left: all she could do was avoid joining in the paeans of praise, using a simple tight smile to pretend agreement.

Emily had never thought she would miss being at sea, but she did now and the option of constant visits to her own family home fell foul of the way they were inclined, indeed eager, to take every opportunity to praise Toby Burns. Her father spoke of his nephew as if his famous bravery was personally connected: had he not done more to raise the boy than his blood father? Her mother, the actual blood relative, would quietly simper in the pool of reflected glory, this while her daughter seethed, she alone being aware that his supposed heroics were a myth, one she was unable to puncture for the very simple reason no one would believe her.

Finally John Pearce was able to observe the frigate on which he sailed anchor at Spithead, before being warped into the quayside of the naval dockyard, the *Guiscard* having been passed over to the agent of the Portsmouth Prize Court for adjudication as to the legitimacy of its capture and an assessment of its value; for him and the men he led it would bring a tidy sum of money. The priests and nuns were taken in by the local vicar, so it was time to find out from Captain John Warren what would happen next and the effect it would have on his friends.

'The crew will be paid off from HMS *Fury*, Mr Pearce and, while the standing officers will stay with her as she enters the dockyard for repairs, only those I trust absolutely to rejoin when called back will be allowed to go home. They are my people, after all, and I would not want to lose them to another captain. The rest will be spread throughout the fleet and that will, of course, apply to those men from HMS *Grampus*, though if there are any Captain Daws values they will no doubt get a scribe to write to him so they can seek service on his next commission.'

'I had hoped that three of my fellows could stay aboard, Captain Warren, until I can get them properly executed protections.'

'You have the order of release from Lord Hood.'

'Do you think it will hold if they are taken up by the press or some crimp?'

The smile was grim. 'No, Mr Pearce, but nor can I leave them aboard a vessel which will, in days, be crawling with dockyard mateys, who, I would not be surprised to find, would sell them for a pot of ale.'

'General's going ashore, sir.'

Warren grinned. 'I can almost feel my liver rejoice. I swear I would be cursed with gout had we had him aboard much longer.'

'So you risked my liver instead,' Pearce responded, with wry humour.

'You had him for a short while, Mr Pearce, we had him all the way from Calcutta, and I can tell you the consumption of wine was measured in pipes.'

'With your permission, I would like to say my farewells too.'

'You got on with the old rogue?' Warren asked, adding when Pearce nodded, 'We all did, you know. He was damn good company.'

There were two carriages and a dray on the quay, a Berlin for the general, the dray for his extensive possessions and an enclosed square conveyance surrounded by broad-shouldered fellows, come to carry the Lisbon bullion to London. The goodbyes were as warm-hearted as Warren had said, the crew lining the rigging to cheer Sir David onto his home soil, for quite apart from his good nature, he had left a goodly sum of money for the hands to share. The old man became quite emotional as he shook each hand, extending an invitation to stay with him as a guest should the occasion of need ever arrive.

'Right, my friends,' Pearce said to the Pelicans, once all three carriages had departed. 'It is the public coach for us, and you are to stay within sight of me at all times. You will not be happy with this when you hear me tell people you are my servants...'

'Sure,' Michael whooped, 'they will not be cheered by the way we address you, John-boy.'

Pearce knew they understood, but he said the words anyway. 'Behave as if you are servants, for there will be people at each post house eyeing you. They are a favourite hunting ground for crimps, on the road from here to London. Wander and they might just nab you and hope for the best.

* * *

Bulstrode Park was a Jacobean pile with later additions, extensive gardens and stretching lawns leading to a fine lake. As they travelled up the drive, passing half a dozen toiling gardeners, Ralph Barclay could not help but imagine himself in possession of such an estate. This was no new dream but a common one amongst his breed: all it needed was a Spanish Plate ship or a great fleet action, followed by the gratitude of the nation, and any naval officer could live like this. Expecting to be received with courtesy, the brusque enquiry as to his business from the liveried, senior footman who manned the entrance put his teeth on edge and made him growl.

'I have a personal communication for His Grace from Admiral Sir William Hotham.'

The superior sniff that received was enough to imply that Hotham might as well be a midshipman. 'And your name again?'

'My name again, sir!' he barked, to no appreciable effect. 'Captain Ralph Barclay.'

'I will inform His Grace's secretary that you are here.'

'Please ensure His Grace is informed personally, my man!'

'That I cannot do, sir, given the duke is not to be troubled by every Tom, Dick or Harry who has a letter.'

'God, how I miss my arm,' Barclay whispered to Gherson. 'Given both I'd box his ears.'

'Your right would do,' Gherson responded, trying,

and not entirely succeeding, in keeping the mirth out of his tone.

'Wait here.'

The footman issued this command as he departed, the two men looking at his back and the gold lacing on his fine livery, in itself expensive enough to keep a normal fellow in food and drink for a month. It was an hour, and a frustrating one at that, before another fellow, just as supercilious but at least not uniformed, came to see them and asked for the letter.

'I was requested, nay ordered, by Admiral Hotham, to deliver it into His Grace's hand.' Seeing the countenance prepare a refusal, Ralph Barclay added vociferously. 'And I will wait here till doomsday if necessary.'

'Very well.'

Another hour passed before they were called for, this by a different and younger liveried footman, following him through chamber after chamber, each with great framed pictures denoting scenes from classical antiquity, each equipped with fine furnishings and deep patterned carpets, until they were admitted into the presence of the owner of the house in a finely proportioned drawing room with long windows overlooking a sloping lawn. Respects paid, the missive was handed over, perused, with the duke looking up at Ralph Barclay.

'This fellow is?' the older man said, meaning Gherson.

'My secretary.'

'Tell him to leave us.' That order, made without so much as a glance at Gherson, was followed by a dismissive wave to his own secretary, who departed, leaving them alone. 'You are aware of the contents.'

'No, Your Grace, but I do not have to guess at the sentiments,' Barclay replied, adding a lie that could do him no harm. 'Sir William and I were quite intimate.'

'You were at Toulon?'

The stump moved sharply, the pain was worth it. 'It is where I lost this.'

If he had hoped for sympathy there was none evident. Long of face with hooded eyes, the duke, sat on a high-backed chair, dressed in silks of the highest quality and bright colour, merely looked back at Hotham's letter. 'Your opinion of the operation?'

'Badly planned and poorly executed.'

'You have a gift for brevity, Captain...' A hand was waved to indicate ignorance.

'Barclay.' The stump moved again, this time with more care. 'It has, of course, cost me my command.'

'And I daresay, when it is healed, you would like another?'

'It is my profession, Your Grace.'

If he was hoping for a positive response, Ralph Barclay was again disappointed.

'There are two things I am plagued by, sir, and the first is those seeking a place. The second is that damned vase my ancestor bought and I let Wedgwood copy, which you had better cast an eye over on the way out. It will save you troubling my door should you ever pass by this way again.'

328

'And your interest should I seek a ship? Admiral Hotham was most anxious that I should be availed of your good offices.'

The reply was given with a sigh. 'Leave your name with my secretary.' The eyes dropped to the letter again. 'Good day, Captain.'

'There is one other matter, Your Grace.'

'Which is?'

The fair copy was produced from Ralph Barclay's pocket with all the flair of a showground conjuror. 'This is a copy of a private letter, not an official despatch, sent by Lord Hood to Mr Pitt.'

Portland lost some of his studied languor then, near to snatching the pages from Ralph Barclay's hand, to be quickly read. 'How did you come by this?'

'By luck!' Ralph Barclay responded: the look he had been given was one of distaste.

'I take it this is for me to keep?'

'It is.'

'Then I think that concludes our business.'

'And the matter of another ship when my wound has healed?'

'I daresay the Admiralty will be able to find you something, Captain Barclay, to please me more than you, so you may rest content. Now, if there is nothing else?'

He did ask to look at the Portland Vase on the way out and, when he gazed upon it, was happy to own it was an admirable piece of virtu, with the black glass and the fine white classical motifs. But having been treated with such disdain, and that by a man whose power and possessions came by inheritance, not ability, Ralph Barclay had to resist the temptation to smash the damn thing to pieces.

Preserved in the bottom of the small ditty bag she had been able to salvage from HMS *Grampus* lay the court martial papers Emily Barclay had taken from Heinrich Lutyens' berth, and each night, after dinner and alone in her marital bedchamber, she would look at them under the light of her candle; not that she needed to read them over and over again, once was enough. The conundrum was what to do with them, for the same conditions applied as had the first time she had perused them: the ripples that would flow from outright exposure.

Finding life at home stifling – when those she spoke with were not on about her wonderful husband or brave nephew – the conversation tended towards the state of the market for sheep and wool or how war was driving up the price of everything. She had also found out that, despite still being only eighteen years of age, her marital status had cut her off from those female friends whose company she had enjoyed prior to her nuptials: the unmarried had not moved on, their talk was still of prospective husbands, not forgetting the ubiquitous hope for a Prince Charming, while the two that had wed in her absence seemed to have given up all love of flighty or amusing gossip at the altar.

Emily knew she had to get away: things were constraining enough now but they would be ten times worse when her husband returned. There was no way she could resubmit to his demands, either domestically or in this room, and that would be a secret not long held, for the house had maids. Maids changed beds and she knew that the evidence of marital abstinence would be obvious, just as servants, finding stained sheets, were always the first to know of a wife or husband committing adultery, at which point, depending on their relationship to the household, they either gossiped and brought about disclosure or indulged in quiet blackmail. She could face neither.

'To London!' exclaimed her husband's eldest sister, in a voice that implied she was setting out on some dangerous adventure. 'You have quite altered my consumption of my breakfast. I shall have dyspepsia all day.'

'Is it not where my husband is at present?'

'Such a journey,' twittered another, though judging by the wedge of butter on her muffin it did not interfere with her stomach.

'One I have made before, ladies, so if you do not mind I will be about the packing of my trunk. I would be obliged if you could send one of the maids down to the Blue Boar to book me a place on the Bath-bound coach.'

The only pleasure Emily Barclay had enjoyed since returning was the ordering of new clothing, all chalked up to an account, which her husband would be required to settle. There was no difficulty in this: not only because of his remitted pay as a captain, but by his letters home and his sisters' chatter, the whole town knew he had taken one valuable prize and was in dispute about an even more fabulous East Indiaman as to whether it was salvage, a case which might take years to settle. Credit, however, was plentiful.

So it was with a full trunk and some money in her purse, as well as plentiful paper, that she set off for Bath, there to catch the fast, two-day coach to London, using the overnight stop to make a copy of the court martial evidence. Once at Charing Cross, she hailed a hack to take her to the home of Heinrich Lutyens, having sent a note ahead to say she was taking him up on his invitation, issued at sea, to stay. Welcome over and tea now cold in the pot, she turned to business.

'Heinrich, I require you to advise me about an attorney-at-law.'

The sharp nose went up in the air and the fish-like eyes narrowed suspiciously. 'I hope you are not about to take any steps, Emily, which are irrevocable.'

'I am not yet decided on what I am going to do, which is why I must consult a lawyer.'

'Will it surprise you to know that I am not acquainted with any who specialise in marital disputes?'

'Then point me towards one whom you trust.'

She had to avoid his eye when she used that word: much as she longed to tell him her purpose, to admit that would be to also own up to theft. Heinrich named a man who he knew from school and sent a note round to him to expect a new client, Emily following when he sent back word that he would be delighted to receive her.

She was brisk, not wishing to enter into any discussion of the state of her marriage. 'Mr Studdert, I need to leave with you this package of papers. You will see I have sealed them so that not even you are aware of the contents. I take it you have a strongbox?'

'A strong room, Mrs Barclay. I am entrusted with many deeds and wills, so a box would not suffice. I take it you wish me to place them beyond common reach?'

'I do.'

'And that is all you require?'

'For now.'

'Then I am happy to oblige.'

'And payment?'

'For such a meagre service we can await that, and I suspect you may have of me other requirements in the future.'

Emily declined to reply to what was an invitation to be open, passing over her sealed bundle. Studdert then led her to the heavy steel door of his strong room, opened it and let her watch without entering as he placed them on a shelf already full of bundles of documents tied with red ribbon. Then he locked the door again, before asking her to sit down once more, producing from his coat pocket a small notebook and dipping a quill once he had opened it.

'Mrs Barclay, it has been my experience in transactions of this nature that the principal, which in this case is you, may want to send for these papers, in short to have them collected and brought to you by another hand. So that I know it is indeed you who is seeing their delivery I require from you a word, a code if you like.'

'One word?' Emily asked.

'Two if you prefer, or more.'

Emily bit her lip in thought, then asked if a name was all right. When Studdert nodded she said, firmly, 'Pelican.'

CHAPTER TWENTY-ONE

Even though Parliament was in recess it took several days to get to see the king's First Lord of the Treasury, days in lodgings during which Pearce had worried for Charlie and Rufus; a time when Michael, free to move around if he kept his eyes peeled for crimps, went back to the Pelican Tavern to find that Rosie had not only gone, but that she had departed as another's bride, and that related cheered Charlie immensely. Pearce had no desire to revisit the place from which he had been pressed, being a tavern he had only frequented once and then in an emergency.

Eventually a messenger came with an invitation to attend at 10, Downing Street, Pitt's official home, where he entered a crowded waiting room of folk queuing to see the man who controlled the executive power of government, all of whom eyed each other suspiciously, as though they suspected everyone else present of seeking to bypass the proper order of admittance. It was dark before he gained the inner sanctum, and telling that he was the last person waiting: when he exited the antechamber it was empty and, making for the cabinet room, he passed as he did so a trio of men he took to be departing ministers.

'Mr Pearce, we meet again, which I did not expect. You know Mr Dundas, of course.'

John Pearce nodded to Henry Dundas, sitting while Pitt was standing, wondering if the pair were joined at the hip: on his last meeting with the man he had come to see Dundas had also been present. He was Pitt's right-hand political ally and, to Pearce, a fellow Scot, the leader of the Caledonian block of MPs in the House of Commons, who voted as he instructed, forming the bedrock of the king's Tory support; he was also a man who had crossed swords with Pearce senior and the feeling of no love lost between the two of them was, the son knew, mutual.

The contrast was strong: Henry Dundas, florid, brimming with confidence and looking like a voluptuary, was the very image of a politician. Pitt looked more of an aesthete with his fine-drawn features, slim build and quiet mode of speech. They had several things in common: they were both rabid Tories, utterly ruthless in their management of parliamentary business, and were both three-bottle men when it came to the consumption of claret. That they were drinking now, but there was no offer of wine for John Pearce.

'You have, I believe, a letter for me.'

'From Lord Hood,' Pearce replied, passing over the oilskin pouch.

'You've become quite a postie, laddie,' Dundas joked, as Pitt broke the seal, 'taking letters one way and another.'

'More, I hope, a winged messenger, Mr Dundas.'

'I heard you had to paddle, not fly, to get here.'

'It is enough that I managed.'

Pitt had obviously developed a way of swift reading, for even at three full pages it took him no time at all to digest the contents. Expecting it to be passed to Dundas, Pearce was surprised when it was not.

'His Lordship also asked me to apprise you of certain other facts.'

'Indeed?' Pitt demanded, his pale-blue eyes open in surprise.

'Lord Hood cannot say in a letter the whole of what concerns him in private.'

'Are you saying he has chosen you as an interlocutor?' Dundas demanded.

'Why you?' Pitt demanded, when Pearce nodded.

'He was anxious that I should back up what he has written with my own observations.'

'His Lordship asks a lieutenant to apply observations?' Pitt enquired.

'He feels his words may not convey the seriousness of his difficulties. Being in writing, he will no doubt feel the need to be circumspect.'

'While you will not be?'

'No.'

'I am curious, Pearce, why has Lord Hood chosen you?'

'Odd as it may seem, sir, he has come to trust me and we share an interest.'

'Which is?'

'I seek redress, as you may recall, for the illegality of my impressment, while Lord Hood wishes you to know the true nature of his difficulties with Admiral Hotham, delivered in a way that could not in any way compromise the government.'

Pitt waved the letter. 'Which are amply outlined in this and, I might add, Pearce, it is not unusual for military commanders to disagree about how to conduct a campaign.'

Dundas laughed out loud. 'Put two generals or admirals in a room and they will emerge with three opinions.'

'In fact, about a tenth of those managed by politicians!' Pearce snapped, catching Dundas draining his glass. 'And all to the detriment of their electors.'

'Mind your tongue, laddie,' Dundas spluttered, his humour evaporating.

'You of all people, Mr Dundas, should not seek that from someone of my parentage.'

'I shut Adam Pearce up more than once, boy, and you are not half the man he was.'

That got Henry Dundas a look of real venom: he had

often wondered who had generated the writs against his father for his attacks on the government – this man sitting before him was as good as telling him he was the prime mover.

'If you care to step into Green Park at dawn tomorrow, you will find, in some respects, I am very much more than the man he was.'

'Now that would be cheering for the *ton*,' Pitt joked, 'to observe a pair of Sawny Jocks seeking to kill each other. Perhaps, given how unpopular your race is in London, I should sell tickets and pay off the national debt.'

Dundas knew it was jest, and responded in kind. 'Which means we would have to leave you English to run the country on your own, a recipe for mayhem.'

'There are the clever Irish to help.'

'That is a recipe for disaster.'

'Or a comedy of errors.'

'Should I leave?' Pearce demanded, given they were obviously indulging in what was an old game of repartee, and a not entirely sober one at that.

'Billy,' Dundas cawed, pulling a face, 'we are being rebuked.'

'I find it hard to believe you have the complete trust of His Lordship,' Pitt said, not jocular now.

'I have performed certain services for him that would lead him to do so.'

'Such as?'

He did not want to sound boastful about his missions

on behalf of Hood, yet Pearce knew he had to build himself up, to make out he was worthy of the attention of the pair he was addressing. So he related the actual events regarding the surrender of the French at Toulon, as well as how close he had come to serious harm, his exploits around Corsica, the missions he had undertaken to La Rochelle, Villefranche, Naples and Tunis, in a way that established without doubt that Hood had come to see him as his messenger of discretion.

'Impressive,' Pitt said finally, and then he turned to Dundas. 'I should avoid Green Park on the morrow, Harry.'

'Quite the warrior,' Dundas responded, though the look that accompanied the words was not praiseworthy, more disbelief.

'So, these private thoughts?' Pitt demanded.

Over the weeks he had been at sea, even sometimes in that cutter, he had rehearsed what he was going to say. So he related with some fluency how the court martial had been fixed by Hotham, with he and the best witnesses sent out of the way by that admiral's order, how the result had been a forgone conclusion. He then added the suspicion that Hotham had, on more than one occasion, sought to put him, as well as the three Pelicans, in harm's way. Yet that, which had all sounded so clear-cut in his head, now sounded like an extended gripe by a man who saw himself and his friends as victims.

'However,' he concluded, 'I admit that to be

speculation and difficult to prove. I say it only to underline that Admiral Hotham will go to any lengths to protect his position. There is no doubt that perjury was not only committed but condoned, if not contrived at, by Admiral Hotham.'

'I am at a loss to know why you are telling us all this?' Dundas asked.

'So that action can be taken.'

'What action?'

'The arraignment of Captain Barclay for perjury and the charge to be levelled against Sir William Hotham of conspiracy to aid in the commission of a felony, which seems to both myself, and I think to Lord Hood, ample grounds for his removal.'

'You do not lack for effrontery,' Dundas scoffed. 'You wish us to invoke the law on your behalf against not only a post captain of some seniority but also a vice admiral held in high regard by many of our political allies.'

'A crime has been committed and if it does not say so in Lord Hood's letter it must be implied.'

'No,' said Pitt softly, shaking his head.

'May I see?' asked Pearce, holding out his hand.

'Most certainly not, you might gossip.'

'I hope you know me well enough to be sure I would say nothing.'

'Mr Pearce,' Pitt guffawed, 'I hardly know you at all.'

'While I know very well how much dispute there

is in the command you mention. It is common talk throughout the fleet.'

'Then let it stay there.'

'I am sure if you saw the papers from that travesty of a court martial you would change your mind.'

'But I do not have them and I am unlikely ever to see them,' Pitt insisted.

'Why not, they are official documents?'

'They will go to the Admiralty and be buried there,' Dundas added.

'You are the king's first minister, you can demand to see them.'

'But why would I want to?' Pitt asked, his voice low.

'For the sake of justice!' Pearce replied in a near bellow, which only got him a smile to tell him he could look for no assistance in this room. 'A case can still be brought.'

'How?' Dundas replied, finally rising from his chair. 'You have no written evidence and the witnesses you require to call are a thousand miles away. You would require a judge to insist they be brought back to England, which would only happen after you had forced the sailors, by legal writ, to give up the transcript of the court martial, and it would have to be established as questionable. The Admiralty will make mincemeat of you, laddie, so I hope you have a deep purse for your legal bills and a few years spare to pursue your hopeless case.'

Pearce had a vision then of the papers he needed falling apart as seawater destroyed them. There was nothing he could do: Ralph Barclay would escape the justice he deserved.

'I will not let this go, Mr Pitt.'

'But I, on the other hand, will let you go,' Pitt snapped. 'Our business is over.'

'Pearce,' Dundas said, 'wait outside.'

'What?' was the reply, from a supplicant clearly confused by the request.

'It is the same as Portland sent us?' asked Dundas, reaching for Hood's letter, which Pitt handed to him.

'Precisely, and it will cost Hood his command. Portland will insist on it.'

'By damn I would like to know how that Whig swine got his hands on it.'

'It matters not, Harry, he will have Hotham elevated because of what he knows.' Pitt sighed. 'With this brought by Pearce's hand its existence and the contents could be denied. Now if I reject the truth of it, given he has a fair copy, I risk losing his support.'

'I don't doubt Hood is telling the truth,' Dundas said. 'Not that it aids us much.'

'Why did you ask Pearce to wait?'

That got Pitt a look of disbelief. 'For a party manager, Billy, you're a sad case. Pearce is a weapon we would be foolish to just dismiss.'

'You're not suggesting we aid him?'

343

'We could use him.'

'Don't speak,' Pitt demanded, 'let me work out your thinking.'

'Thank the lord for that,' Dundas replied, sitting again and filling his glass with claret. 'All that arguing the toss with Pearce has given me a deep thirst, but I would say just one thing, and it hurts me to do so given that young man's parentage. I think he is speaking the truth. Oh, and another, he is not as clever as he thinks he is.'

William Pitt paced up and down the long room for several minutes, his head bent, occasionally stopping by his claret to take a sip from the glass. Without stopping he looked up and began to speak.

'Portland will demand Hood's head, which we must give him, but a hint at certain irregularities will need to be established before we can agree to elevate Hotham.' The nod and satisfied quaff from Dundas was enough of an agreement. 'Portland will ask what they are but we must say they are so unproven as to require the recall of Hood on, say, the grounds of ill health.'

'That I had not thought of, but I agree.'

'The duke is bound to make enquiries of his own and if he has any sense he will smoke what it is we are after and try to ensure we do not find out the truth, but if you are right about Pearce we already have it and the evidence will be in those court martial papers.'

'Your father would be proud of you, Billy.'

'Meanwhile we ensure Portland finds out the

truth. To protect himself he is bound to cover up for Hotham...'

'Which leaves him exposed in the future and, perhaps, as a political ally, more malleable. The facts, passed on to Fox, would bring him low given he sets himself up as such a paragon.'

'The Admiralty will lose the transcript.'

'They cannot kill the witnesses.'

'The French might.'

'Not all of them, Billy, and we have the power to insist they be brought back to England for an enquiry.'

'It would not destroy Portland.'

'We do not need to destroy him,' Dundas insisted. 'In fact if we did that we would harm ourselves. What we need to do is make him cautious.'

'Pearce?'

'We need to get Hood to agree to take leave on the grounds of ill health. He comes home and after a decent interval retires from active service. He is, after all, in his seventies.'

'And you think Pearce should return to the Mediterranean with that message.'

'If he will agree, which I doubt.'

'So much for your plan, Harry.'

'Unless you offer him your backing in the matter of the case for perjury.' Seeing Pitt look surprised Dundas added, 'Dammit, Billy, you don't have to mean it.'

Pitt nodded slowly, having lost any fear of spouting untruths the minute he took up politics. He went to the door himself and called Pearce back in, aware, as he did so, that he was the object of deep suspicion. Dundas spoke before he could.

'I don't warm to you, laddie—'

'Stop calling me laddie!'

'And I doubt many do, but old Hood seems to have done so, and we require you to aid him in return.' Dundas held up the letter. 'You see, boy, we had already read this letter before you ever came through that door.'

'How in the name of—?'

'You're not, I hope, with an atheist for a father, going to invoke God. It was copied, and that must have been when it was in your possession.'

Stunned, John Pearce could not reply, and it was obvious from his expression he was wondering when, even if he was less doubtful about the whom.

'It was then shown to the Duke of Portland,' Pitt continued, 'and he, knowing it would embarrass us, passed it on. The trouble is, with all these complaints about Hotham out in the open, and the Duke of Portland knowing we are dependent on his support, Lord Hood is vulnerable and he needs to be told that is the case, but with discretion.'

'You're not asking me to act as your messenger again?'

'There you go, Billy,' Dundas cried, slapping the table hard. 'I told you he would smoke your wiles.'

'Naturally, we would not expect you to do this without reward,' Pitt said, looking piqued.

'The case against Barclay!' Pitt nodded and that air of being found out changed to a smile. 'What has changed in the last fifteen minutes? You were sure it was impossible then.'

'No, Lieutenant Pearce,' Pitt replied, using his rank for the first time, which did not go unnoticed by the recipient. 'I told you I was not prepared to pursue it, but it has become plain to me I need your services once more and I am not fool enough to seek them without payment.'

'I think we should be honest with you, Pearce,' Dundas lied, 'it will not be easy. We must proceed with care, for the slightest hint of our aim will bring about the very situation we are seeking to avoid and block for ever any hope you have of redress.'

'But with a fair wind and us at your back,' Pitt hinted.

A hoot came from Dundas. 'Damn me, Billy, a nautical simile.'

Throughout the conversation John Pearce's mind had been racing: he did not trust these two one little bit – they might be truthful in what they were saying or they might not – but with that set of papers at the bottom of the sea the answer to his problem did not lie here in London, it lay back out there in the Mediterranean. There was also the knowledge, which he had been gnawing at for some time, of his own lack of prospects, as well as that of his companions. While he could not decide for them, he could for himself and aid them in the process.

'I agree, with conditions.' Pearce enjoyed the way

the two politicians reacted, as though they had just discovered someone had stolen their watch. 'I require two warrants for arrest squashed and three protections from impressments guaranteed by you.'

'The Admiralty issues those,' Dundas protested.

'They will grant them quickly on your demand. I also wish to choose the vessel on which I travel.'

'You pose a stiff price.'

'Take it or leave it.'

Pitt was walking again, head down in a brown study and moving from side to side.

'Billy,' Dundas said, only to be silenced by a raised hand.

'I agree,' Pitt said eventually. 'Leave the details, the names and crimes, with my clerk and call upon me tomorrow, and let us hope, Mr Pearce, that what we are about works out for the best.'

John Pearce nodded and left, leaving the two politicians looking at each other for several seconds until they were sure the sound of footsteps had faded. Then they burst out laughing, Dundas filling their glasses with yet more claret, both then raised in a silent toast.

'That was easier than I thought,' said Dundas. 'We should get hold of Sheridan and ask to appear at Drury Lane.'

Eventually, having taken a deep drink, William Pitt replied, 'If only our political opponents were as biddable as Lieutenant John Pearce, life would be so much easier.'